ALSO BY KERSTIN HALL

Star Eater

THE MKALIS CYCLE
The Border Keeper

SECOND SPEAR

KERSTIN HALL

A TOM DOHERTY ASSOCIATES BOOK

NEW YORK

SECOND SPEAR

Cover art by Jaime Jones
Cover design by Christine Foltzer

A Tordotcom Book
Published by Tom Doherty Associates
120 Broadway
New York, NY 10271

www.tor.com

Tor® is a registered trademark of Macmillan Publishing Group, LLC.

ISBN 978-1-250-25016-2 (ebook)
ISBN 978-1-250-25017-9 (trade paperback)

First Edition: 2022

For Stephen Hall

Second Spear

Chapter One

The amber walls of the city caught the moonlight and dis-
torted it into eerie, shifting patterns; shapes that morphed and
twined like long grass in the wind. Tahmais, the City of the
Spinelight, gleamed in the darkness. It stood alone on top of
the plateau, and the sharp ridge of the mountainside curved
away below it, the steep granite slopes veering outwards to a
shadowed plain.

At the gates of the city, a single beacon flared to life. Mo-
ments later, the shrill blast of a horn cut through the air. More
lights appeared—a ripple of fiery sparks that swept over the
length of the wall.

In a dimly-lit room deep within the city—beyond two more
sets of translucent walls, past gardens and houses and night mar-
kets bustling with people, midnight rendezvous and secret affairs,
groves of hollow trees, whispering libraries and hidden lairs below the orange streets—a woman pretended to be asleep. She
was scarred and wiry, her skin writ with intricate tattoos and her
long hair pulled back into a braid. Her left arm lay across her
chest, the bone broken just above the elbow.

Tyn watched Twelfth Healer Abathei from beneath her eyelashes. Oblivious to her attention, he moved around the room
and quietly restored it to order; he returned bottles of cutroot
sap and vinegar to the cabinet, folded gauze and linen ban-
dages, washed the empty vase of terjic clay in the basin beside

the door. Occasionally, he glanced toward the window. The beacons burned in the distance, and the wail of the horn carried on the breeze. When the door opened, he jumped.

"Are you finished?" whispered Ninth Healer Davet. "Uban wants us in the hall. He says it's urgent."

Abathei moved to the basin and pumped water from the spigot. "Do we know the cause of the alert?"

"Not yet, but Res Lfae has returned from the 200th realm. They are meeting with the First Spear in the War House now."

Abathei set a glass of water at Tyn's bedside. She kept her breathing deep and even, her face slack.

Go on, she urged him. *Hurry up.*

"What a night," he murmured to himself, then turned. "All right, I'm coming."

The door closed with a gentle click, and the murmur of the Healers' voices subsided. When all was silent, Tyn opened her eyes.

The recovery room was situated on the ground floor, a small, quiet chamber with sky blue walls. Coloured glass tokens, scrolled with terjic wards, hung from hooks in the ceiling. Outside the window, a warm wind stirred the leaves of the trees.

She slid her legs out from beneath the bed sheets. From her shoulder to her wrist, Abathei had packed a thick sleeve of yellow clay. Currents of strange electricity pulsed beneath the cast—living hexes that knitted her flesh and bone, worked their way through her muscles like miniscule tadpoles, correcting, realigning. The sensation made her nauseous, and when she stood her arm hung awkwardly at her side, heavy and stiff as a club. Still, at least it was dry. She could move.

Crouching, she found her boots beneath the bed and clumsily pulled them on. At any moment she expected to hear footsteps in the corridor. The window creaked when she pushed it open; she swung her leg over the ledge and climbed through.

The Sanctum, Res Lfae's private residence, filled the guarded heart of Tahmais. The bustle of the outer districts faded inside the compound; within the walls it remained peaceful and secluded and unchanging. Eleven buildings were scattered amongst the ramble of tiled pathways and wild cherry trees, and moonlight touched their roofs with silver. Night birds sang and insects chirruped, and the ever-present sound of water hushed at the edge of hearing.

Tyn moved swiftly, heading east through the trees. The Sanctum was as familiar as her own skin and she melded with the darkness, a ghost amongst the leaves. Her thoughts ran in hopeless, anxious circles.

If the emergency beacons had been lit, then someone was dead. Either an ally or an enemy, the border keeper or Kan Fanieq. By now, the fight between them would have been decided. Res Lfae had returned from the 200th realm and triggered the alert, and Tyn did not know whether that meant her ruler was bracing for Fanieq's attack or some other unforeseen danger. If the goddess had emerged victorious, then she would be sure to want Lfae's head—after six hundred long years plotting her vengeance, she would be eager to make an example of the demon. But if the border keeper had won, then why sound the alarm?

For better or worse, she needed to find out what had happened.

An intricately carved stone bridge arched over the Sanctum's deep, slow-moving river. Below the surface, sleek watercats wound through the currents. A few, curious, approached the surface as Tyn drew near; their wide, white eyes shining like lanterns. She passed the animals without a second glance. Up ahead, pale light spilled out of the slatted window shutters of the War House.

Lfae would disapprove, but she had already disgraced them; she could hardly surpass that shame. Soundless, she crept around the side of the building. Yet her ruler had brought her home, even after she had damned the border keeper. They had demanded that the Healers fix her. Even after the damage she had caused, they had refused to say one word against her.

She could hear voices. The rough-plastered walls muted the conversation, reducing words to an angry inaudible murmur. She eased the back door open.

". . . shadowline might fall. Midan is as good as dead if the Ageless breach the boundary while she's unconscious."

"Then is it possible to revive her?"

The wards over the door bristled as Tyn passed below them. She muttered a phrase and they subsided again, hexes coiling back on themselves like snakes. She held her breath as she crept down the corridor, and her arm throbbed dully. Through the entrance to the Assembly Chamber, she glimpsed Lfae's shadow as they paced.

"The injuries to her Mkalis body are too severe," they said. "Waking her now is almost certain to kill her."

Tyn sidled into the gap between the door and the corridor wall. Through the thin crack, she could see the whole room.

The Assembly Chamber was circular; the walls sloped outwards like a bowl and the high ceiling was ribbed with massive, curved tusks. A brazier burned in the middle of the room, and the smoke curled upwards and darkened the rafters around the vent. Fleeting images swirled in the air around the fire.

A tall demon with waves of platinum hair stalked the floor. Res Lfae's skin possessed a luminous quality, a terrible, unearthly glow. Even furious, they remained starkly beautiful—if anything, their anger seemed to accentuate their features, to make the strong angles of their face more pronounced. A little apart from them stood a hard-boned woman. From her angle, Tyn could only see First Spear Vehn's back, rigidly upright, her hands clasped at her waist.

"How did it come to this?" snarled Lfae. "Midan *knew* it was a trap, she knew Kan Fanieq had prepared. Why didn't I stop her?"

"With respect, your Reverence, I doubt she would have appreciated that."

"And so? I should have at least tried." They came to a halt beside the window and stared out into the darkness. For a moment, they were silent.

"Call off the alert, but double the watch," they said at length. "I need to leave the realm. When I return I'll bar the channels."

A slight pause. "All of them?"

"Kan Fanieq had allies. They will know Midan is weakened now. If I were in their position, I would take the chance to press that advantage."

"Your Reverence, isolating yourself is going to look like weakness. The other rulers—"

"Are you questioning me, Vehn?"

The First Spear stopped talking.

"Midan came here because she trusts me." Lfae turned around. "Thus I will keep her safe even if it means war with every god in Mkalis. Do I make myself clear?"

The front of Lfae's shirt was soaked in blood. A small gasp escaped Tyn's mouth, but the crackling of the brazier covered the sound.

"Understood," said Vehn.

"While she is still clinging to life, I won't risk her enemies infiltrating my realm." The heat left Lfae's voice. "Perhaps that is foolish, but it's my decision."

"I apologise."

They sighed. "No need for that, just be sure to double the watch. You're dismissed."

Vehn pressed her fists together in acknowledgement, then walked to the main doors of the Assembly Chamber. But at the threshold, she hesitated.

"What is it?" asked Lfae.

The silence yawned. Tyn wondered for a moment if the First Spear had somehow detected her presence, but when Vehn spoke again her voice was quite different.

"I won't ask where you are going," she said, without turning around, "but would you like me to come with you?"

A pang of some strong, painful emotion crossed the demon's face, then disappeared.

"Thank you, First Spear, but that won't be necessary," they said. "I'm going to demand a Tribunal of the High for Kan Buyak's impeachment. It would be faster to go alone."

"I see," said Vehn. "You consider the god such a threat?"

"I know he's ruthless, more so than I am." Lfae shrugged. "And desperate people are always dangerous. With Kan Fanieq defeated, he will know his time is short."

"Then why don't you just kill him? He cannot harm us if he's dead."

"Because I want him to suffer."

Tyn shivered. The images dancing over the brazier grew brighter: a figure scything a machete into another's skull, bodies falling, birds tumbling from the air.

"Be cautious, your Reverence," said Vehn.

Lfae did not answer her. Once she had left the chamber, they sighed and leaned back against the wall. They watched the swirl of smoke and illusion. The blood on their shirt had eaten through the fabric, and the skin beneath looked scorched and raw.

"You should be in the infirmary, Upstart," they said.

Tyn jumped.

"Go, before I decide to take proper notice of you." They tilted their head back and shut their eyes. "As far as I'm concerned, you were never here."

"Understood," she whispered.

Chapter Two

With dextrous fingers, Abathei peeled off the layer of clay covering Tyn's arm. The hardened cast pulled away with a reluctant hiss, and the Twelfth Healer narrowed his eyes. He probed the bone.

"It feels better?" said Tyn.

"Hmm. Res Lfae wants you to make a complete recovery." Abathei drew the elbow straight, then manipulated it towards Tyn's chest. "That means no stress on this arm for the next week."

"But I can go?"

"Flex your wrist. How is the pain?"

"It's much better than yesterday."

"Turn your hand to the left. Now right." He watched the bones shift. "You'll need to be careful."

"Of course."

He sighed. "In that case, you may go. But let me fit you with a sling first."

Midday, and the confusion of the previous night already felt remote and unreal. Small bright birds swooped between the buildings, chirping wildly. Res Lfae had returned to the 194th realm before dawn; Tyn had overheard two Healers discussing the matter. Without bothering to explain why they had left in the first place, Lfae had gone straight to the border keeper's bedside. An hour later they emerged from her room, gathered all the tribe Firsts, and declared that a guest of the realm had been granted empane status.

A bold choice, suggested the Eighth Healer disapprovingly. The kind of choice that might have significant consequences if Res Lfae wasn't careful.

Then she noticed that Tyn was listening, and after that the Healers hushed and grew tight-lipped and tense. When Tyn asked how the border keeper was recovering, they refused to say anything at all.

Their secrecy was justified. Still, she could not help feeling slighted by the way they excluded her. She was only a dweller, insignificant beside the larger clashes of power and influence that governed Mkalis. They were right, of course, that she did not *need* to know. But she didn't have to like it.

The path from the infirmary to the Sanctum barracks cut through a shaded corridor of jacaranda trees, and the ground was carpeted in their fallen purple flowers. Curling strips of copper wire and old painted bones hung from the branches. Femurs, vertebrae, ribs; some wrapped in strands of precious stones and pearls. They served as mementos to Spears who had fallen while defending Tahmais. Past them, the barracks stood two storeys high; a rust-coloured building that curved outwards over the western tributary of the river. The first Fifteen of the Kisdja Tribe held chambers on the upper floor, and the newest Spears shared quarters below, where they stayed until they could be assigned roles elsewhere. A clean-swept yard extended from the trees to the front door. Tyn had almost reached the building when a loud crash shattered the peace.

"I don't belong here!"

The voice—angry, male, edged with petulance—was new. The front door swung open to admit Tyn, and she walked inside. Battle masks glared down from the wood-panelled walls; the ornate helms carved from the skulls of the desert elk. Soot stained the tips of their horns.

"You're lying!"

Another crash. The argument was coming from inside the kitchen. Tyn followed the noise to the end of the corridor.

Matir knelt on the floor and gathered up the pieces of a broken bowl. His broad, muscled shoulders were stiff with suppressed irritation.

"I understand that you feel confused," he said, his voice low and honey-smooth. "It's perfectly normal."

The other man in the kitchen, slight and wild-eyed, stood with his back to the corner. His skin was light brown, and his features had an odd kind of delicacy, as if they had been moulded from porcelain. When Tyn entered the room, he bared his teeth in a snarl. His eyes did not match, she noted. One tawny brown, the other dark green.

"Let him be, Matir," she said.

Matir glanced over his shoulder and his expression brightened at the sight of her. She resisted the urge to grin back.

"Yes, Second Spear," he said, dipping his head. "It is good to see you again."

"Who is this?" spat the stranger. "Who are you?"

Tyn ignored him. She leaned against the doorframe. "Has Res Lfae spoken to the tribe?"

"To Vehn, I think. I don't know about anyone else. But I heard that the channels have been barred."

"All of them?"

"It seems that way."

"I asked you a question!" The man took a step toward her, his fists balled. "You will answer me!"

Tyn met his gaze. "Why? Do you plan to attack me?"

Her bluntness threw him. His eyes darted to Matir.

"No, look at me," she said. "You're new to Mkalis, right? Let's see if I understand this correctly. You're frightened and angry. You feel like your old memories have slipped just out of reach, like they're fading even as you try to grasp hold of them. You keep forgetting where you are and how you got here, and you assume some kind of cruel trick is being played on you, because you keep forgetting that you died. Does that sound right?"

"You know nothing about me."

"True, but neither do you. What's your name?"

He opened his mouth to answer her, but instead there was only silence. A shudder ran through him.

"He has been named Rion," said Matir.

In response, the man grabbed another bowl from the counter and slammed it down on the floor.

"I guess we'll leave you to that, then." Tyn turned back to Matir. "Listen, I've been told that I'm not allowed to, uh, stress my arm. Would you mind giving me a hand with something?"

"Don't dismiss me!"

For a moment, Tyn thought that Rion might burst into tears. His jaw trembled and he stared fixedly at the shattered pieces of ceramic. She softened.

"It gets easier," she said. "You'll see. You just have to—"

"What's going on here?"

Vehn stood in the doorway to the dining hall, frowning. Tyn had not heard her approach, but that was unsurprising— the First Spear moved with the silence of the dead. Vehn had stormcloud eyes and a braided rope of thick black hair, and she ruled the Spears with pitiless, brutal efficiency. For five years, she had served as Lfae's right hand, rising to the position after crushing her predecessor in combat. Since then, the role had stripped her of every remaining trace of softness and sentiment.

"First Spear." Tyn bowed her head. "I knocked over a bowl. I apologise, it was clumsy of me."

"Out of the infirmary already?" Vehn's lips thinned. "Too soon, apparently. Clear away this mess, and meet me on the roof."

"Yes, First Spear."

"And you," Vehn addressed Rion, "will be quieter."

Rion scowled. The First Spear waited until he averted his gaze and she was satisfied that he understood her. Then she spun around and disappeared into the hall.

"I'll handle it," said Matir under his breath. "Don't keep her waiting."

Tyn nodded. "Thanks."

The barracks' central staircase lay open to the air, a curving spiral of pale yellow stone. Tyn hurried upwards. The fact that the First Spear wanted to speak privately did not bode well. Vehn would probably demand to know *exactly* what had taken place inside the 41st realm, and even the idea of describing her own abject helplessness filled Tyn with dread.

But worse, it would also mean talking about Vasethe—which she didn't feel ready for, not yet. That pain lay too close to the surface.

Nevertheless, she steeled herself and walked out onto the roof. Vehn stood straight, her hands folded on the balustrade. She gave no indication that she heard Tyn's approach.

"You wished to speak to me?"

Without turning, Vehn beckoned. Tyn allowed herself a

small grimace and joined her leader at the edge.

The yard yawned below. The effect was immediate: with heart-hammering intensity, the memory of hanging in the air over Addis Hal Rata flooded Tyn's mind. Fear. The terrible, blessed lurch of Fanieq's power yanking her back towards the windows.

"You are suspended," said Vehn.

With effort, Tyn breathed out. Vehn's words reached her slowly. Not what she had anticipated.

"On what grounds?" she asked. "And for how long?"

"On the grounds that you endangered our ruler's life and reputation. And for as long as I see fit."

Another breath. The barracks roof had never bothered her before. Her vision narrowed, and sweat broke on the back of her neck.

"Understood," she said. "I won't disappoint you again."

"Words are easy, Upstart." Vehn finally turned to look at her. "I will not tolerate weakness in the tribe."

"Yes, First Spear."

Vehn's eyes remained cold. "This is for your own good too."

Tyn nodded. There was a bitter taste in her mouth. "Yes, First Spear. I understand."

"You are dismissed. Go well."

The fear waned as she turned from the edge and walked towards the stairs, careful not to rush or betray any sign of anxiety. Vehn resumed her study of the Sanctum grounds.

Only once she was out of sight, did Tyn let her guard slip. She leaned her back against the wall of the stairwell, and rested her forearm over her eyes.

"Dammit," she muttered.

The roughness of the plaster dug into her shoulders. Suspended. She had not given much thought to punishment, but suspension was probably generous under the circumstances. Res Lfae had threatened war with another ruler because of her impulsiveness, and she had led the border keeper's consort—or whatever Vasethe was—straight into a trap. In another realm, she would be lucky to escape torture and execution.

"Suspended!" said Matir.

"Under the circumstances—"

"Oh, come on, Tyn." He rolled his eyes. "This is ridiculous. For how long?"

"She declined to say."

"So until Res Lfae intervenes."

"I hope not. Vehn won't appreciate having her authority undermined."

"Who cares what she appreciates?"

"Don't be like that. Besides, it doesn't make a difference at the moment anyway; I'm supposed to be recovering."

They were lying on Matir's bed with the shutters half-drawn over the windows. Bars of afternoon light fell across the sheets and their bodies, bisecting scars and tattoos, her pale skin crossing his dark. Tyn's head rested on Matir's stomach, and rose and fell with his breathing. He toyed with the end of her hair, winding it between his fingers.

"You seem pretty well recovered to me," he said.

She jabbed him in the ribs with the elbow of her uninjured arm.

"Ow! All right, all right, you're still on the brink of death."

"Better," she said.

"You are okay though, aren't you?" He let go of her hair. "You scared me when you disappeared. What happened?"

She was quiet for a while.

"Tyn?"

"I'm fine." She sat up. "It was just a broken arm."

"I was—"

"I'm fine."

He breathed out heavily. "Right. Of course."

Don't do this, Tyn implored silently. *Don't get serious.*

It was of the utmost importance that their trysts remained secret: from the tribe, from Res Lfae, and most especially from Vehn. Not that fraternisation was expressly forbidden, but it complicated matters. Matir understood that. Had always understood that, and it was why their arrangement worked— anything more meaningful threatened to disrupt the hierarchy of the tribe.

But in the past few weeks, he had begun taking her side over Vehn's. Little things, small gestures. He never quite disobeyed the First Spear, but rebellion fomented below the surface of his smooth-faced obedience, and it was only a matter of time before Vehn noticed.

And the worst part was that Tyn could not return his feelings. She liked Matir, she trusted him, and she enjoyed his company, but they both knew his affection ran deeper. If she were kinder, she would have ended the affair already. Instead she lingered, and her guilt tightened like a noose.

"Forget that I asked, all right?" he said. "Whatever happened to you, there's no pressure to tell me about it."

"Is that an attempt to goad me into sharing the details?"

"Nothing of the sort. Although, if it works . . ."

She laughed and lay back down beside him. The light reflecting from the river cast rippling patterns over the ceiling. Through the gaps between the shutters, Tyn could see thin, patchy clouds.

"When I arrived in Tahmais," she said, "was I like the new Spear?"

"Who, Rion?"

"Yeah. I can't really remember." She traced her fingertips over Matir's forearm. "He seems so unhappy."

"It's different for everyone, but we all needed time. Some more than others." He stared at the ceiling. "It was generous of you to lie for him in front of Vehn."

"Probably a mistake."

"I don't know. I doubt he'll forget that." Matir scrunched up his face. "Let's see, when you arrived . . . I don't recall much smashed crockery, no."

Tyn gave him an exasperated look. He smiled fondly.

"You really don't remember?" he asked.

"Only parts. I remember meeting Vehn."

"And me?"

She shook her head.

"It was on the Orasion Wall. Vehn was showing you around Tahmais. You were thin and wide-eyed and your hair was short. I remember thinking that Res Lfae must have assigned you to the wrong tribe; you didn't look the part at all."

"But I wasn't like Rion?"

"No. No, not exactly. You were . . ." Matir fell silent, thinking. "Quiet. Watchful, like you expected us to turn on you— you were far more paranoid than most. But there was also this strange air about you, like you were waiting for something."

"But I was less angry than Rion?"

"Oh, definitely. I'd say you seemed more sad than anything else. You kept to yourself for a long time, that's all. Why the sudden interest?"

"Just wondering." She drew a spiral over his arm. "Do you

ever think about your past life? In Ahri?"

"I suspect it was nothing spectacular. But who knows?" He grinned suddenly. "Maybe I was a prince."

"I doubt that."

"You wound me."

"More likely a criminal. Perhaps a thief."

"Because I've stolen your heart?"

"A conman, then."

"Ouch. And who do you suppose you were? Queen? Assassin? Farmer?"

Scholar.

"I don't know," she lied. She made herself smile, easy and careless. "What does it matter anyway?"

Except, maybe, it did.

Chapter Three

Even suspended from her position, Tyn was permitted to keep her quarters at the barracks. She suspected Vehn was trying to avoid drawing Lfae's attention to the situation—an idea which she found obscurely pleasing. It also meant that she retained access to the usual chains of rumour and gossip that flourished in the dining hall.

"They're fighting," said Koitu. She was Fourth Spear, bloodthirsty and loyal, with little respect for other people's personal space. She stabbed a stewed beet with her fork, and crammed it into her mouth. "Dunno what about, but Res Lfae's mad."

The dining hall was an oval chamber with copper-coloured walls and wide windows. Two giant iron helms, relics from a long-past conquest, were mounted on podiums beside the entrance to the kitchen. For luck, Spears threaded wildflowers through the visors. Four old tables stood in a square in the middle of the room.

"It strikes me as incredibly ungrateful," said Seventh Spear Hale. He was a large man, taller and more heavily built than anyone else in the tribe, and he possessed a slow, ponderous way of pronouncing words.

Tyn gave him a hard look. "We don't know the circumstances."

"Res Lfae barred the channels. Our allies are furious, and for what? The border keeper is not worth this much trouble.

Not to mention that they granted her empane status."

"You're jumping to conclusions," said Matir. He reclined in his chair, arms resting behind his head. "Tyn's right; we have no idea what their argument is about."

"Yes, *we* don't." Koitu leaned forward. "But our Second Spear probably has a clearer view than most. What happened after you vanished, Upstart? You can't keep it a secret forever."

"I think you'll find I can."

"Oh, come on."

"It's not my place to say." Tyn folded her arms. "Res Lfae will explain everything in due course."

"But that could take *months*!"

"I suggest developing a little patience, then."

"Yeah, quit nagging," said Matir.

"I'm not nagging, you sycophant. And by the way, just because you agree with everything Tyn says, doesn't mean she's going to sleep with you."

Hale snorted. "Settle down, children."

Tyn took a nonchalant bite out of a slice of spicegrass bread and studiously avoided looking in Matir's direction. "Whatever their disagreement, I'm sure the border keeper and Res Lfae will make amends."

Hale set down his glass. "I still say that she should show some respect."

"Give it a rest, Seventh."

"You're suspended. You can't tell me what to do."

"Hah!" Koitu laughed, delighted. "Once Tyn's reinstated, there's going to be so much pain in your future."

"Me? Vengeful? What, do you think I'm taking notes for future reference?"

"Well, *now* I do . . ."

Matir nudged her foot beneath the table, and cleared his throat. Tyn followed his line of sight. Vehn stood in the doorway, her expression stony. As others in the room noticed her, the murmur of conversation died away.

"Oh, what now?" muttered Koitu.

The First Spear's cheeks were uncharacteristically flushed, and her mouth was a thin, severe line. She stalked over to their table.

"Res Lfae wants to speak with you in their private chambers," she snapped at Tyn.

The silence in the room deepened. Koitu and Hale exchanged a look. Everyone had noticed the deliberate emphasis that Vehn had placed on the word "private."

After a second, Tyn knocked her fists together in a gesture of acknowledgment. She stood up and collected her plate, keeping her gaze lowered. "Thank you for passing on the message."

"Don't keep our ruler waiting."

Tyn set her chair straight, and bowed her head lower. "Of course not. I'll head to their quarters directly."

Matir's deep voice carried through the dining hall.

"While you're there," he said, "why not discuss the matter of your suspension?"

Stifled gasps from other tables. Matir remained seated. He smiled faintly. A fruit knife dangled loose within his grip; he twirled the blade between his fingers.

"Quiet, Eighth Spear," said Tyn.

"It was just a thought."

She wanted to shake him, to grasp him by the shoulders and demand that he stop smiling; he was going to ruin everything. Why do this? Why risk Vehn's anger over nothing at all? And yet she stayed rooted to the spot. Hale and Koitu both stared at Matir as if wondering whether their friend had lost his mind.

Vehn's expression did not change. With great deliberation, she placed her hand on Matir's shoulder. From anyone else, the gesture might have seemed friendly. From her, it was a threat.

"Consider this your only warning, Eighth Spear." She leaned forward, lowering her voice. Her breath stirred his hair. "I will not be tested."

Matir continued to stare ahead. The knife spun, spun, and came to a stop. He nodded.

"Good." Vehn withdrew her hand and straightened. She turned to Tyn. "Why are you still here, Second Spear?"

Tyn muttered an apology. As she left, she saw Vehn take the seat she had vacated next to Matir. Koitu caught her eye and mouthed something. It was not until Tyn reached the yard that she deciphered the words.

Still calls you Second Spear.

Thick grey clouds obscured the sky. It had rained during the night, and glinting beads of water dripped from the trees. The Sanctum was quiet; a few dwellers from other tribes hurried between the buildings. Tyn came to a stop below the low-hanging eaves of the War House, where no one would see her. Pulse racing, she balled her right hand into a fist and punched the wall.

"Stupid!" she snarled.

She struck the wall again. How could she have let it come to this? A thin trickle of blood rolled down her knuckles and over her fingers. She pressed the graze to her mouth.

She needed to end things with Matir, soon, before Vehn uncovered the truth. Ruler's blood, the way he had looked at her in the dining hall; the complete trust on his face and the knife in his hand. Did he believe that he stood any chance in a fight against the First Spear? Did he believe Tyn did?

She breathed deeply and waited for her heart to slow. Weak sunlight cut hazy shadows over the grass. The heat of her anger faded.

Res Lfae would be waiting for her.

In contrast to the opulence of their banquet halls and guest palaces, the demon ruler's home within the Sanctum was modest. The house stood within a web of wooden walkways and tree-shaded paths, the rear of the building overlooking a fork in the river. The steep peaks of the roof rose above the trees, and iridescent blue feathers thatched the slopes.

Tyn followed the path through the old elm grove. From the shadows of the branches, sinuous creatures of metal and coloured glass watched her. Lfae's roaming eyes. To safeguard the autonomy of their dwellers, the demon had taken the radical decision to set rules against themselves. They could not possess a subject without explicit permission, nor could they blood-compel a dweller to follow their commands. Instead of borrowing living eyes and ears, Lfae constructed mechanical aids to pad through the city on silent paws, feline bodies swathed in rippling chains of hexes.

A door slammed up ahead. A moment later, Tyn glimpsed a wild-haired woman limping down the eastern path. She breathed in sharply.

The border keeper favoured her right leg, and her chest was bound in white linen. Her face appeared almost normal; her bruises blended into the shadows of her cheekbones. Not fully recovered from her fight with Fanieq, but alive and intact and, by the looks of it, very angry.

A sudden recklessness seized Tyn. She stepped off the walkway and called out through the trees. "Border keeper!"

The woman stopped. When she saw Tyn, a strange expression crossed her face.

"Oh, it's you," she said. "What is it, Second Spear?"

God-slayer. Destroyer of Realms. The Quiet Before the Shatter. The border keeper was not like Lfae, or any of the other rulers. She looked human. She looked *vulnerable*. But the thoughtless, brutal ease with which Fanieq had fought was branded upon Tyn's memory. The woman standing before her had withstood that violence. Surpassed it.

Tyn bowed her head.

"Forgive me, your Reverence," she said. "May I speak with you?"

The border keeper frowned.

"Eris is fine," she said. "Or Midan, considering that Lfae insists on it."

The idea was so absurd that it took Tyn a second to understand what was being proposed.

"I—I can't use your given name," she said.

"Why not?"

"It would be disrespectful."

"I'd think arguing with me is worse. What do you want?"

In Tyn's imagination, this conversation had played out differently. She gathered herself. "I wanted to apologise for the trouble I caused."

A pause.

"That's it?" said Eris.

"Yes. I'm very sorry."

"Huh." The border keeper's gaze roamed over the trees, then returned to Tyn. "You know, by performing a Questing on

Sethe, I was able to see some of what occurred inside the 41st realm."

At the mention of Vasethe, Tyn's pulse fluttered. "So you could see that I was powerless against Kan Fanieq."

"I saw that you were far braver than you had any right to be." Eris' black eyes glinted, cutting through Tyn's defences like gossamer.

"That wasn't—"

"Second Spear, I'm glad that you brought the Compass to me, because Sethe would be dead if you had refused. I know you felt compromised. But your shame isn't justified, and you owe me no apologies."

How easy for her to say, how easy to suggest that Tyn's guilt could simply be laid aside. How could she ever understand? Like an avenging scion of justice, the border keeper had descended upon Fanieq's realm and struck the goddess down. What did she know of weakness?

When Tyn had stumbled back into Kan Buyak's realm, every step had felt like a betrayal. She could still recall the way the God Compass had adhered to her skin; ice-cold inside her clenched fist. And before she had even reached the top of the Jifui Pass, the border keeper had found her.

"Lfae will be here soon." Eris' eyes had possessed a glazed, faraway quality. As if she had been caught half-dreaming, and now stood torn between wakefulness and the dark.

"I'm sorry."

"Hush." With gentle hands, she had taken Tyn's wrist and raised it, looping the chain of the Compass between her own fingers. "It's all right."

Then, like the fall of a stone through water, the border keeper had vanished. And ever since, shame had plagued Tyn.

She had fought to repress it, but now the secret well of her guilt finally rose up and spilled over.

"Res Lfae was covered in your blood," she said. It came out harsher than intended. "Your wounds—"

"Were not as severe as Fanieq's."

"You almost died."

"Almost. It happens." Eris gestured to her bandaged torso. "In a few days, I will have recovered. If anything, I feel fortunate. I expected to lose that fight."

"It was my *fault*."

"No." Eris shook her head. "It wasn't."

Tyn averted her gaze. She had anticipated anger from the border keeper. Not this.

"Listen to me," said Eris. "No one blames you, not me, not Lfae. The circumstances were outside your control."

"But how did you win? Against . . . against her?"

"That would be telling."

"Is the goddess dead now?"

"Oh, very dead. I made sure, since apparently I didn't kill her enough the first time around."

Eris' tone caught Tyn off guard. *Was that a . . . joke?* Her surprise must have shown, because a smile broke across the border keeper's face; the harsh angles of her features softened and she appeared much less severe, much less cold. Even marred by the marks of her recent battle, that smile was disarming. Warm and hard, like winter sunlight on tarnished metal.

She's beautiful, Tyn realised with an unexpected jolt.

"I'll be fine," said Eris. "I have my regrets, but Fanieq won't harm anyone else now. Speaking of which, how is your arm?"

"Oh." Tyn glanced down. "The Healers have taken care of it."

Eris extended one hand, and looked at her expectantly.

Since she had left the infirmary, the swelling around the bone had reduced and the skin no longer felt as hot. Uncertain, Tyn slipped off the sling. Eris reached out and traced her fingers over the bandage.

Then, without explanation, she spat into her palm and laid it flat against Tyn's wrist.

"What are you . . . ah!" A jolt of electricity ran from Tyn's fingers to her collar. The border keeper's eyes flashed blood red, and the pain disappeared.

"Better?" she asked.

Tyn raised and lowered her arm experimentally. There was no indication that it had ever been broken. She curled her fingers into a fist, relaxed them again.

"You should not have done that, your Reverence," she said.

"Don't mention it."

Tyn rolled her shoulder. Strong. Possibly stronger than before. "Thank you."

"You can thank me by using my name."

"I . . ."

"Please?"

"Thank you, Eris."

"There you go, and look: the realm didn't fall apart." The border keeper nodded in satisfaction. "Good. I have to return to Ahri now, but I expect I'll see you again in the near future."

"Of course. I'm sorry for delaying you." Tyn's throat constricted. Her one chance, slipping away. If she didn't speak now, she might not get another opportunity. "But could you— may I ask if Vasethe is all right?"

The effect was instant and uncanny. Like a door slammed

shut, Eris' face closed off and all traces of her previous humour vanished.

"I haven't heard anything," Tyn added quickly. "I just wanted to know, after I left Fanieq's realm—"

"Lfae hasn't told you?"

"Told me what?"

Eris pressed her lips together.

"Sethe's fine," she said. "For now. But he's done something spectacularly stupid, and I need to fix it."

"He's in Ahri?"

"Yes. Until matters are resolved, it would be unwise to say more than that. Yes, he's alive."

"Okay." Tyn's skin prickled with unease, but at the same time it felt like a massive weight had lifted off her shoulders. He was alive. Whatever else was going on, at least he had survived.

"You were worried about him." Eris' gaze was piercing. "You care for him?"

"I'm glad he's safe."

"But it's more than that." The border keeper scowled abruptly. "You know, don't you? About who you were before, about Raisha. He told you."

Tyn nodded.

Eris made a frustrated sound. "That fool."

"I won't tell anyone else."

"No, you misunderstand. He should never have placed that burden on you." She narrowed her eyes. "And it *is* bothering you, isn't it?"

"No, I can handle it." Tyn was taken aback by the border keeper's concern. "Really. But if it isn't any trouble, could you tell him . . ."

She trailed off. Tell him what? Thank you? That she was sorry? That she wished to talk to him again, because she could not find her way back to the person she had been before that night in the temple?

"I'll tell him that you said hello," said Eris, after the silence grew too long. Her expression was guarded. "Anything else, I think you should say yourself, Second Spear. But now I believe your ruler is waiting for you."

And has been, for some time already. Tyn pressed her fists together and bowed her head. A thought struck her.

"Border keeper, given that you requested I use your given name, would you like to use mine?"

Eris smiled again. "I would like that very much. Tyn."

She might be the Slayer of the High, Tyn thought, but up close it was easy to understand how Vasethe had fallen for her.

Chapter Four

Res Lfae's door opened as she approached, and the smell of iron and spice wafted out into the cool morning. The demon's quarters were always perceptibly warmer than the rest of the Sanctum, as if Lfae's presence heated the air.

"You're late, Upstart," they called from somewhere within the house.

Tyn stepped inside. The entrance chamber held seven ancient bloodroot trees, their slim grey branches woven into a domed canopy overhead. The bark's sheen gleamed with mirror-brightness. Encircling them, the glass walls of the room glowed faintly; rich threads of blue light shifting slowly.

"I was not provided a specific meeting time, your Reverence," she called.

"Excuses, excuses. You were too busy charming the border keeper."

She smiled to herself, and followed the passage. Metal tracks ran over the floor and ceiling; rusted old spheres slid along them without a sound. Small stone medallions rotated in the air; they shivered when Tyn passed them.

Lfae sat on a jade-green bench in the conservatory, before the towering bow windows that overlooked the river. Their hair tumbled across their shoulders, collecting on the ground in a pool of sunlit platinum. They wore a shawl of gold spear-tips, with black velvet gathered at the neck. When they glanced over their shoulder, it was with a studied air of nonchalance, but Tyn recognised that their expression was troubled.

"You've made a strong impression on Midan," they said. "She likes you."

"Are you fighting?"

"Yes."

"Is it serious?"

They made a non-committal gesture. The spear tips clinked together like coins. "The disagreement won't last; our history matters to her. She is just very angry at the moment."

"Angry at you."

"Unfortunately, yes." They turned back to the river. Tyn followed their gaze. Two birds tussled along the pebbled shore, wings flashing in the sunlight. "We will get through it. We always have."

"And if you don't?"

"We will."

"Your Reverence . . ."

"Don't be so concerned, Upstart. It doesn't become you." They rose and stretched. "Besides, I didn't summon you here to interrogate me on my relationship with the border keeper. I hear Vehn suspended you. Do you want me to intervene?"

"No, thank you."

"Wise. But if the situation continues too long, I will."

"She wants what's best for the tribe."

"That doesn't mean I'll allow her to act the tyrant indefinitely. It serves no one."

"I understand," she said. "Did you really grant the border keeper empane status?"

"A graceless attempt to change the subject. No. I did not."

"Oh? Then—"

Lfae sighed. "I granted it to Vasethe."

He was here? "Why?"

"Because the Ahri-dweller is weak as a kitten, and Midan would murder me if any harm befell him."

"Is he . . . does that mean he's in danger?"

Lfae studied their nails. Again, attempting to look unconcerned. Something had rattled her ruler, and Tyn did not like it.

"It's only a precaution," they said. "For Midan's sake. A gesture."

It seemed like more than a gesture to Tyn. She was only aware of her ruler granting empane status to one other person in the last two centuries. It was a rule; empane status conferred the demon's protection to a guest, so that none of the dwellers of the 194th realm could wilfully harm that person without inflicting the same injuries on Lfae themself. The ultimate act of hospitality—and incredibly dangerous. It was one matter to extend that protection to the battle-hardened border keeper, but another entirely to offer it to Vasethe, who was all but defenceless.

"I wouldn't presume to question your judgement," said Tyn cautiously. "But are you sure—"

Lfae smiled. "I'm sure. Why, have I lost favour with the tribes? Do you think revolt is likely?"

"No, of course not."

"Spoken like a true conspirator. But I didn't summon you to discuss Vasethe either. Buyak's Tribunal is next week."

Despite herself, Tyn shivered. The face of the slick, smiling god rose in her memory, accompanied by a hot rush of shame.

"Oh," she said.

"Don't make that face." Lfae reached out and lightly brushed her cheek with the back of their hand. "He's locked up in a High realm now. Powerless."

"So you were successful, the night of the alert? The High heeded you?"

"The night you spent obediently recuperating in the infirmary?"

"When you failed to notice me, yes."

"You're lucky Vehn was distracted." Their humour faded. "Yes, the High listened. And apparently Buyak didn't even put up a struggle; he just let them take him away."

"You expected him to fight?"

Lfae did not answer her. They got up and walked over to the cabinet in the corner of the room, where they picked up a red scroll bound in reed and unfurled it.

"'Kan Buyak, God-King of the 200th Realm, Lord of Fluttering Wings and Speaker of Absolutes, will hereby be tried before a Tribunal of the High on charges of aiding his deceased conspirator Kan Fanieq, Ruler of the 41st Realm, Jasper Wreathed of the Nine, White-Crowned, in the forging of one or more God Instruments. May the truth serve the realms of Mkalis, may all voices be heard on this day.'" They let the parchment curl closed again. "It's going to take place in the 5th realm. Kan Helquas' domain."

"Interesting that the High selected a goddess's realm for the trial."

"Helquas isn't so bad. She's served as a Tribunal host before, so it was probably the most neutral decision under the circumstances."

"That must make her ancient."

"Quite." Lfae strolled back over to the window. "Until the

Tribunal commences, her channels have been suspended. No one goes in, no one leaves, and she'll establish new temporary channels to admit the attendees of the trial. Buyak is cut off."

"Then why are you so worried?"

They gave her an irritated look, but shrugged. "I'm not sure. I suppose I was just expecting something. Some resistance. Buyak's a coward, but he is not stupid; he knows the penalties when it comes to God Instruments. It's far better to die before ever going to trial."

"In that case, he must expect to win."

"It's a possibility." They rested their hands on the windowsill, drumming their fingers on the stone. "But we cannot allow that to happen. Buyak knows that I instigated the Tribunal against him; if he gets acquitted, he'll seek revenge. He would find allies to make that fight bloody."

"You'd still crush him, your Reverence."

They smiled slightly, a little sad. "Perhaps, but I have all of you to think about. Besides, it's the sort of war that has the potential to escalate. Reignite the old arguments, and gods will turn on demons once more. Which is why Buyak *must* lose the Tribunal." Their hands stilled. "I want you to testify."

Tyn's stomach dropped.

"I realise that it is a lot to ask," Lfae added. "You can take some time to consider."

She slowly shook her head, turning over the implications. The image of Buyak's face grew clearer in her memory. She could see his sneer as he mocked her ruler.

"No," she said. "No, he insulted you. I want to do it."

In the next room, one of the medallions flipped over in the air and fell to the ground with a hard clink. The smooth walls of the conservatory flickered with purple lights, and

Lfae's forehead creased.

"Trouble at the barracks," they said.

Matir. Tyn struggled to keep her face impassive. No doubt he had pushed Vehn too far. "May I . . . ?"

Lfae stared into the middle distance. "Don't worry, the situation has already been contained. No one is hurt. But yes, go. Use my Gate."

"Thank you, your Reverence."

"One more thing." Lfae's gaze cleared. "The newest member of the tribe? Please watch over him. He's struggling."

Tyn knocked her fists together, then hurried out of the house.

Lfae's Spinelight Gate stood a hundred feet from their door. Translucent orbs crisscrossed along the curved rails of the machine; the spheres transitioning from one colour to another. Milky green to pink to bronze and gold and blue, their movement gradual but ceaseless. The Gate produced a low hum, broken by small clicks when the orbs slipped onto a different set of rails. A famed property of the 194th realm, the Spinelight consisted of myriad invisible currents running over the mountainside and across the plain beyond. Lfae manipulated the currents into a series of short permanent channels, which allowed them to easily traverse the city and wider realm via their Gates.

A maroon sphere cycled around the widest of the tracks; Tyn reached out to touch it. When her hand met the glass, she vanished, only to immediately reappear in the yard in front of the barracks.

The smell of smoke assaulted her. Black clouds rose from the rear of the building; within, she heard indistinct shouting. *A fire?* She hurried inside. A grey haze hung in the air, and water pooled on the floor. Other Spears rushed to open windows, coughing and cursing, their clothes sodden.

When she reached the dining hall, she found it in shambles. The window drapes smouldered and the rugs were drenched. One table lay on its side, and all the benches had been knocked over.

In the midst of the chaos, Rion thrashed on the floor, restrained by Hale and Ninth Spear Saa. His face was smeared with blood; a thin cut bisected his right eyebrow.

"I'll make you regret this!" he yelled. "You have no idea who I am!"

Vehn stood at his feet, her hands clasped behind her back.

"You are nothing," she said.

"People will come for me, then you'll see." A thin sheen of sweat covered Rion's skin. His chest shuddered as he gasped for breath. "This place will *burn*."

"You are nothing," Vehn repeated, without inflection. "Seventh Spear, please escort Rion to the run-off. I will retrieve him tomorrow."

Hale hauled Rion upright in a single movement, pinning his arms behind his back. "Yes, First Spear."

"Let go!" Rion's mismatched eyes were bloodshot and wild, wide with anger and pain. He tried to kick Hale, but stumbled. "I said, let go!"

Vehn stood aside and gestured towards the door. She noticed Tyn.

"Something the matter, Upstart?" she asked.

Tyn shook her head. Hale passed her, manhandling Rion out of the hall.

"I hate you! I hate you all!"

"As you might have gathered, our newest recruit tried to

burn the barracks down." Vehn brushed loose hair back from her face. "Please assist with the clean-up."

"Of course."

Vehn opened her mouth as if she wanted to say something else, but changed her mind. Her shoulders were tight, and her hands were stained with ash. Small burns marked her fingers and wrists.

"Good," she said. "Carry on."

Tyn moved to the door, then wavered.

"Vehn, listen," she said. "I know I'm suspended, but if there's anything you need—"

"If I needed anything from you, I would ask."

The coldness of her voice stalled the words forming on Tyn's tongue.

"Yes, First Spear," she muttered.

Chapter Five

Lfae's new channel to the 5th realm opened in the Passage of Scarabs.

Soot covered the ground and glittered with flecks of bright saffron. The walls rose high, the colour of burnished chrome and soft as melting wax; so tall that their summits were lost in the haze of the sun-soaked sky. Thousands of jewel-coloured beetles—each easily the size of Tyn's fist—burrowed through the wall's surface, producing an unsettling and persistent chorus of scratching.

"I've only been here once before," said Lfae cheerfully. "It looked the same three hundred years ago."

One of the beetles crawled toward them and spread its iridescent green wings. It spoke with an eerie, thin voice; dry river reeds over smooth metal.

"The tithe, interloper," it whispered.

Vehn, to Lfae's right, held out a bloodstained hessian sack. A swarm of beetles detached from the wall and delicately lifted it from her grasp.

"Adequate," said the first beetle. "Welcome to the Realm of Submerged Fire, where dwells the Burning Empress, Fifth of the High."

"May her fire lay waste to those who speak against her name. May she be fed, always," intoned Lfae. "We are honoured and humbled."

The scarabs drew the sack into the wall. The surface bubbled and re-formed around the mass.

"We gather in the Chamber of Reckoning," said the beetle. "Follow, interlopers."

Tyn glanced past Lfae to Vehn. The First Spear appeared composed; her gaze sweeping the walls, ready to respond to any threat to her ruler. Her skull mask was newly painted with whorls of ochre dye, and the thin gold chains hanging from the horns clicked together when she moved like the warning of a rattlesnake.

"The Tribunal should be brief." Lfae strolled after the scarab. Their sheer black robes brushed the soot-covered ground. "If everything goes as expected, we'll be able to return to Tahmais in a matter of hours."

The ground sloped downwards as they exited the passage, and a shock of hot air filtered up from the hillside beyond. The scarabs buzzed through the air, polished wings gleaming. Tyn's breath caught.

"It's quite something, isn't it?" said Lfae.

Heat radiated from the city below. The metropolis smouldered like a burning coal; the great sweep of orange towers and bridges and roads and domes seared Tyn's vision, and it was *moving*, the buildings melding and re-forming, colossal palaces growing flaming buttresses, roofs banking low and folding into red-hot walls. Figures moved through the city, spindle-limbed creatures of fire with manes of yellow hair. Hundreds of them, howling over the streets; they frolicked and danced and fused together only to split apart in showers of white sparks. Clouds of scarabs swirled on the thermals above them.

It was dizzying. Tyn took a step backwards. Even Vehn

looked a little awed; through the slits of her mask, her eyes were wide.

"She *is* beautiful," said Lfae. They sounded wistful. "That's the nature of the High, I suppose."

"Come, interlopers," said the scarab. "You are expected."

For a confusing moment, Tyn thought that their guide would take them down to the city. But instead the scarab hovered before Lfae, swaying from side to side. The air beneath its wings shimmered.

With a tremulous ringing sound, a translucent golden dais appeared below the scarab. The insect dweller buzzed forward a few feet, and the platform grew larger.

"Follow," it said.

Lfae stepped onto the dais, which held firm beneath their weight.

"Where exactly is the Chamber of Reckoning?" they asked.

"You are expected."

"Not the greatest conversationalist, are you?"

Tyn followed Lfae and Vehn. The surface of the dais felt curiously liquid, as if the air had gained the consistency of dense mud. She bent down to touch it and her hand passed through a pliant film. She quickly withdrew her fingers.

The scarab flew higher, and the dais rose smoothly after it. Tyn's stomach lurched as the ground fell away. She froze up; once again memories of Addis Hal Rata rushed back to her, new and crisp and detailed. The blackened courtyard below Fanieq's windows, the yawning expanse beneath her feet, Vasethe shouting her name, and the cold fear that filled her mind, the panic that pushed aside every other thought and feeling, the terror that said: *you will die.*

"Eyes up, Tyn," murmured Lfae.

They spoke quietly, only for her. The demon did not say anything else, or even look in her direction. They continued to stare down at Helquas' city, an expression of polite appreciation and interest on their face. But they knew. They would hold her upright, if she needed it.

Tyn swallowed, glad for her mask. At least Vehn could not see her face.

Above them, a colossal stone cylinder descended from the sky. Its colour blended with the clouds, peach and yellow and pink, and hundreds of windows glinted along its curves like snake scales.

"Ah, so that's the Chamber," said Lfae.

The surface of their dais spread and darkened from pale gold to black, obscuring the city below. With a sharp clicking sound, it came to a stop. The scarab landed and folded its wings.

"Cross the bridge," it said. "Await the attention of the Burning Empress."

"Do you have any idea how long she'll be?"

"Cross the bridge."

A slender black ribbon extended from the edge of the dais, stretching out towards the cylinder. It widened to form a path. Tyn felt sick. Standing still was bad enough; the idea of walking across that narrow channel was intolerable.

"First Spear, if you would lead the way?" said Lfae.

Vehn strode forward without hesitation. She did not even afford the drop a glance.

"Let me take over, Upstart," said Lfae quietly. "I'll guide you."

"That's not necessary, your Reverence."

"I know you *can* do it yourself. But let me help. Close your eyes. Do I have your permission?"

She wavered, then nodded. Lfae's presence brushed against her mind, the touch light but unmistakably strong. Their concern radiated through the connection, and she closed her eyes.

Her legs moved. The wind drew swelteringly hot air upwards, but Tyn tried to relax and imagine that there was only solid ground beneath her. At her back, she could hear the rustle of Lfae's robes. She gripped her spear tighter.

Then Lfae's presence retreated from her mind and she came to a stop. She opened her eyes. The cylinder was in front of her.

"I am Res Lfae, Ruler of the 194th Realm, Marquis of the Spinelight and Wielder of the Machete," said Lfae. "I will heed the Tribunal of the High for Kan Buyak's impeachment."

A pause.

"You will heed," whispered the smooth, pale wall. The stone folded back to form an oval entranceway.

The chamber within was large and cool. Set into the walls and floor were transparent channels filled with slow-moving lava. Other rulers wandered around the room, pausing to speak to one another or to stare out the windows. Kan Moi was talking to his ghost child attendant, and Res Durani sat in a corner, humming to herself. A beige-skinned ruler Tyn did not recognise was sewing a strange, many-limbed ragdoll out of grey leather and gut-twine.

"Looks like half of Mkalis wants to watch Buyak burn," said Lfae. "Although it would seem the High are making themselves scarce. They must be planning to generate a spectacle."

"They're actually conferring on one of the higher floors."

Eris stepped through the entrance behind them. Her limp was gone. She was wearing a white tunic and skin-tight breeches, a long gold chain hanging from her neck. Lfae tensed as she drew closer.

"It seems there's a disagreement," she continued. "I'm not sure the nature of the argument, but it doesn't bode well for us."

Lfae bent their neck in greeting. "Border keeper."

"Don't look so stricken, Lfae. I won't bite."

They cracked a thin smile. "Are you sure? There was that occasion in Res Bekjan's domain—"

"Bekjan had it coming." She glanced over her shoulder, then sighed. "Look, I know my request was unreasonable."

"But you haven't forgiven me."

"I'm trying."

"I can wait. For what it's worth, I am truly sorry."

"No, save your apologies," she said, and looked over her shoulder again. "I haven't run out of options yet. But another time."

A slim, dark-eyed man stepped through the entrance, and Tyn made an involuntary sound. Vasethe nodded to Lfae, a slight smile hovering at the corners of his mouth.

"I feel like I'm always being healed by demon rulers," he said. "I'm in your debt."

"It was the efforts of the Terjia Tribe, not me." Lfae suddenly seemed to grow even more uncomfortable—as if uncertain, or perhaps even pained. "I'm glad the surrogate body could be salvaged."

"Your dwellers are a credit to you." Vasethe's eyes flicked towards Tyn. "Although I suppose that goes without saying."

She desperately needed to talk to him, but this was not the time, not with other people around, and definitely not while she was supposed to be serving as her ruler's aide. The whole situation had a strange atmosphere, as if hidden undercurrents rippled through the conversation, as if everyone was communicating in channels she had no access to.

"You are always welcome in the 194th realm." Lfae's tone struck her as almost deferential; they spoke to Vasethe like he was their equal. "It is the least I owe you."

Vasethe glanced at Eris, who nodded.

"I appreciate that," he said. "Although I'm not sure you owe me anything at all."

A stir spread through the crowd of rulers. The wall on the far side of the chamber had opened. A hooded man with unnaturally broad shoulders and a belt of keys walked through the gap. Behind him, manacled and serene, followed Buyak.

"The bastard arrives," murmured Lfae.

The silver-eyed god looked around the room and smiled benignly. He did not appear in the least concerned; if not for the restraints, he could have been another observer of the Tribunal. Other rulers drew away from him.

In unison, Tyn and Vehn stepped in front of Lfae. The movement caught Buyak's eye; his gaze alighted upon their ruler and then travelled to the border keeper.

He said something to his jailer.

"Why is he allowed this much liberty?" asked Lfae. "Surely a cell, some kind of cage filled with flesh-eating locusts—"

"He hasn't been found guilty yet," said Eris.

The jailer nodded. Buyak walked across the room. Hatred rushed through Tyn, but the feeling was laced with fear. The god's confidence disturbed her.

"Border keeper," Buyak's voice emerged smooth as oil. "I had hoped to see you before the start of the Tribunal."

Eris stared at him. Her expression was ice-cold and impassive, and she suddenly appeared taller.

"Nothing to say to me?"

"You are beneath her notice." Lfae's anger was palpable; the atmosphere grew close and dark in its wake, like all the air had been drawn out of the chamber.

"But evidently not beneath yours, Lfae," said Buyak. "Protective as always. Although I'm hardly a threat right now, so you might want to call off your guards. One of them has demonstrated a certain overzealousness in the past, and I'd rather not be assaulted."

"You should be more worried about *my* capacity for violence, god."

"Is that so?" Buyak laughed. "Well, I've heard the stories, but I assumed you'd matured since those days."

"For you, I'm willing to relapse. What do you want?"

Buyak spread his hands in appeasement. He had long, elegant nails, encrusted with tiny jewels. "I just wanted to offer my regards to the border keeper and her Ahri friend. Vasethe, was it?"

Eris' face grew even colder.

"Tell me, Vasethe," Buyak continued, "did she claim you? Or have you staked your claim in her?"

The suggestive lilt in his voice, the deliberate way his gaze travelled down Eris' body, left no doubt as to Buyak's meaning. For a split second, Tyn was certain that the god had gone one step too far. Eris became very still, and a painful ringing filled the room.

Vasethe brushed the back of the border keeper's wrist.

"Speaking of claiming, Kan Buyak," he said, clearly and with equal smoothness, "have you chosen a successor for the 200th realm? You might want to consider it prior to the Tribunal."

Buyak's smile did not slip. "A quick tongue you have there, mortal."

"I've heard it compared to silver."

From higher within the cylinder, a deep gong rang out. Tyn started. Without realising it, she had been holding her breath.

"It seems that the main event is about to begin." Buyak offered a low bow and turned on heel. "Please excuse me."

The border keeper did not blink, even as the god strolled back to his jailer. She seemed a hair's breadth from violence.

"Eris," Vasethe murmured.

"He knows," she said, unmoving as stone. "I should kill him now, and let procedure be damned."

"He said it himself, he isn't a threat. All he wants is to get under your skin. It's his best shot of surviving the Tribunal."

She finally looked away from Buyak. Vasethe met her gaze evenly.

"He's gloating," she said. "He knows he'll be cleared."

"Or he's bluffing," said Lfae. "Vasethe is right, Buyak is probably gambling on you making a mistake."

She was silent for a moment. Around the room, other rulers resumed their conversations and began to move towards the stairs at the centre of the chamber.

"I hope you're right," she said.

Chapter Six

The amphitheatre arena had no floor. Below the rows of stone seats lay the burning city, shimmering and shifting with heat. A bulb-shaped cell hung from a chain set into the distant ceiling. Buffeted by the winds, it swayed from side to side. Suspended between the bars of the cage was Kan Buyak.

He hung limply, his limbs swallowed within a tangle of black cords and braided ropes. A fly caught within a spider's web, waiting to be devoured. Only the lower half of his face was visible; pale against the darkness of the restraints. Despite his imprisonment, he was smiling.

"You may not accompany her inside the Avowal, physically or otherwise," said the scarab. "But you are permitted to occupy the adjoining box for the duration of the Tribunal."

Lfae's expression darkened. "As her ruler—"

"It is the will of the Burning Empress. You are permitted to occupy the adjoining box for the duration of the Tribunal."

Lfae had already been displeased when Helquas' insect dwellers escorted Vehn to a higher, closed-off region of the tower. Along with other rulers' attendants, the First Spear was forbidden a seat at the trial itself. The second revelation—that Tyn would face questioning alone—threatened to push the demon over the edge.

"I'll be fine," said Tyn.

They sighed and looked down at her.

"Are you sure, Upstart?" they asked. "You can change your mind; you don't need to do this."

She smiled and removed her mask. "I'm very sure, Your Reverence. Let me do my part."

They held out their hand and took the skull from her. "You know I'm proud of you, don't you?"

"I like to hear it."

The scarab rubbed its forelegs together in an impatient manner. "The Tribunal will begin shortly."

"Yes, yes, I'm going," said Lfae. "Honestly, I don't remember you lot being *quite* this annoying last time."

Tyn stepped into the Avowal. The room was small and open to the air at the front, where a straight-backed chair waited for her. Beyond, she could see the whole of the cavernous chamber; hundreds of stepped terraces ascending into the cylinder's core. A single lantern hung at the top of each terrace so that, looking upwards, the vault appeared studded with stars.

She took a deep breath and walked to the chair. Buyak's cage hung level with the Avowal. He slowly rotated within the cell. Although a web of ribbons covered his eyes, Tyn had the creeping sense that he could see her.

He looks smug, she thought. She leaned her spear against the wall and took her seat. The eyes of hundreds of rulers followed her movements. She could hear them calling to one another in the upper reaches of the vault, the inhuman shrieks and roars of their voices.

Where the wall of the amphitheatre curved away on the right, the border keeper occupied a second Avowal. Eris leaned over the balustrade and studied Helquas' city, apparently absorbed in her own thoughts. Further to her right, Vasethe occupied the third Avowal. He watched Buyak, arms folded.

With a click, the door closed behind her. The scarab flew over to the balustrade, neatly folding its wings as it landed. The vault quieted. Buyak's head tilted to the side, as if he was listening closely.

Then the city spoke.

"You are gathered, rulers of Mkalis," it said, in a voice like the cracking of dry wood in a bonfire. "The Tribunal is begun."

The words echoed all around and vibrated within the confines of Tyn's chest. Her skin itched. She leaned forward, gripping the arms of the chair. Far below, the city shimmered with heat, a fiery jewel set into the valley. Alive. Observing.

"Today, we decide the fate of the God-King Buyak, Ruler of the 200th Realm, Lord of Fluttering Wings and Speaker of Absolutes." A pause, as the goddess drew breath. "I, Helquas, sanctify this Tribunal."

A swarm of scarabs rose from below and ascended into the vault. They swirled around Buyak's cage in a glimmering, buzzing cloud. Then they drew into a single, tight mass and hovered at the level of his face.

"Kan Buyak, you are said to have conspired to forge God Instruments." The swarm hissed with Helquas' voice. "If this is so, you will be stripped of your realm and cast to the Lightless, which will tear your soul asunder. Speak. All lies shall be known."

The swarm dispersed with a whisper. Buyak was quiet for a moment. Then he laughed.

"I confess, I expected worse," he said. "'All lies shall be known.' How fitting; that mirrors my own realm's principles."

The vault was silent.

"Yes, the truth," he continued, unperturbed. "I am Kan Buyak, accused of conspiring an Instrument into existence. I wonder, will we hold Tribunals for merely thinking of Instruments in the future?"

The swarm circled around the cage.

"Are we now held accountable for our desires, or actions?" he said. "Because if it is the former, none of us will be found innocent. Nevertheless, I submit to this Tribunal. Ask what you will—I am not afraid."

"Truth," murmured the swarm.

From one of the lower terraces, a ruler stepped forward. Even stooped, he stood well over ten feet tall. His entire face was covered with eyes, although all but one had been stitched shut with red thread. It shone like a lamp in the middle of his forehead.

"I am Res Mirwich, Seer of the Thaw, Ruler of the 32nd Realm," he said. His mouth was set into the sagging skin of his long neck. "At the request of Kan Helquas, I will voice the questions of the assembly. We will hear from the accusers in turn."

Abruptly, the Avowal went pitch black. A moment later, a soft green light flared overhead.

"You will await the assembly's attention," said the scarab on the balustrade.

"I'm not permitted to hear the other testimonies?" Tyn got up and pressed her hands to the darkness in front of her. "Who speaks first, the border keeper or the Ahri-dweller?"

"You will await the assembly's attention."

"Right." She glanced at Helquas' dweller. "What did you think of Kan Buyak's response?"

The scarab did not deign to speak. After a few minutes, Tyn returned to her seat. She waited.

When the darkness peeled away, the sun had set and the

land beyond the city was shadowed. Bright eyes gleamed from the terraces above. Tyn's stomach clenched.

"Declare yourself," said Mirwich, in a rumbling baritone.

The web of black ribbons that swathed Buyak's cell now obscured him from view entirely. The other Avowals were cloaked in darkness. Had they given their testimonies already? Tyn wished she knew what had happened; she felt exposed and small and tongue-tied. She wet her lips.

"Revered Ones, I am Second Spear Tyn, dweller of Res Lfae of the 194th Realm," she said

"Lie," murmured the swarm.

"Sorry." Her heart sped up as the vault filled with whispering. "I *was* Second Spear, but I have been suspended from that role. Currently I'm just Tyn of the 194th Realm."

Mirwich blinked and spread his arms, gesturing for silence. He wore torn rags, and his pale grey skin showed through the rips in his shift.

"You attended Kan Buyak's convocation?" he asked.

"I did."

"It was your first time in Demi Anath?"

"Yes."

"And during the celebrations, you attacked a guest. This guest, according to the Ahri-dweller Vasethe, was the goddess Fanieq."

"I was not aware of that at the time, but yes." She cleared her throat. "As punishment, Kan Buyak proposed my execution. Res Lfae argued against this, and then the border keeper accused Kan Buyak of forging a God Instrument."

"At which point, she broke the rules of the realm by telling a lie."

Tyn nodded.

"What happened subsequently?"

"I departed the convocation with Res Lfae, the border keeper, and Vasethe, and we returned to my ruler's quarters within Demi Anath." Her tongue felt leaden and dry, but she strove to continue. "I was ashamed because I knew myself to be partly responsible for the border keeper's discomfort. I left my ruler's side."

That raised a stir through the upper terraces. Tyn's cheeks flushed.

"You disobeyed your ruler?"

"I—"

"This has nothing to do with Buyak's crimes!" Lfae's voice rang out from the terrace to Tyn's left. She could not see them from her angle, but they sounded furious. The lights above the terraces dimmed. An uncanny, rippling sound pulsed through the vault, then faded.

"Hold your tongue, Res Lfae," said Mirwich. "The questioning has begun; it will continue until the assembly is satisfied."

Tyn clenched the arms of the chair. She was disgracing her ruler. Again.

"Yes, I left Res Lfae's side," she said. "While they never specifically forbade me from doing so, I knew that they disapproved."

Low conversation, a murmur of gossip and scorn.

"And at this point, you entered Kan Fanieq's realm?" asked Mirwich.

"That occurred after Vasethe came to find me; we crossed together."

"Why would you enter the goddess's realm?"

"I failed to notice the channel."

"How?"

"It was . . . disguised. Very well disguised; I could not sense it. By the time I discovered the truth, we had already left the 200th realm."

More muttering. The rulers mistrusted her, Tyn could tell. Or believed that she was stupid. She burned with shame.

"This is in keeping with what we heard from the other accusers," said Mirwich after a pause. "We shall move on. Did Kan Fanieq ever specifically mention Kan Buyak in your presence?"

"Yes."

"Her words?"

"That I would find the channel back to Kan Buyak's realm in the antechamber of her throne room. It emerged in the Jifui Pass of the 200th realm."

"And you left via this channel."

"I did."

"Did Kan Fanieq say anything else with reference specifically to Kan Buyak and God Instruments?"

Tyn was silent for a moment.

"No," she said. "But the channel did emerge in his realm."

"That is not the matter we are concerned with. Did you see any other sign of Kan Buyak, or indication of his presence, in the 41st realm?"

But the channels, she wanted to insist. *Fanieq's plan could never have succeeded without Buyak's assistance.*

"I don't think so."

"Is there anything else you want to share with the assembly?"

There was an impatience to Mirwich's voice now; she had told them nothing new, nothing they had not already heard from Eris or Vasethe. She had been an idiot to think that she could help.

"No," she heard herself say. "No, that's all."

Mirwich opened his sunken mouth wide and an eerie cawing emerged from his throat. The darkness clouding the windows of the other Avowals cleared, and the net of black ribbons unfurled around Buyak's cage, falling away like dead petals. The god raised his head at the sound.

"We have listened," said Mirwich. "And now we shall ask questions of the accused."

Tyn tried to read Eris and Vasethe's expressions. The border keeper's face was blank, but Vasethe seemed perturbed. He caught her eye, and shook his head slightly. His testimony had not gone well either.

"Kan Buyak, you were in contact with Kan Fanieq during the period when the goddess was believed dead," said Mirwich. "You concealed your knowledge of her survival. Why?"

"The answer should be sufficiently obvious," said Buyak.

"Explain."

The god sighed. "Fanieq approached me four hundred years ago. I perceived that she was alone and afraid, perhaps even terrified, that the border keeper would discover she still lived. I offered her safe harbour."

"Why? How did that benefit you?"

"I pitied her. We formed a relationship over time."

"An intimate relationship?"

"Of a sort. She was vulnerable. It was difficult not to feel protective after she placed her trust in me."

Eris laughed loudly.

"Border keeper, be silent," said Mirwich.

"It's absurd," she said. "I'll admit that I despised Fanieq more than most, but this is an insult to her memory. Vulnerable? Terrified? Does anyone find this credible? Did any of you ever *meet* her?"

"Border keeper, you will be silent or you will be removed from the Tribunal."

"First's blood, the insinuation that she would sleep with this spineless invertebrate." Eris scowled and sat back in her seat. "Carry on, then. I'll be quiet."

Mirwich stared at her for a long moment.

"We remind you that the accused's lies will be known," he said.

"The accused is leading you."

Mirwich returned his attention to Buyak.

"You felt protective," he repeated.

"Yes. I did." Buyak's voice was controlled and calm.

"Were you aware of her plans?"

"I was aware that she wanted to . . . end the border keeper. To finally feel safe. As to the methods? No."

"You were not aware that she had forged a God Compass?"

"No. I had granted her access to all my channels; she could use them at will. She took advantage of that trust and my allies suffered."

"Your 'allies' were tortured to death, along with their dwellers," interrupted Lfae loudly. "Do you mean to suggest you knew *nothing* about that?"

"Res Lfae, you will not be warned again," said Mirwich.

Tyn had a terrible sinking feeling in her stomach. With Helquas' rules set against him, Buyak could only be speaking the truth. But her instincts screamed that this was wrong, that the sneering god opposite her was guilty.

"I will ask again," said Mirwich. "Kan Buyak, have you ever forged or possessed a God Instrument of any kind?"

"No."

"Did you abet Kan Fanieq in forging or acquiring a God Instrument of any kind?"

"No."

His refutations hit Tyn like physical blows. Buyak had rotated within the cage, and now he faced her. A hideous smile scored his face.

"Is there anything else you want to share with the assembly?"

"Only that I commend the border keeper's viciousness," he said. "What she did to Fanieq was . . . artistic."

Eris' jaw clenched. She stared at Buyak, and there was a murderous gleam in her eyes. Murmurs echoed in the heights of the vault, gathering in volume.

Then the darkness slid down once more, and Tyn was cut off from the scene. She held still, body tensed, expecting the vault to reappear and for someone to explain that there had been a mistake. The silence mocked her.

He had won. Again. He was innocent of every charge levelled against him. If the High had no grounds on which to impeach him, Buyak was as good as free.

Tyn realised she was shaking.

How? How did he do it? She pressed the base of her palms against her eyelids. *It's impossible; he* is *guilty.*

The scarab buzzed loudly, and she jumped.

"Welcome to the Realm of Submerged Fire, where dwells the Burning Empress, Fifth of the High," it said.

"What?"

The scarab rocked sideways on the edge of the balustrade. "Welcome to the Realm of Submerged Fire, where dwells the Burning Empress, Fifth of the High."

Tyn got to her feet. "Why are you saying that?"

It dropped, landing on its back on the Avowal floor. Its legs scrabbled at the air.

"Welcome to the Realm of Submerged Fire, where dwells the Burning Empress, Fifth of the High."

She knelt and tried to turn the scarab over. The needle-sharp claw at the end of its foreleg sliced her hand. She swore. Drops of her blood flecked the ground, and a line of red ran across her palm.

"Welcome to the Realm of Submerged Fire, where dwells the Burning Empress, Fifth of the High."

"Stop that, I'm trying to help you." Tyn managed to tip the dweller over.

It hissed at her, spreading its shining wings wide. Then, almost immediately, it flipped onto its back again. The frantic thrashing of its legs resumed.

Her skin crawled.

"Welcome to the Realm of Submerged Fire, where dwells the Burning Empress, Fifth of the High."

"Please stop saying that." The scarab's behaviour unnerved her; the expressionless, hollow quality to its voice. She walked to the door, and tried the handle. Locked.

"Welcome to the Realm—"

"Stop!"

The scarab fell silent. Its legs ceased moving, and only its antennae twitched.

"Let me out."

No response.

"The Tribunal's done. Please, just let me out." She tried the door again. It did not budge. She pushed against it harder.

A soft sigh. Silence.

Tyn looked over her shoulder as the door swung open.

"The Tribunal is finished," said Lfae brusquely. "The High will hold further conference before making a final decision, but Buyak's won. It's over."

She did not move.

"What's the matter?"

The scarab had disappeared. She stared at the ground where it had fallen. "It's gone."

"Tyn, I'm running very low on patience right now."

"There was a scarab in the chamber with me," she said. "One of Helquas' dwellers. It was behaving strangely, and then it . . . vanished."

"No doubt Helquas has summoned the creature home," Lfae said impatiently.

"But it kept saying the same thing over and over."

"And? This is what concerns you, after Buyak has succeeded in making us look like fools? After he has, yet again, cut Midan down in the eyes of the other rulers?" Lfae stalked away down the corridor.

"Your Reverence—"

"I don't want to hear it. Where is Vehn?"

Lfae's dismissal stung her. Their steps echoed on the floor, and their head moved angrily. She hurried after them. A goddess drifted by, trailing streamers of mist. Her heavy-lidded gaze found Tyn, and something between disapproval and amusement reflected in her eyes.

"First Spear?" barked Lfae.

Of course Lfae was angry. The Tribunal had been a disaster, and even if it had succeeded, Tyn had still shamed them before the entire assembly with her admission of disobedience. She had made them a laughingstock.

"I'm sorry," she said softly.

Lfae did not hear her. They reached the end of the corridor, where they spied Vehn.

"First Spear!"

Vehn turned. Her mask was in her hands, and she looked curiously distant.

"My apologies, your Reverence," she said. "I was distracted."

"Are you going to tell me about the habits of Helquas' dwellers too?" growled Lfae.

She bowed her head. "I don't follow, your Reverence."

"Never mind. Let's just get out of this place before I kill someone."

Tyn followed in their shadow. Guilt weighed down her every step.

Chapter Seven

In the quiet predawn stillness, Tyn slipped out of the barracks. Stars lingered in the lightening sky, and the pathways of the Sanctum were illuminated by the gently shifting colours of the walls. She wore plain clothes, nothing overt to mark her tribe or position. Her breath misted in front of her mouth.

She took the half-forgotten paths, through the wilder trees and across the river where it ran shallow. As the first birds roused and began to sing, she reached the Sanctum's western Spinelight Gate.

The mechanism whirred and clicked, and the rotating orbs pulsed with faint light. Of the five Gates within the Sanctum, this one was the least used, which was exactly why she had chosen it.

Six years, and she had never left the Sanctum without permission. She had never felt the urge to. But since returning from the Tribunal—or maybe before then, maybe ever since she had heard the bone snap in her arm, like she was made of porcelain, like she could be shattered with a thought—her sense of suffocation had grown steadily more painful.

The orbs clinked. Tyn hesitated, then placed her hand on an amber-gold sphere. The Sanctum vanished.

Within the space of a breath, she stood at a crossroads within the Sunlit Downs.

The rough-cut stone walls of the tunnel curved on either

side of her, and pools of light drenched the mossy ground below the ceiling vents. The warren of passages looped through the south side of the city's outer district. The passages flooded frequently in the winter, but their inhabitants did not mind. The Ilisa Tribe were the tenders of the waterways, listeners of the currents, and a flood marked the beginning of their season of dominance.

Tyn headed downhill, ducking around curtains of hanging spire-reed. Clumps of weeds blossomed in the cracks between stones; small, round flowers and sprays of apricot grass. From one of the smaller passages, she could hear the trembling chords of a water harp. A signal to rise—the tunnels would grow busier soon.

Would her absence be noted? Not for a few hours at least, and she could return before then. Besides, if she was suspended, surely she could do as she pleased? There was no reason she should be missed.

A man appeared at the door to his home, bleary and yawning. Like others of the Ilisa Tribe, his head was covered in a mussed crown of feathers and his eyes were over-large and yellow. He nodded to Tyn in greeting as he pulled on his boots.

"You all right there?" he asked. "Lost?"

She smiled. "No, I'm fine. Just taking a walk."

He yawned again, revealing a second row of serrated teeth. "Go well."

She carried on south, and the tunnels dipped deeper into the mountainside before rising again. More dwellers stirred from their homes; those she passed turned to watch her. Their attention wasn't unfriendly, but she was an oddity in their territory, especially for this time of the morning.

The passages converged on a broad city square. The intricate pattern cut into the ceiling of the Downs cast curving shadows over the ground. Beyond stood the Tedassa College. The edges of the building melded with the tunnels and the earth around it, and ancient trees snaked across the façade, heavy with hanging pink flowers. The front doors stood wide open.

Tyn drew up the hood of her coat. This was stupid. She knew she should just return to the Sanctum. What did she think she was going to accomplish here? If she left now, she could be back in the barracks before it was even time for breakfast.

The small foyer was dim and smelled of old paper. A pale woman with short blond hair sat at a desk, legs propped up on the surface. An assortment of strange potted plants obscured her view of the entrance, and she stretched to see over them when Tyn walked in.

"Hello. I don't believe I've met you before." The woman set down the book she had been reading. "How can I help?"

Tyn blinked, letting her eyes adjust to the gloom. "Is this the Tedassa College?"

"A small part of it; mostly general storage, with a few specialised laboratories. The main artefacts depository is in Yasebo End and the scholars' living quarters are in Three Locks. If you're looking for administration, you should probably have tried the main entrance; we're a bit out of the way down here."

"I just wanted to look around. If that's all right?"

The woman smiled warmly. "Are you interested in applying?"

"Sorry?"

"Are you interested in applying for admission to the College?"

Tyn thought, for a second, that she had misheard. "I could do that? I could be a scholar?"

"Certainly, although you would require permission from the ranking members of your own tribe. A number of scholars at the College are from Ilisa, more from Terjia. You are?"

"Kisdja."

"Huh. A Spear." She seemed impressed. "Unusual, but why not?"

Tyn felt rather stupid. "I thought Scholars were all from the Falei Tribe."

"All Falei are Scholars, but not all scholars are from Falei." The woman got up from behind her desk. "If you can balance the research with your obligations of the Spears, it shouldn't be a problem. What's your name?"

For an awful moment, Tyn's mind went blank. She should not be here, this wasn't her place—

"Raisha," she said.

The woman inclined her head politely. "I'm Naamkis. If you're interested, I could show you around?"

Vehn was going to be furious when she found out about this.

"I'd like that," said Tyn.

The building was far larger than it appeared from its exterior in the Sunlit Downs and, as Naamkis explained, most of the College was actually built on street level. The underground facilities were used for storage or more sensitive research, or for the benefit of dwellers with an aversion to sunlight. As the Falei Tribe was observing a weeklong fast, the corridors were quieter than usual and many of the laboratories had been locked up.

"It's a bit lifeless at the moment," Naamkis explained, a little apologetic, as she led the way upstairs. "Normally it's far more interesting."

They emerged in a corridor crowded with large, angular boulders of a dark blue stone. The rocks' surfaces gleamed and threw back slightly delayed reflections, two steps behind Tyn. She peered at them, intrigued.

"You'll want to keep away from those," said Naamkis. "They do strange things to your dreams and we aren't sure why. Scholar Lesell insisted she'd have them moved, but then she took a trip to the Besiva Fjord and we haven't heard from her since."

"What sort of strange things?"

"Oh, prophetic visions, a sense of impending doom, the conviction that you are being stalked by malign forces. Although the effects are temporary, I've heard they're quite alarming."

"Right." Tyn stepped back.

"I'm sure someone will remove them at some point."

The upper halls were brighter. Morning sunlight flooded through the high-peaked windows of the corridors, and warm drafts of air drifted in from the overgrown courtyards. Naamkis led her through observation chambers and seminar rooms and laboratories. She explained the ongoing projects of prominent Scholars: testing the quantities of different minerals in terjic clay, documenting the movements of the mountain and the city over time, recording changes to the ambient air temperature around Lfae's channels—how it varied depending on the strength of their diplomatic ties with the ruler in question. In the Inventory, she showed Tyn the skeletons of animals predating Lfae's rule of the 194th realm; massive creatures with thick, fibrous black bones, the cracked exoskeleton of a species of giant crustacean. They visited the Historical and Artistic Preserve ("this is only a small collection, the most important artefacts are kept in Yasebo End"), where annals and manuscripts and paintings regarding Lfae's overthrow of Kan Temairin and rise to rulership were stored in polished glass cases. A portrait of Lfae during their Ascension caught Tyn's eye.

"They had dark hair," she exclaimed. "And it's *short*."

Naamkis laughed. "Well, yes. Although by many rulers' standards, Res Lfae's personal body alterations are rather plain."

The blunt, unexceptional features of her ruler struck Tyn as impossibly strange. The person in the portrait had close-cropped mousy brown hair and weathered skin, lines branching out from their eyes and mouth. In her mind, Lfae had always been ageless and unchanging. To see them like this made her feel vaguely uncomfortable.

"How old were they when they defeated Kan Temairin?" she asked.

"We are not entirely certain, but we think they had lived in Mkalis for around forty-five years? They say they've forgotten." Naamkis smiled fondly at the painting. "I'm inclined to think they just don't want to tell us."

"Huh." Tyn stared at the portrait.

"Shall we carry on?"

"Sure." She dragged her eyes away from Lfae's face. "Of course."

They left the Preserve and climbed a flight of stairs into a new building, or perhaps a higher floor of a building they had already visited—Tyn struggled to maintain her sense of direction; the College seemed to wind back on itself, each department connected by endless corridors and passageways. Here was where Scholar Olase was conducting research on Spinelight weather; through that door was Restricted Experimentation—they had recently uncovered a hex that could permanently erase memories, very controversial, the whole College was talking about it. The ethical implications alone . . .

Through the windows, the sun blazed down. Midday. It was far later than Tyn had expected.

"Everything all right, Raisha?"

She flinched. "Uh, yes. Sorry, I was distracted. Where are we now?"

Naamkis reached a pair of doors with curved bronze handles, the metal worn smooth by thousands of hands over hundreds of years. She pushed them open.

"This is the library," she said.

The black cherry wood shelves ran in neat rows from one side of the hall to the other, and the air was full of whispering. Tables piled high with books stood between the stacks, and mist lamps shone down on the texts, catching on gold-embossed spines and metal casings. Stone statues of grotesque creatures perched on top of the shelves.

"It's the heart of the College," said Naamkis, stepping inside. "The Scholars' Haven."

Tyn cast around. "Where does the whispering come from?"

"Oh, the library talks to itself."

"The books?"

"No, I don't think so." Naamkis looked thoughtful. "It's more like memories are conversing. You learn to ignore it very quickly."

The low susurration of murmurs rose and fell like ocean

waves, like breathing. Tyn walked forward slowly. At the end of the hall, she could see more doors, and archways leading to reading rooms and studies. The place was enormous. There didn't appear to be anyone else around, but for all the space, it didn't feel lonely.

"It's beautiful," she said.

Naamkis gave a small laugh. "Not so much during the exam season. But it's home."

Tyn's chest tightened.

"Do you think—" She stopped. Took a breath. Her voice came out small and guilty. "Do you think Res Lfae ever assigns dwellers to the wrong tribe?"

Naamkis did not rebuke her or seem shocked. She leaned against a shelf.

"A better question is whether anyone is ever assigned to the right tribe," she said. "Not to become too philosophical about it, but who could ever perfectly embody the essence of a Spear or a Scholar? Everyone is infected, in some way, with complication. Parts that don't fit."

"But maybe some of us could fit better elsewhere."

"Maybe. Maybe not. In the end, maybe all we are is where we are—a place and a time and the people around us."

Tyn was silent.

Naamkis straightened up. "Why don't you stay a while? Browse the books. Even if you're not admitted to the College, you're welcome to visit whenever you like."

She patted Tyn on the shoulder as she left. Sweet and honest and perceptive. The doors closed with a quiet click and her footsteps faded down the corridor. Tyn gazed around the room, taking it in, listening. The voices ran over one another, and none spoke in any language she recognised. She wandered down the first aisle, not touching the books.

I was a scholar?

One of the best, whispered Vasethe's ghost.

"So much for that," she said aloud.

The air was cool and dry and still, and she was entirely alone. Each shelf was set with bronze plates detailing the subject matter of the tomes: undersea dwellers of the Fathomless Lake, agricultural practises of the Ghedhi Tribe, insects of Tahmais and the Spinelight Region. Whole shelves devoted to the most obscure minutiae, the kind of thing that she had never given a second thought. And then more books, books about other realms, other times, gods and demons she had never heard of, witches, obscenities, and miracles.

She passed into the next room, then the next. It would be easy to get lost here, drowned in knowledge. The whispering continued, but Naamkis had been right; Tyn hardly heard it after a while. She paused before a shelf on the Kisdja Tribe, glancing over the titles, then continued. How many years had the Scholars devoted to building this place? An inexplicable sadness trailed after her, a kind of yearning nostalgia.

The library grew less orderly as she pressed deeper; piles of books collected on the floor, cobwebs tied volumes to their shelves. Mist lamps burned dimmer, and the light from the windows caught the dust that she stirred up as she walked. Parasitic Dwellers of the 124th realm. Private Languages of the Scabclad Alliance. Ruler Courtship of the Blessed Era.

A spiral staircase tucked into the corner of the hall caught her eye. The wooden banister was cracked and a stack of books barricaded the way. Tyn stepped over them and climbed. The door at the top stood slightly ajar, and a colder draft blew through it.

She peered inside. The attic was small and crowded, some kind of storeroom. A broken ottoman leaned against the wall, feathers poking out from a rip in the upholstery. Shattered mist lamp globes gathered in a wicker basket hanging from the grip of a snub-nosed stone statue, and a single bookcase stood against the far wall.

Tyn cocked her head to one side. The whispering had stopped.

She glanced over her shoulder and then stepped inside, closing the door behind her. She could not have said why, but she felt drawn to this place. A narrow, grime-streaked window above the ottoman cast hazy yellow light over the room. The silence felt heavy after the soothing murmur of the rest of the library; she was aware of every sound she made, creaking floorboards, the rustle of her clothes.

The shelf was half-empty and the books themselves were falling apart, bindings frayed and pages slipping free. Apart from the manuscripts in the Preserve, nothing in the College had looked this old. Tyn leaned close to read the titles, her breath lifting dust from the leather covers.

Crisis Strategies of the War of Black Sands. Verified Observations on the Nature of the Lightless. Dweller Subjugation: Methodologies and Mistakes. Pain and Fear: Altered Rules, Altered Forms. The Means to Control a Witch. God Instruments and Their Makers.

She shivered, both disturbed and intrigued. These could not be Lfae's books, and they didn't seem like the kind of research they would condone either. Although perhaps, earlier in their rulership ... She ran her fingertips over the spines. More likely, some Scholar had smuggled them into the realm without Lfae's notice. She picked up *God Instru-*

ments and Their Makers.

The book was heavier than it looked. She turned it over in her hands. No author. The supple vellum cover was scorched on the back, as if it had been rescued from a fire at some point. She gently prised apart the pages. The ink had faded to a pale brown, difficult to decipher against the yellowed parchment. She moved closer to the light to read the preface.

God Instruments. So named because of their capacity to bridge the divide between Dweller and Ruler, to replicate the power of blood-command, to wield the ability to alter. Or indeed, in the hands of a Ruler, to amplify that ability. Here within, we describe the known forms that such Instruments may take, the Wielders who have so designed them, and the methods by which these tools may be forged.

With God Instrument in hand, a Wielder stands amongst those who rend sharply through the staid ties of history to revise the world according to their Will.

A part of her wanted to close the book and return it to the shelf. There was something wheedling in the writer's tone, an insidious slant to the letters. Tyn turned to the contents page, running her eye down the list of chapters until she found the section on God Compasses.

The first successful forging of a God Compass dates back to the Damasked Era, when Kan Rodan of the 84th realm captured and subsequently slew Res Alyne of the 433rd realm. According to the records of his Principal Observer, Kan Rodan took sixteen months to craft the Compass. His efforts were likely hampered by sundry allies of the late Res Alyne attempting to invade his realm, and it may be assumed that under ideal conditions the process could be expedited.

The God Compass grants its Wielder the capacity to move freely between all the Realms in existence without the consent of the Rulers of such Realms. In addition, it also bestows the Wielder with the ability to unfailingly Quest the souls of others – irrespective of whether such souls have passed through the veil of death or not. This dual function is unusual, and highly sought after amongst the Ambitious and the Vengeful.

Kan Rodan's work was later replicated by other rulers, including Kan Ibe, Kan Berthiermis, Res Phenea—

A sharp pain flared at the base of her neck. Tyn lost her grip on the book, but she grabbed it automatically before it could hit the floor.

For a moment, all she felt was confusion. Then fear surged through her. That was the alarm hex. Her tribe was in trouble.

She shoved *God Instruments and Their Makers* into her satchel and raced from the room. The pain pulsed just above her shoulders, thudding in time with her heartbeat. As she sprinted through the stacks, she could hear raised voices outside the College walls.

She threw the library doors open and careered out into the corridor. No time to return to the Sunlit Downs, she would leave via the front doors; it didn't matter if she was recognised. Through the tall windows, she could see the warning flares flicking to life over the top of the city wall.

A few Scholars milled around the foyer, anxious and uncertain. She ran through their midst and out into the early evening. When had it gotten so late? How had she spent so much time here? Someone called after her; she ignored them.

The pain in her neck suddenly blazed—one bright, sharp stab. Then, coldness. Tyn gasped.

A ranked Spear was dead.

Chapter Eight

The streets of Tahmais were in turmoil. Tribe leaders called dwellers into fortified buildings, and district runners combed the streets for stragglers. Tyn cut through their midst, swerving around abandoned rickshaws and carts, running at a dead sprint. Dread clenched around her heart like a closed fist.

She reached Oracle Square, where the Ducaift District's Spinelight Gate sedately rolled and clicked. Clasping a stitch in her side, she reached for the maroon orb. Her palm met the surface of the sphere and she closed her eyes.

Nothing happened. The sphere rolled away down the rails.

With increasing apprehension, she tried other Gates to the Sanctum, Gates that had always been open to her. Again and again, she was denied. She snarled, and grasped the orb to the Turolt District Gate instead.

The world blinked and she stood in the shadow of the Sanctum. The sun reflected blood red on the ring of crystal walls; warning flares gleamed purple against the sky. Here, there were no dwellers; the district had gone to ground already.

Tyn ran up to the gates of the Sanctum.

"Second Spear Tyn," she gasped. "Open."

The command did nothing; her authority was no longer recognised by the hexes. She pounded on the doors.

"Let me in!"

She hammered on the wooden surface, and the sound

echoed across the square. A flock of birds flew up from the rooftops. No response.

Tyn rested her forehead and arms against the smooth grain of the wood, chest heaving.

"Okay," she whispered. "Think. *Think*."

Pain flared at her neck again. Another Spear dead. Her breathing hitched. Why had she left the Sanctum? Why was this happening now?

She turned and continued running. Her legs burned from exertion. There were no other gates to the Sanctum, but if she could access the run-off—the underground system that channelled the river below the city—she might still be able to get inside. She glanced up in time to see the emergency flares turn white gold. The signal to evacuate.

The sun blinded her as she rounded the wall's southern corner, but there, mercifully, was the storm water drain. It was set into a recess next to the road, nondescript and easy to overlook, no different from countless others throughout Tahmais. However, if she was right, this one should lead to an escape route through the waterway—Lfae had told her about a hidden switch inside the tunnels. She gripped the metal bars and heaved.

The grate hardly moved. Tyn swore. She braced her back against the Sanctum wall, tightened her grip, and pulled again. The muscles in her arms and shoulders protested, but this time she managed to shift it a few inches. She paused for breath, her heart pounding.

The third attempt was enough; she made a gap that she could squeeze through. With a grunt, she let go of the bars.

The rungs of the ladder below were freezing cold and beaded with moisture. Tyn clambered down the shaft. Ilisa

Tribe hexes marked the walls, and grew brighter to illuminate the space as she descended. The muted roar of the Sanctum river echoed through the shaft.

She dropped to the ground and shrugged off her satchel and coat, leaving them beside the ladder. Sweat chilled her exposed skin. It appeared that no one had used the tunnel in decades; a thick layer of dark green algae covered the floor and abandoned blackfur moth cocoons hung from the ceiling. Tyn hurried to the door at the end of the chamber. The handle stuck; she shoved it downwards.

She was battered by sound. The run-off falls, thirty feet high and almost as wide, poured down from the inlet at the top of the wall. The torrent pooled in the cavern before flowing out into the city's network of tunnels and pipes, diverted and funnelled through the subterranean maze until it reached the overflow, where the water cascaded freely down the slopes of the mountainside.

There was only a narrow ledge before the basin. Tyn kicked off her boots, took a deep breath, and stepped into the pool. The water wrapped around her legs eagerly, its touch bone-achingly cold. She set her teeth to stop them from chattering and waded forward. Under her bare feet, the stones were smooth; the ground sloped steeply downwards and water rose up to her waist. Spray misted in white plumes below the falls.

There is a switch at the top of the run-off, and another at the base, Lfae had explained, laying out emergency procedures for her. *On the Sanctum side, it's accessible via a hidden chute. On the city side, you'll have to swim.*

Treading water, Tyn deepened her breathing.

If you dive under the falls, you'll find a tunnel.

She plunged her head beneath the water. The roar of the

run-off was instantly muffled. She swam forward.

It isn't large. It would be easy to miss.

The pressure of the falling water drove her downwards. The animal part of her brain resisted; urged her to turn around, away from the terrible, ceaseless thundering rush. The water seethed with bubbles, and she moved blindly. Kicked. Her fingertips found the rear wall, and she worked her way sideways until she came to an empty space.

At the end of the tunnel, you'll find a lever.

Using the walls of the passage, Tyn pulled herself out from beneath the falls. Opened her eyes. The tunnel was coal dark. She swam forward, fighting her intensifying sense of claustrophobia, navigating by touch.

Her hand closed on a metal bar. The lever. She gripped it with both hands and wrenched sideways. The bar swung left with a dull shriek.

Limbs tangled, Tyn managed to turn and kick off the rear wall of the tunnel, propelling herself back towards the falls. Her skin was freezing, but her lungs burned; lines of fire seared her air-starved limbs. Under the crushing torrent once more, and then she burst through the surface, gasping.

A path will open.

The falls had parted, leaving a thin channel between two cascades. Iron rungs glinted silver-blue in the hex-light.

She had her way into the Sanctum.

Tyn swam over to the ladder and grabbed the lowest rung. The roaring made her head spin, tonnes of raging water crashing down on either side of her. She heaved herself out of the pool—half-deaf and shaking—and climbed.

At the top of the run-off, a small crawlspace slanted into the roof. There was light on the other side. Tyn pulled herself through the gap and into the room beyond, and collapsed onto her back. Straw covered the floor; it stuck to her wet hair. She squeezed her eyes shut and panted, trying to catch her breath.

The pain in her neck was muted now, an ominous buzz at the edge of her awareness. Whatever had killed her tribemates still lurked within the Sanctum. With a grimace, she sat up. Her clothing clung to her, but it was warmer here. Uniform rows of barred cells ran the length of the chamber, and flickering lamps hung from the rafters.

She rolled over and got to her feet. Seldom used, the prison had a faintly musty smell, an undercurrent of dryness and long decay. The walls were shaped from solid slabs of dark-red stone, and set with centuries-old defensive hexes. Water thrummed beneath the floor.

Her cell door was unlocked. She hurried to the stairs, leaving a trail of wet footprints in her wake.

When she emerged from the prison entrance, concealed behind the fringe of ancient willow trees, the twilight sky had faded to lilac. The Sanctum had fallen quiet, the birds and insects vanished, and only the low gushing of the river disturbed the silence.

Tyn listened for a few seconds. Then, keeping to the shadows of the trees, she crept forward. The path past the barracks would be the fastest route to Lfae's house, but it left her with almost no cover. She moved in the direction of the infirmary. Better to remain unseen for now. The water covered the sound of her footfalls.

The first body lay below the trees, like a root protruding from the soil. The Healer's head was turned towards Tyn, but he stared unblinking at the ground. A trickle of blood stained his lips. Judging by the trail of crushed undergrowth, he had been fleeing from the infirmary. And by the stab wound just below his shoulder, he had been attacked from behind. A single wound. It had not been a fight.

Tyn crouched beside him and mechanically checked for a pulse. The man's skin was already cooling. His glazed eyes felt like an accusation.

"I'm sorry," she whispered.

Up until then, the situation had retained an element of unreality. She had believed, somehow, that it had all been a mistake. Tyn shut the man's eyes.

She needed to find Lfae.

Another Healer lay slumped against the wall of the infirmary, her throat opened and her blood splattered across the wall. A third body had fallen across the doorway, but Tyn could not see the person's face.

How many? she wondered, numb. *Where is my tribe?* The Spears should have defended the other dwellers in the Sanctum; it was their duty, their purpose. Had the attack occurred too quickly for them to prevent it? She sidled around the building. Why was no one else *here*?

The grove surrounding Lfae's house stirred in the breeze. Tyn moved from the shadow of the infirmary into the trees, and crouched in the undergrowth. Her heart beat quicker, but she kept her breathing soft. *There should be more noise; it's too quiet.* She stole closer to the walkways, and winced when something small and sharp dug into her heel.

Fragments of coloured glass littered the damp soil. Lfae's mechanical creature appeared to have shattered; small golden cogs were scattered amongst the grass. Tyn pulled the splinter from her foot. A smart move, to take out her ruler's eyes. The wind hushed through the grove. A calculated move.

The walls of Lfae's house were visible through the branches. Tyn crept closer, padding from one tree to the next. A coppery scent reached her nose. Blood. Everything was still; she could detect no movement through the windows. She edged along the wall of the building until she could see the front door. Her heart sank.

Third Spear Chitanda lay across the walkway, her right arm brushing the earth. Her face was slack, and blood dripped steadily through the gaps between the wooden boards beneath her.

Tyn ducked back behind the wall, breathing more heavily. Chitanda, quiet, focussed, with an easy, unexpected laugh. She had held her position almost as long as Vehn. When Tyn took the role of Second Spear, Chitanda had woven a wreath of flowers and hung it from her door, to prove that the Third Spear harboured no ill feelings.

Tyn closed her eyes, steadied herself.

Chitanda's spear had rolled into the yellow grass. Tyn picked it up and carefully stepped over the fallen tribeswoman's body. A stab wound through the heart, a quick death. Once again, only a single injury, and no obvious signs of a struggle.

Tyn entered the house.

The bloodroot trees stood sentinel over the room, casting the faintest of shadows on the floor. Through the canopy, the sky had darkened to navy blue. Lights fizzled and sparked across the glass walls, bursts of sickly yellow and muddy orange. Tyn rolled Chitanda's spear within her palm. A long streak of blood ran from the centre of the bloodroots through the passage and out to the conservatory.

She readied the spear and strode through the doorway.

Hale was propped up against the jade bench below the windows. He stiffened when she appeared and then his fear melted into relief.

"Tyn," he whispered. "Ruler's mercy, you scared me!"

She hurried to his side. His right leg was streaming with blood, his clothing soaked with it, and his skin was ashen and filmed with perspiration. He grasped her hand.

"Where *were* you?" he demanded.

Explanations died on her tongue. "What happened? Where is Res Lfae?"

"They're gone, I think." He grimaced as she peeled away the fabric covering his thigh. "I think everyone else is too, everyone from the Sanctum."

The light through the windows was low; she set down the spear and peered closer. "I need to staunch the bleeding until I can find help."

"Chi and I were teaching initiates at the stables when we felt the death. Got back here just as the beacons were lit." He shuddered as Tyn applied pressure to the gaping wound in his leg. "The Sanctum was already deserted; we were left behind. Chitanda—"

"I saw." She took his hand, made him press it to his own leg. She pulled her wet shirt off and looped it around his thigh to make a tourniquet. "Who did this, Hale?"

A flash of light sheared past Tyn's ear, and an unearthly howl ripped through the air. Hale jerked once, his head snapping backwards against the bench as his eyes grew wide. A red gash split the centre of his forehead.

Tyn screamed. A breath later, pain flared and froze over her shoulders.

"I see that the lure drew in larger prey."

Footsteps behind her. Tyn grabbed Chitanda's spear and scrambled to her feet.

"Lfae's little favourite. It seems fortune shines upon me."

Buyak stood silhouetted against the doorway. He held a sword in his left hand, and his normally groomed hair hung loose around his face.

She lunged at him, swinging her spear around to cut across the god's midriff. With another ear-splitting shriek, his sword deflected the attack. The force juddered up Tyn's arms. She shifted her weight backwards and drove her weapon towards his throat. Blocked again.

"Why were you left behind?" he asked pleasantly.

She snarled, drove her heel down, and struck as hard as she could. Buyak flicked his sword, and the blow glanced aside. The blade of his weapon seemed to morph in the shadowed observatory, changing colour and size, the air around it shimmering like a heat haze. It screamed with every movement. A woman's voice.

Buyak casually rotated his wrist and the sword snapped forward like coiled lightning. A lock of Tyn's hair fell to the floor. She stumbled backwards.

"Your ruler has something I need," he said. "Where are they?"

She was not going to beat him like this. Tyn feigned an attack to his right flank, then followed the motion of her swing and rushed past him. She leapt through the doorway and down the passage to the bloodroots.

"Step and turn, tear asunder and reform," she said breathlessly, and fell through the shadow of the trees. Colour vanished from the room; her vision was reduced to sharp-edged shades of grey.

"That's a nice trick. A property of the Spinelight?" Buyak followed her into the room, unhurried.

Tyn stifled her breathing. The god would only catch glimpses of her when she moved; so long as she crossed between the shadows of the bloodroots, she would remain hidden. A gambit Lfae had built, an added advantage if the Sanctum were ever invaded. She stepped forward, and was on the other side of the ring. The spear was warm in her hands. She aimed.

"Still, it won't help you."

Putting the full weight of her body behind the movement, Tyn threw. Chitanda's spear soared through the space between her and Buyak, true and fast and deadly, straight for his heart. No time for him to react, no way for him to anticipate the attack.

His sword howled and split the spear in two.

Impossible!

Buyak raised his weapon. With a lazy gesture, he cut through the air.

The bloodroots, centuries-old and hex-fed, crashed down in an avalanche of falling branches and silver leaves, and colour snapped back into the world. Tyn stumbled out of the way.

"See?" he said.

She ran for the front door, but it slammed in her face. Something heavy and blunt collided with the back of her head; she staggered and fell to her knees. Lights danced before her eyes.

Footfalls behind her. She had to move. She had to get up. Buyak grasped her shoulder and roughly cast her onto the ground.

"I'm not going to kill you yet," he said. "Consider it thanks for your help in disposing of Fanieq."

The god's face swam above her. His silver eyes gleamed through the darkness like twin moons.

"If you want to stay alive," he continued, "you'll find your ruler and tell them to cooperate with me. Deliver them to me, and I might decide against grinding this realm to dust."

Despite her pain and fear, Tyn couldn't help but feel scorn for him; an instinctive sense of revulsion in his presence. He was no god, no ruler—pitted against Lfae, Buyak was nothing at all.

He must have seen her thoughts written on her face. A second later, an invisible force drove into her midriff.

"Don't take my generosity for granted. You will live only so long as you are useful to me," he said.

May as well die, then, she wanted to reply, but she was too winded. She wrapped her arms around her stomach. Had to get up.

"Lfae has a simple choice to make. The channel to my realm remains open to them." He reached into his pocket and drew out a single pearl-white egret feather. He dropped it in front of her. "Speak my name to this when you've found them. I want you to know that Lfae can come of their own accord, or I can conquer them. But if I'm forced to take the latter option, it would benefit you to be in my good graces."

He turned and the front door swung open before him.

She had to stop him. With shaking arms, Tyn pushed herself to her knees, used the wall to rise. It was so hard to breathe. She shambled after the god, and her sight dimmed at the peripheries of her vision. Chitanda's body lay across her path, blood drying, coagulating now.

"Come back," she wheezed, but Buyak could not hear her. He strode away down the walkway, his sword glinting quicksilver bright. Tyn lurched down the path. Her legs tangled and she fell again.

When she looked up, Buyak was at the Spinelight Gate. Then he was gone.

Chapter Nine

Inside the infirmary, three more bodies.

The dead of the Terjia Tribe: First Healer Uban, Sixth Healer Lendeso, Seventh Healer Teo, Twelfth Healer Abathei, Thirteenth Healer Parl. The dead of the Kisdja Tribe: Third Spear Chitanda, Seventh Spear Hale, Eleventh Spear Jevin. Eight ranked tribespeople, murdered by Buyak.

Tyn applied a mask of terjic clay to the lump on the back of her head, slathering the yellow mud over her hair. She was no Healer, and the hexes worked sluggishly. Fragments of shattered vases were strewn across the recovery room. One of the walls had collapsed, and plaster and rubble covered the ground. It looked like Buyak had ransacked the building. The Healers had probably just stood in his way.

She wiped her hands clean on a rag and stood up, testing her balance. Better. In a few hours, she should be able to fight again.

The emergency beacons had burned out at last. Throughout the city, Lfae's dwellers would begin to emerge from hiding, anxious and confused, hungry for answers. Tyn descended to the infirmary basement and fetched a shovel from the Healers' store. The city would wait for daybreak. She wasn't ready to face it yet.

In the Kisdja memorial grounds, beneath the jacaranda trees hung with bone and copper wire, she dug.

A rich yellow moon rose over the Sanctum wall. The soil was soft. She rested from time to time; whenever the dizziness grew too strong, she stopped to drink from the river. Her progress was slow, but steady. The terjic clay eased the swelling on her head, and formed a scratchy cake of hair, sweat, and mud. Her clothing dried.

The top layer of soil was loose and fine; it took a few hours to clear the earth up to the corners of her pit, enough time for the moon to climb to its full height. But the next seam was harder, pitted with rocks and the snaking roots of the jacarandas. By the time Tyn stood knee-deep in the hole, she was spent.

She leaned against the trunk of a tree, taking a moment to breathe. Her hands hurt. Dirt streaked her skin and, in spite of her exertions, she felt chilled to her core. While she was occupied with the ceaseless rhythm of digging, she could keep her thoughts at bay, keep her feelings contained. One shovelful of dirt bled into the next. But, standing still, the image of Hale's face returned to her.

Where were you?

A twig snapped. Tyn's eyes flew open; she dropped to a crouch, snatching the shovel out of the grass and swinging it up to strike—

Rion raised his hands in alarm. "Don't hurt me!"

The sudden, violent surge of adrenaline sent Tyn's head spinning. She stumbled back, dropping the shovel, and braced herself against the tree.

"You can't surprise me like that," she said hoarsely.

"I wasn't trying to!"

"Then be more careful." Her legs trembled, and she sat down. "I could have killed you."

His lantern dazzled Tyn's eyes. "You don't look like you could kill anyone."

Now that the rush of fear was receding, relief edged in to take its place. She was not alone. Another Spear, even a new, untested one, another person from her tribe.

"You're still here," she said.

He shrugged.

"Are you hurt?"

"I stayed hidden from that god, if that's what you're asking." He tried to cross his arms, but the lantern made it awkward, so he uncrossed them again. "I wasn't going to be slaughtered like the others."

"You were left behind."

"Clearly didn't make the cut." He shifted his weight to his other foot. "And you? You thought you could kill him?"

She exhaled. "Didn't really think anything, to be honest."

"Yeah, and look at you now. What's wrong with your head?"

"Nothing. I'm a little tired, that's all." She picked herself up. "Thank you for the light."

"I never said it was for you." He set it down on the path. "You should rest. You can't keep digging all night."

"I'm almost finished."

"And then?"

"And then," Tyn climbed back into her pit and set the point of the shovel to the earth, "I bury my friends."

Rion watched her in silence. She left him to his sullenness; his hostility did not bother her. Anything was better than being alone. She dug. Pushed the heel of her foot onto the shovel. Lifted away the earth.

Rion scoffed and stomped away. But he left the lantern behind. By its shallow pool of light, Tyn worked free stones and roots, and the mound of earth beside her grew taller.

He returned with a second shovel.

"You're going to help me get out of here," he said.

Tyn turned away so that he would not see her face.

Dawn spread across the sky by slow, imperceptible degrees. Cautious birds landed in the trees and on the roofs of the Sanctum buildings, singing softly as the sun touched the edges of the plains below the mountain.

They replaced the last of the soil. Tyn's hands throbbed, bleeding from open sores on her palms. She set down the shovel. It wasn't much of a burial, but she hoped the dead would understand. Carrying them down to the memorial grounds, she had silently said her goodbyes, her apologies. Now she felt hollow. Rion stood with his arms crossed and glared at the ground. His uncalloused palms were blistered and weeping.

"What now?" he asked.

Tyn brushed dirt off her trousers. "I'm going to speak to the tribe leaders in the city. While I'm there, I need you to fetch something for me." She gave the turned earth a last lingering look. "Then we're going to the 213th realm."

Rion nodded once, and did not ask for an explanation.

When she pushed open the gates to the Sanctum—rearmed, composed, clean—a crowd was waiting. Rion stuck to her heels. Tyn tried to project calm as she walked out onto the square. The people stared at her with wide-eyed fear.

"Res Lfae is secure," she called. "I am Second Spear Tyn and I will explain the situation to your representatives."

"Where is Res Lfae?" someone shouted.

She spread her hands in appeasement. "They're safe. I can't say more than that right now."

The representatives met her in the Spiral Cloister, all of the highest ranking members of Terjia, Ilisa, Falei, and Sonn. The tribes beyond the city were absent; word would be sent to them by Sonn's messengers. In as clear and concise a way as she could manage, Tyn outlined the attack. She did not falter, even when the Terjia Tribe's representative blanched at the news of the First Healer's murder. In plain words, she described her own encounter with Buyak and the message he had asked her to deliver.

"You were hurt," murmured the Ilisa representative.

His concern threw Tyn off-balance. She had expected remonstration.

"Take time to rest and recover, Second Spear," said the First Scholar. "You have suffered a loss. We can send for reinforcements from the Nteke Gulf; the Spears there will come to fortify Tahmais' defences. Others can search for Res Lfae while we will prepare to evacuate to the Fyorin Keep."

"The Terjia Tribe will care for you," said the Eighth Healer forcefully.

They did not understand, Tyn realised. They did not understand the power Buyak wielded, or the urgency of the situation. Instead of reassured, she suddenly felt acutely alone.

"You are too kind," she said. The weight of responsibility for the realm's future bore down on her shoulders.

Rion met her outside the Cloister, her satchel at his feet.

"Are we leaving now?" he asked.

She picked up the bag and opened it. *God Instruments and Their Makers* was still inside. She retied the straps and slung it over her shoulder.

"Come on," she said.

The Spear initiates at the d'wen stables were anxious, but

when she arrived a fierce, possessive pride entered their eyes. They hurried to ready Pax and fill saddlebags with supplies. Tyn leaned against her animal's heavy flank, stroking the soft line of paler fur at the ridge of her spine. Pax chattered and nudged her. Her feathers lay neat and flat against her sinuous neck, and she smelled of camphor and sawdust.

"Can you fetch Hermoz too?" Tyn asked.

The initiate blinked, uncertain. Hermoz was Chitanda's mount, a gentle, even-tempered female with black hooves.

"Please?"

The woman nodded and hurried off. Tyn turned and beckoned to Rion, who was standing as far away from Pax as the stable would allow.

"What is that creature?" he asked.

"This is Pax." Tyn's d'wen crooned at the sound of her name. "And you're going to ride Hermoz. We'll reach the Midplain outpost by nightfall; the channel out of Lfae's realm is at the crossroads."

Rion muttered darkly.

"She's not going to bite."

He refused to move. "How am I supposed to ride one of those things?"

"It's quite intuitive." With one hand, Tyn guided Pax towards the door. "And they're herd animals, so Hermoz will probably follow me. You'll only need to hang on."

In the sunshine of the yard, she swung herself onto her d'wen's back. Dizziness struck again, but she hid it from the other Spears by leaning forward to stroke Pax's feathers. She needed sleep. Pax greeted Hermoz with a cheerful yap as the second d'wen poked her head out the door.

"Would you like us to ride with you, Second Spear?" asked

one of the senior initiates. Another assisted Rion onto Hermoz's back.

Tyn shook her head, but softened the refusal with a smile. "No, stay here. Help the rest of the tribe to protect Tahmais. I hope to return soon."

The initiate pressed his fists together. "Go well."

She returned the gesture and directed Pax out of the yard with her knees. The shining stretch of the road fell in elegant, pale blue curves down the mountainside, unspooling like a satin ribbon. Beyond, the plains grew wild and rolling with spicegrass, and ancient baobabs towered hundreds of feet tall. Flocks of red swallows circled their canopies.

Keep moving. Don't stand still.

Pax's hooves rang clear on the road, and the wind whipped through Tyn's hair. She leaned forward and let air flow into her lungs. The sun was warm and high, and it dredged the chill out of her body. Behind her, Hermoz yipped quietly and loped after Pax, while Rion grimly hung onto the d'wen's neck.

They made good time. Rion showed a surprising aptitude for riding; rolling with the motion of the animal, keeping his knees loose. After a while, he relaxed—away from the Sanctum, he appeared more at ease. A shame, Tyn thought. Maybe this was what he had needed all along. A little space. Neither of them spoke, leaving the other to their private thoughts.

They passed oryx herds, and lone ox-beetles shuffling through the grass. A clouds of tiny copper-coloured hummingbirds cut across the road ahead of Tyn. She found her focus wavering; the steady roll of Pax's strides pulled her eyelids down.

Where were you?

She forced her eyes open again.

A small ring of buildings crowned the low hill ahead. Smoke from stove-fires rose above the roofs, and stray goats wandered the fenced enclosure beside the road.

"Is that the outpost?" asked Rion.

Tyn nodded.

"And the channel is out here? It seems strangely remote."

"Most of Res Lfae's channels are a little out the way." She slowed Pax. "The 213th realm belongs to Res Tahirah. I haven't encountered them before, but Res Lfae has implied that they're an eccentric."

"Great." Rion's scowl returned.

"Eccentric is usually better than malicious."

"Just get me out of this forsaken place."

The crossroads led west towards the Nteke Gulf and northeast to the Twin Lakes. A thorn tree stood in the centre of the road. Small white flowers bloomed in its highest branches and its spreading network of black roots snaked over the ground. A smaller footpath led up the hill to the outpost.

Tyn could sense the channel; the hairs on the back of her arms were standing up. She climbed down from Pax.

"And now?" asked Rion.

She unhooked her spear from the clip on Pax's saddle. "Because of my senior role within the Kisdja Tribe, I am what is known as a Bequeather. I have the authority to access Res Lfae's channels, and to grant others permission to do the same."

"So you can leave whenever you like?"

"I suppose."

"And these channels, they can take you anywhere?"

"Oh no. Only to realms where Res Lfae has formed an agreement with the ruler." She had half-forgotten Rion's newness, the fact that the most ordinary and obvious laws of Mkalis might be unknown to him. "The channels are a bit like pathways built out of consent. They allow movement between realms, but they also leave rulers vulnerable to betrayal and invasion—once consent is given, it's extremely difficult to retract. Rulers can life-bond a channel so that it collapses when one of them dies, but that isn't typically done; most channels survive long after the rulers involved are dead. So a god or demon's realm can also be invaded via channels that their predecessor established."

"Is that how the god got in?"

"Kan Buyak?" His face loomed out of the darkness in her mind. "I don't know. Until recently, Res Lfae *did* have their own channel to the 200th realm, but they had barred the entrance even before the Tribunal took place. It would have been extremely painful for Kan Buyak to withstand those hexes, especially as a lower ranked ruler. But one of his allies could have allowed him to use their channels, let him in via their realms."

Rion slid awkwardly off Hermoz's side. "Your ruler is higher ranked than the god? That makes them more powerful?"

"Well, yes, in a fair fight. But Kan Buyak had—"

She broke off. Someone was slumped beneath the tree.

"What is it?"

Tyn gestured for Rion to be quiet. Shadows made it difficult to see the individual's face, but they seemed to be asleep; their head resting on their chest.

Her heart sped up and she hurried closer. "Vehn?"

The First Spear jerked up at the sound of her name. A second later she was on her feet.

"*You,*" she said, and her voice held a terrible blend of anger and disbelief.

With her clothes crumpled and her face haggard, Vehn looked like an entirely different woman. She had none of her usual composure; her hair hung lank around her shoulders, and her hands were balled into fists. Tyn came to a sharp stop, taken aback by the venom in her leader's voice.

"I . . . I thought you'd left with Res Lfae," she stammered.

"Of course. Of course it's you. Ruler's blood, I deserve it, but of *everyone*—" Vehn swallowed. "Who is dead?"

"Jevin, Chitanda, and Hale." There was a lump in Tyn's throat. The joy of finding her leader alive, of finding someone else who would *understand,* was strangled by the raw hatred on the First Spear's face. "And five Healers."

Vehn turned away in disgust. She breathed hard. "Res Lfae?"

"They evacuated with everyone that they could."

"But not you."

"I was in the Ducaift District when the alarm hex triggered; I returned too late." She could not quite keep the bitterness from her voice. "And you, First Spear?"

That hit close to the bone; Tyn saw Vehn recoil, a flash of shame on her leader's face. For a moment, it was almost satisfying—the knowledge that she could hurt Vehn too. Then the First Spear's mask slid back down.

"Res Lfae had sent me to investigate a sensitive matter," she said flatly. "When I felt the first death, I was halfway to the Nteke Gulf. I rode through the night to get here." She gestured at the outpost. "Now my d'wen is exhausted and the Midplain Spears are caring for him. For all that's worth; given that I'm too late to help anyone. Tell me what happened in Tahmais. And why is the initiate with you?"

What sensitive matter?

"I agreed to guide Rion out of the realm," Tyn said. "I take full responsibility for him."

"You'll probably only get him killed."

Rion glared at Vehn. "That's a risk I'm willing to take, so long as she gets me closer to Ahri."

Vehn made a contemptuous sound, dismissing him. She turned back to Tyn. "The city. What happened?"

For the second time that day, Tyn recounted the attack on the Sanctum—the failing Spinelight Gates, the dead bodies at the infirmary, Buyak's sword and his threats. With every word, Vehn's expression grew darker. When Tyn finished her report, she shook her head.

"He let you live," she said. Her face twisted. "He killed the others, but he let you live. Ever the tool of a god, aren't you?"

Tyn felt like she had been punched.

"And now you'll find our ruler and throw them to Kan Buyak's mercy," continued Vehn. "Is that right, Second Spear? Is that your plan?"

The d'wens pawed the ground, disturbed by the tone of her voice.

"No," said Tyn softly. "No, I wanted to try to re-establish the Demonic Concord."

For a moment, Vehn appeared taken aback.

"Res Lfae needs allies," said Tyn. "I thought that if they had the support of the Concord—"

"Then they could crush Kan Buyak." Something kindled in the First Spear's eyes.

Tyn nodded. "It would give them the means to fight back."

Vehn was silent for a moment, but she held a new energy now. It radiated in the air. A spark, a small violent hope.

"Very well," she said under her breath. "Let's try that."

Chapter Ten

The God Sword, first forged by Kan Himaya during her 800-year reign of the 29th realm, is perhaps the most powerful and dangerous of all God Instruments. As its Progenitor and first Wielder, Kan Himaya succeeded in the conquest of every Realm she desired, before eventually falling prey to the combined efforts of the surviving High. Following her death, the Council of the High set forth their edict prohibiting the creation of God Instruments. The Ruler's Decree to eliminate the forging of Instruments altogether, however, ultimately failed to meet muster.

The God Sword has also been named The Sword of Intention.

Tyn read by flickering candlelight. Dawn would come soon. Rion slept by the door to the stablemaster's kitchen, his back to her. Vehn had her own room.

The God Sword is capable of fulfilling the exact violent Intention of its Wielder, regardless of the Wielder's combat ability. It is no exaggeration to say that even a child, possessed of this weapon, could topple Empires.

For no defence can be mounted against the Sword. It moves as its Wielder wills, it strikes as its Wielder desires. Similarly, the Wielder need fear no retribution. With Sword raised, no strike shall fall against them that shall not be parried. Invincible, unstoppable, the Sword of Intention is capable of crushing realms to dust.

Outside the window, one of the outpost dwellers called for their goats. Vehn had decided they would spend the night here before crossing into Res Tahirah's realm. The delay made Tyn uneasy, but, after a few hours of sleep, she felt more in control of herself. She shut the book, tucked it back into her bag, and rose from her borrowed sleeping mat.

The stablemaster had the d'wens rested, fed, and saddled by the time the sun touched the mountaintop. Tyn rode Pax to the crossroads. After yesterday, she had feared that Vehn would remain bitter and angry, but the First Spear—now astride the grey-feathered Indebe—had reverted to her usual self. Distant and cool, she treated Tyn with her customary curtness.

"You're so desperate for her approval," muttered Rion. "It's pathetic."

Tyn shot him a warning look.

"Not that I care." He smoothed Hermoz's feathers. Since waking, he had been in a good mood; eager to leave the realm behind. "It's none of my concern."

"What is your plan? Once you get to the 213th realm?"

"I'll find someone to take me to Ahri," he said, with absolute conviction.

"And if that doesn't work?"

The channel to Res Tahirah's realm unfolded from the long shadow of the thorn tree. Vehn watched the shadows as they paled and rose from the ground to form a latticed passageway. She walked her d'wen forward.

"You can doubt all you want. I'm going back." Hermoz ambled after Indebe. Rion twisted around to speak to Tyn over his shoulder. "Anyway, I definitely don't want to be here when that god returns."

"I'm curious why you believe your life in Ahri was so wonderful."

"I wouldn't expect you to understand," he sniffed.

Tyn took a final look back at the sunlit plain, breathing in the smell of the spicegrass and smoke. The mountain shadow stretched long across the land.

She followed Vehn and Rion into the channel.

The greyish weave of the passage grew denser, like a giant spider's nest or a cocoon, and the threads snapped crisply beneath Pax's cloven hooves. Vehn sat straight-backed and stern, her gaze fixed ahead, one hand resting on the shaft of her spear.

Was what Rion said true—did she really crave the First Spear's approval? Was it that obvious?

A gust of wind blew through the tunnel. Sheets of fungi grew from the walls and floor, patterned with spreading rings of colour—pale blues melding into dark brown and dull bronze. The breeze shook free a fine haze of spores. Pax sneezed. Ahead, the passage brightened where it opened into the 213th realm.

The channel emerged on a stone plateau. Knife-edged cliffs fell into valleys overrun by vegetation, great sprawling blankets of lush green and yellow. Trees stooped beneath the weight of creepers and clusters of fungi, and the air danced with clouds of spores, feather-light flecks of colour that spiralled above branches. Across the rolling landscape, massive golden spheres were sunk into the ground. Hundreds of feet across and draped with vines, they lay like forgotten relics of a former age. Holes pitted their upper curves, and flying creatures darted in and out of the apertures.

Hives, Tyn thought.

A peculiar, warbling cry echoed amongst the trees, and the undergrowth rustled. A squat figure scrabbled up the side of the cliff on thin, double-jointed limbs.

"What is *that*?" asked Rion.

"Quiet." Vehn walked Indebe forward as the creature reached the plateau. She pressed her fists together in greeting.

The dweller had skin that undulated with growths and nodes, colours that bloomed across its chest like war paint. Blackcap mushrooms dotted the ridges of its joints, and rippling silver gills formed delicate grooves across its ribs. It stooped; its arms almost touched the ground when it walked. Translucent golden needles bloomed over its arms and shoulders and skull, interspersed by bright teal clusters of lionsmane spines. Its liquid eyes shone curious and dark.

Tyn stared in open fascination. There was something beautiful and disturbing in the creature's riotous appearance; life seemed to overflow from its misshapen body. In its wake, it left a trail of wet prints on the ground.

"We are representatives of Res Lfae," said Vehn. "Marquis of the Spinelight, Wielder of the Machete, and Ruler of the 194th Realm. We humbly seek an audience with Res Tahirah on their behalf."

The dweller raised both arms above its head in a salute. It spoke, pale lips parting to reveal pointed teeth.

"To win an audience with Res Tahirah, Bright of the Faded, Speaker of the Demonic Concord, guests must submit to the trial. This is known."

"Is this what the rest of Mkalis is like?" asked Rion. "Is this normal?"

"I submit to the trial," said Vehn.

"I submit to the trial," echoed Tyn.

The dweller lowered its arms. "You will be accommodated."

"I do *not* submit to any trial," said Rion.

The creature made a peculiar huffing sound. It was laughing. "You will also be accommodated. Please, this way."

A pathway cut from the plateau into the valley, twisting back and forth down the sheer slope. The dweller moved along the track in fluid bounds; the surface of its hands and feet adhered to the rocks. The d'wens also navigated the course easily, but the drop to the valley floor made Tyn uncomfortable. The memory of Res Lfae's support before the Tribunal was fresh and painful in her mind; their absence gnawed at her.

They reached the floor of the valley. Humid air rose from the sprawl of dripping plants and rotting leaves, and Rion turned his nose up at the earthy smell. The ground grew wetter; the d'wens' legs sank into puddles of brown water, and the croaking of frogs bubbled up between patches of swamp grass and peat. Through the trees, one of the realm's giant spheres loomed. The golden structure captured and reflected light, spilling rainbows over the undergrowth.

The dweller came to a halt at the base of a weathered stone ledge, a half-submerged terrace in the middle of a glade. It turned and spoke to Vehn and Tyn.

"You may leave the animals here with your friend," it said.

Tyn dismounted and reached for her spear.

"You won't need a weapon."

Would be nice to have one though. But she nodded and tucked her hands into her pockets instead. Pax wandered over to a clump of large yellow mushrooms, and poked at them curiously.

"Are there any rules we should be aware of for the purpose of the trial?" asked Vehn.

The dweller huffed again, its chest inflating like a bellows. "Act as you see fit. You may approach the sphere to begin."

"You won't tell us the nature of the trial?" she pressed. "Can we work together to complete it?"

"I wish you good fortune."

Vehn glanced at Tyn, then climbed onto the terrace. She scanned the ground and trees. Tyn followed her. Her scalp itched; she had the sense of many tiny creatures brushing over her skin with invisible, twitching legs. Spores tickled her throat. Out of the corner of her vision, she saw a flicker of movement.

"First Spear, I think there's something—" she began.

Her vision abruptly turned white. Tyn gasped and stumbled. Jagged red lines of lightning burned over her sight.

"Vehn!" she shouted.

Then the realm re-formed.

The First Spear was gone. So was Rion, the d'wens, and their guide. Tyn rubbed her eyes, trying to scrub away the bright afterimages. The ordinary sounds of the wetland continued. The sky through the canopy remained unclouded and blue.

"Vehn?"

She was alone. The smell of ozone hung over the terrace. Tyn's forehead creased.

"All right," she muttered. "Part of the trial."

The stone path looped through a maze of rotting trees and small islands of drier ground, where quilts of yellow and blue flowers grew plump and bright. Tadpoles danced away from her shadow as she made for the shining sphere. It towered over the trees, its base swallowed by the forest floor, and as she drew closer she could see that the gold surface was not smooth, but covered in thin, needle-sharp bristles. The path ended at its base.

Tyn craned her neck upwards. What now? There didn't seem any obvious way inside, not from the ground anyway.

She picked up a stick and prodded the bristles. They parted like hair.

"Can anyone hear me?" she called. "Is someone listening?"

She was met with silence. A butterfly wove over a moulding log. A lizard sunned itself in a shaft of light falling through the leaves.

"I don't know what to do!"

The waters were still. Tyn turned back to the sphere. Approach it. That was all they had been told. She bit her lip, then reached through the bristles.

In an instant, the spines pivoted and sank into her wrist. She cried out, more surprised than hurt, and then the world went black. Beneath her heels the ground tilted, pushing her forwards, driving her towards the sphere. For a moment, she managed to keep her balance, rising onto her toes, but gravity won. She threw her free arm in front of her face as her feet left the ground.

The sphere swallowed her. But there was no pain.

With a sliding sensation, the spines withdrew from her wrist. She hugged her arm to her chest, skin stinging. Even with her eyes wide open, she could see nothing. She drifted in a void.

"Where were you?"

She breathed out and the sound rattled all around: echoing, repeating, *huh, huh, huh.* Streaks of light like starbursts flashed in the distance.

"Where were you?"

Hale's voice whispered through the dark. Tyn stretched out her arms, searching, but there was nothing around her.

"Hello?" she called uncertainly.

"Tyn, I'm running out of patience with you right now."

Res Lfae's voice sounded far-off and broken. Tyn shivered.

"I don't want to hear you." Their words, closer, then distant again. "This is your fault."

"Your Reverence?"

"All your fault. Buyak is going to kill me, and it's all your fault."

What is this? She tried to propel herself forward, kicking air. The darkness seemed to tighten around her, growing closer and denser.

"Ever the tool of a god, aren't you?" Vehn this time, every word dripping with disdain. She could have been right behind Tyn. "You are the weakness in my tribe."

Tyn jerked as something warm and smooth nudged her right calf.

"Desperate for my approval." A flash of light, in the distance. The smell of smoke and lilies. "Res Lfae wants to speak to you in their bedroom, Upstart."

"Shut up," Tyn snapped. She drew in her legs.

"You thought you could fight me?"

Fanieq's voice, razor-edged and commanding, made Tyn's blood run cold. She balled her fists. The goddess was dead. This was all a distraction; she needed to complete the trial. What was the trial? An unseen hand pulled her hair and she lashed out at the empty space behind her.

"You were a scholar before, one of the best."

"Stop it," she muttered. "Not him."

"But now you aren't," Vasethe said softly. Disappointed. There was no venom in his voice, no malice or disdain or impatience; he was not like the others and yet his sadness cut so much deeper. "Now you're just a soldier. I guess I was right to leave you in Mkalis."

The trial, she had to complete it. She would re-establish the Concord and none of this would matter.

"Raisha was the first person I ever fell in love with."

She knew everything that the voices said, had heard it all before in other places at other times, but it became so much colder and more bitter to swallow now.

"But you aren't Raisha."

"Just stop," she begged.

"You're everyone's second choice," said Vasethe. "Second to Vehn. Second to Raisha. Second to the border keeper. You'll never be good enough."

"I know!"

The darkness broke and light flooded her vision. With a violent jolt, her body was dropped knee-deep in the cool water of the wetland. Tyn swore.

"The trial is over," said the realm guide.

The sudden rush of sensation and colour disoriented her. She squeezed her eyes shut.

"I failed, didn't I?" she said.

The creature laughed. They were perched on the edge of the terrace, slender legs hanging over the side, feet hovering above the mud. On a dry knoll a little way off, Rion sat with his arms folded. The d'wens wandered between the trees.

"Your companion has not yet returned," said the dweller. "Perhaps she will succeed."

Of course Vehn is doing better than me, Tyn thought, and then immediately felt stupid. She splashed out of the pool, and drained the water from her boots. Their plan now relied on the First Spear's success. Lfae's survival, maybe the realm's survival, relied on Vehn.

"Sit with me," said the dweller. They touched the terrace

beside them. "We may be waiting some time, and your other companion is unwilling to share my company."

Rion methodically pulled flowers from the ground by their roots.

"I'm sorry about him," said Tyn.

"He is new to Mkalis, is he not? And he looks to you for guidance."

"I'm not sure about that."

"It is what I perceive." The dweller tapped Tyn's knee gently with powder-soft fingers. "May I ask what business you had with my ruler?"

Rion threw the flowers into the water. He caught Tyn watching him and scowled.

"We seek aid," she said slowly. "Two nights ago, the 194th realm was attacked by Kan Buyak. Res Lfae has fled and we are alone."

"Why would they run from a lower-ranked ruler?"

"Because Kan Buyak possesses a God Sword."

Res Tahirah's dweller seemed to shrink. The fungi of their shoulders bristled like animal fur.

"Are you certain?" they asked.

"I saw it with my own eyes. I don't know how, but Kan Buyak has deceived the High." Tyn gripped the edges of the stone slab, her knuckles turning white. "Even if Res Lfae sought help from the border keeper, they would still be defeated. Buyak would only need to think them dead."

Gauging the dweller's feelings was difficult, but they seemed anxious. "That is troubling." The frills on their skull rippled. "Very troubling."

"That's why we have come to petition Res Tahirah to re-establish the Demonic Concord. As Speaker of the Concord, it would fall to them to issue the summons."

The dweller made a soft whistling sound.

"*Former* Speaker," they corrected. "The Concord is no more."

"Then it must be re-formed; Res Lfae needs the old guard. If the demons bind together now, they might still be able to stop Kan Buyak."

The creature rocked from side to side.

"If you could ask your ruler—" she began.

"Too much was lost," they said. "You are so young. You will not understand. But the last time the Concord unified against the gods, it cost . . . too much."

"But this time the Concord doesn't have to unify against the gods. Just one god specifically."

"It always starts that way."

"Res Lfae is alone." She felt her patience slipping. "And we are desperate. How can other demonic rulers justify abandoning them? I know the stories of the War of Black Sands as well as anyone; my ruler fought every battle to defend members of the Concord. If demons have a shred of honour left, they will come to Res Lfae's aid now."

"It is not so simple."

"They are going to *die*!"

Rion looked up, and the d'wens' heads rose from the undergrowth. Pax whined.

"We will lose everything." Tyn lowered her voice again. "But we will only be the first casualties."

"This I know," said the dweller. They had not flinched at her outburst, but had shrank smaller still. Their voice was heavy. "And yet the first to support Res Lfae will be the next marked for destruction."

"Have all demons been reduced to cowards?"

The creature was quiet. Below the dangling soles of their feet, small white mushrooms pushed through the mud, growing with unnatural speed.

"The old guard will not heed a summons," they said at last. "The War of Black Sands is a wound unhealed. That terror is still too near."

Tyn felt as though a vice were closing around her chest.

"Then you sentence us all to death, your Reverence," she said.

The mushrooms swelled and darkened, their edges crumbled, they formed fissures and collapsed. The panic Tyn had held at bay since Hale's death now threatened to overwhelm her. If the Concord could not be re-established, if Lfae really was left without allies or an escape, then all hope was lost. Her ruler, her guardian and leader and the centre of her world, was lost. The idea clawed at her insides.

Res Tahirah laid a hand on her knee again.

"You speak of allies," they said. "But no ally alive can reliably thwart a God Sword. Not the border keeper, not the Concord, nor even the High."

"So abandonment is justified," she said bitterly. "What a comfort."

"I am saying that what you lack is not an ally, but a *tool*. By whatever treachery, Kan Buyak has his God Instrument. Where, then, is Res Lfae's?"

She recoiled. "They would *never*—"

"I am not suggesting that you forge one, Second Spear," they added quickly, and withdrew their hand. "But what if the tool already existed? The High did not destroy every God Instrument following the issuing of the edict. Some were too difficult to break. Others were too useful. When the High seized the Concord's cache of Instruments, there were rumours that a few ended up sealed within the 12th realm, Domain of the Architect."

Her heart sped up. "They're still there?"

"Possibly, although I am unsure which Instruments the High believed worth preserving. For fear of it falling into the wrong hands, I doubt they would have kept anything that might serve as a weapon."

Her wild streak of hope faded. "I suppose that would be too much to expect."

"No matter the Instrument, it is better than facing Kan Buyak empty-handed—Res Lfae will need to use what tools are available."

"And the First Spear and I might be able to deliver those tools to them."

The demon inclined their head. "I believe it represents their best chance of withstanding Kan Buyak's assault. Of course, I will help you as much as I am able."

And what will you take in return? Tyn thought. A cache of God Instruments, even a single Instrument, would make Res Tahirah vastly more powerful. Might turn them from an eccentric ally into a new threat.

"Res Lfae doesn't have a channel to the 12th realm," she said guardedly. "They've never even mentioned it before."

"The Architect had few allegiances to begin with, and almost all the old channels have atrophied by now."

"Who are they?"

The demon raised their gaze to the treetops and was quiet. Eventually, they shrugged.

"The ruler of the 12th realm is known as the Architect. The

Architect has no other titles. The High have shunned the Architect. The Architect designs and builds and devours. There isn't much more to be said, because that is all I have ever heard. I doubt anyone has visited the 12th realm in centuries, and the High considered it a secure haven to lock away the God Instruments. That in itself speaks volumes."

Fingers of cold trailed across Tyn's back. "If the channels are gone, then how are we to reach the realm?"

"Not all of the channels have fallen; at least two still remain. Kan Sefune of the 355th realm, and Kan Meiralle of the 124th realm. You would need permission from one of them to cross."

Invincible, unstoppable, the Sword of Intention is capable of crushing realms to dust. The words from *God Instruments and Their Makers* lingered in her mind. Perhaps this was the only option available: to counter the Sword with a second Instrument. Buyak could hunt Res Lfae down at any time. If this gave her a way forward, the slimmest of chances, it was at least *something*.

Res Tahirah rose. "Your companion is returning."

Vehn. "Did she succeed in the trial?"

They huffed once.

"What?"

"Surely you've realised by now that you did not fail?" The demon spoke with a certain amusement. "I place trust in those who are capable of acknowledging their own uncertainties and fears, because there is strength in recognising weakness. That does not mean you should allow your insecurities to grow too powerful, Second Spear. You will need to be stronger than your doubts if you are to save your ruler."

Chapter Eleven

Vehn emerged from the trees, pale and drawn. Her wrist was circled by a band of dried blood. Tyn searched her face. *Who did you hear? Did you feel anything? Or did your resilience prove your failing?* The answers remained locked behind the stone-cold wall of the First Spear's eyes.

"The trial is over," said Res Tahirah.

Vehn bowed slightly. Said nothing.

"For tonight, the hospitality of the 213th realm is yours."

"Will Res Tahirah call for the old guard to re-establish the Concord?" Her voice was low and gravelly.

Silence.

"They will not," she said. There was no hint of accusation; she spoke as if this was what she had expected all along. "Then the Concord will not rally. I see."

"The situation is complicated."

She nodded, agreeing. For all the blankness of her face, Tyn noticed that Vehn's fists were clenched. In the diffuse light under the trees, her skin looked waxy and bloodless.

"There's another way, First Spear," said Tyn quickly. "It isn't—"

"Why bother?" Rion had gotten up and walked over to join the conversation. "I saw what that god could do. This is all pointless."

Vehn did not react to him. Her gaze strayed to Tyn.

"We can still fight back," said Tyn.

Traces of feelings shifted behind those slate-grey eyes. The rigidity of her jaw softened a degree.

"There's always another way," she said quietly.

"Oh absolutely. Another way to get killed," said Rion.

"Perhaps." Vehn was still for a moment. Then she motioned to Indebe, and the d'wen obediently approached. "But we might still earn useful deaths. Second Spear, I hereby retract your suspension; you are reinstated to your role."

Tyn gestured acknowledgement. This time, she would prove herself worthy.

"So that's it," said Rion. "You're just going to throw your lives away."

"If that's what is necessary." Vehn mounted her d'wen. She was all control and focus now, but there was a brittle edge to her movements, like a river only half-frozen. Indebe pawed the ground. "That's how our tribe lives. To protect each other and our ruler."

"Oh, so it's *honour.* Forgive me, there I was thinking this was straightforward stupidity. Tyn, you too?"

Tyn clicked her tongue to get Pax's attention. "I know my duty."

Rion made a face.

"Dweller of the 213th realm, we are grateful for your ruler's hospitality," said Vehn, turning Indebe with the light pressure of her knees so that she faced Res Tahirah. "Will you convey our thanks to them?"

"Your thanks are heard," said the demon smoothly. "If it pleases you, I will take you to the Hollows, where you may spend the night and recuperate from the trial."

Vehn nodded. "We would appreciate that."

The ruler bowed from the waist, then set off down a concealed, fern-covered path, away from the sphere and back towards the cliffs. They moved like a ghost, hardly seeming to touch the ground, leaving undisturbed the water and mud and feather-fine tendrils of spiritweed.

Lfae had said that Res Tahirah was eccentric. Tyn watched the curious figure as they traversed the forest ahead. Eccentric enough to conceal their identity behind the guise of an ordinary dweller. Still, they seemed kind; in an unfathomable, stilted sort of way. She didn't entirely trust their motives, but that could not be helped—at least they were willing to provide information.

The demon delved deeper into the forest, where the plants grew dense and ancient, through strangling webs of vines and between walls of white-fan fungi. Rion, riding ahead of Tyn, had subsided into a sulk. From time to time, he shot resentful looks back at her. The old path wound through the trees and then along dripping, algae-draped cliff walls, until it ended at an arched bridge.

"This is the Hollows. I hope that you'll be comfortable here," said Res Tahirah. "It is safe."

The bridge rose over sedate pools of black water. Frogs croaked below. Beyond, warm lights shone through a veil of low-hanging branches and vines. The cliff wall was the colour of burned caramel, and scored with caves. Slim cracks in the rock formed doors and windows and vents. Chimes dangled from the tops of crevices; they rattled and clinked when the breeze swelled.

Tyn imagined Lfae here in the bygone days of the Concord, and strangely it was their portrait in the Preserve that she recalled. She shivered.

"Could you pass word of Kan Buyak's attack on the 194th realm to the High?" she asked.

Res Tahirah led the way across the bridge. "I will see it done. However, given that the Tribunal was so recently decided in Kan Buyak's favour, I believe that the High are unlikely to react without more substantive proof of a God Instrument's influence. They will assume this is ordinary warfare."

Vehn climbed down from her d'wen. "Is Res Lfae no longer considered a credible witness?"

The demon raised and lowered their shoulders, and the rows of gills on their back flared slightly. "As it was your ruler who called for the previous Tribunal, their authority to demand another is lessened."

"Then is it possible to reach out to the border keeper?" asked Tyn. "If she took the matter to—"

"The border keeper won't help us," Vehn interrupted.

Tyn frowned, but held her tongue. The First Spear's vehemence surprised her—for some reason, the mention of the border keeper had touched a raw nerve.

"Under the circumstances, Res Lfae will have already tried to reach her," said Res Tahirah, looking at Vehn askance. "If she were to listen to anyone, it would be them."

"The witch won't save us." Vehn removed Indebe's saddlebags and slung them over her own shoulder. "We will have to take the fight to Kan Buyak ourselves."

Rion made a sound of exasperation. He slid off Hermoz's back none too gracefully. "What, just you and Tyn? Do you realise how ridiculous—"

Vehn moved faster than Tyn thought possible. The saddlebags hit the ground and her spear arced through the air as she swung it towards Rion. The blade came to rest at the curve of his windpipe. He inhaled sharply.

"The Second Spear may have patience for you," said Vehn, with perfect steadiness, "but mine has expired. Cross me again and I will end you."

Rion held dead still.

She withdrew her weapon. "You can return to the 194th realm tomorrow. The tribe will have work for you, so that you may serve a useful purpose."

She was halfway up the path to the caves when Rion found his voice.

"What honour?" he spat. "You protected no one; all you want is power."

This time, Tyn managed to intercede. She lunged forward and shoved Rion out of the way. The shaft of her own spear rose to block the swing of Vehn's blow. The force reverberated in her bones. A killing strike.

"Vehn!" she gasped. "Vehn, *stop.* What are you doing?"

The First Spear's breathing had stilled. She drew her spear back smoothly, a viper recoiling, and Tyn thought that she might attack again. Then the impulse died behind her eyes. She averted her gaze and lowered the weapon to her side.

"I think I need some space," she murmured.

Tyn did not know how to respond. She had never seen Vehn lose control quite this badly before; if Tyn had not blocked the attack, Rion would have been cut down. Her skin crawled. He might be untried and arrogant and selfish, but he was still a member of their tribe. An *unarmed* member of their tribe.

"Then go," she said, shaken.

Vehn nodded, the barest movement of her head, then brushed past Tyn back in the direction of the forest. Rion flinched, but Res Tahirah merely stood aside, their hands folded at their waist. They watched Vehn, their feelings inscrutable. Their eyes found Tyn's.

"Let me show you inside," they said.

Insects hung over the water. From somewhere higher up the cliffs, a falcon screeched, and the cry echoed over the trees. Wordlessly, Tyn followed the demon. Rion trailed after them.

"What was that?" he muttered.

A reed-curtain, stained with blooms of bright orange fungi, hung over the widest entrance to the caves. Res Tahirah lifted it aside. The chamber beyond was bright with phosphorescent mushrooms; red and yellow globes that ranged from the size of Tyn's finger nail to the size of her fist. It smelled damp. A dark brown couch covered in a woven blanket stood against the wall. Through the arch to the next chamber, she could see a cook stove and rows of sleeping pallets heavy with furs.

"We should wait for the First Spear to return before discussing matters further," said Res Tahirah.

"Yeah." Tyn dropped her bag and sat down on the couch. Through the holes in the opposite wall, shafts of sunlight filtered into the room. "I'm sorry for the inconvenience."

"I understand the strain that you are under." They paused. "I must make an enquiry elsewhere. Would you excuse me?"

"Of course."

Rion stood in the entrance, arms crossed and sullen. Res Tahirah drifted past him, light as smoke, out of the chamber.

"She's crazy," said Rion.

Without acknowledging that he had spoken, Tyn took out *God Instruments and Their Makers* and reclined on the couch.

"She tried to kill me."

Tyn cracked the book open to the index page and ran her

finger down the chapters.

"Are you listening?"

"You should stop talking until you've considered what the First Spear is going through," she said without looking up.

"What *she* is going through?"

"She has lost three of her tribemates." Tyn continued to scan the contents page. "A First Spear is named First because that is the order in which we are supposed to fall. First the strongest. Last the weakest. And yet three of her subordinates were murdered while she was too far away to save them. Her ruler has vanished, so she cannot protect them either. Vehn bears the weight of safeguarding an entire realm, and she is quite prepared to die trying to fulfil that duty. That does not mean she *wants* to die. She just expects to. So maybe, maybe, you should stop and *think* before you accuse her of failing to protect anyone. You don't know what you're talking about, and you don't know her at all."

"You're on her side."

"Of course I am."

"But she—"

"I don't want to hear it, Rion."

He shivered at the sound of his name. For a moment, he was quiet.

"She tried to kill me," he said, as if that settled the discussion.

Tyn sighed and returned to her book. Rion stood in the entrance and fidgeted. When it became clear that she was not going to talk to him further, he disappeared into the next room.

God Bolt. God Brush. God Cage. God Chalice. God Coin. God Compass. God Drum.

She felt distracted. She felt alone.

God Hammer. God Hatchet. God Hook. She ran her hand over the page. Somewhere here, there had to be an answer. The silence drew close around her.

Chitanda's blood dripping from the walkway. The way Hale's eyes widened as the sword pierced his forehead. The weight of their bodies. The coldness of the earth as she buried them.

Tyn rubbed one hand across her eyes. Not now.

The afternoon dimmed into evening, and *God Instruments and Their Makers* drew her away from the world by slow degrees, until the sounds of the forest outside were only a whisper at the edge of her awareness.

God Mantle. God Mortar. God Needle.

To think that rulers had forged every one of these tools, macabre and strange. Each entry represented thousands of lives, each word standing for hundreds of the dead. The instructions were all there, alongside lovingly detailed descriptions of the tools themselves and the histories of their makers. How to build a forge. How to shape the materials. And how the strength of the finished work would vary according to the power of the sacrificed ruler's blood.

The illustration of the God Cage lingered with her—a horned woman with massive wings huddled within a hanging cell. It reminded her of Buyak's cage during the Tribunal, down to the dark ribbons poised to bind the prisoner. But a more complex system of bars ringed the exterior, and the annotations suggested that they could move under the direction of the Cage's wielder. Lines of cruel spikes curved inwards and upwards, driven through the soles of the woman's feet.

The rustling of the reed curtain startled her, and Tyn closed the book with a guilty snap.

Vehn took in the room. She propped her spear against the wall.

"What are you reading?" she asked.

Nothing. Tyn resisted the urge to try to hide the book.

"I borrowed it from the Tedassa College Library," she said. "It's about God Instruments. I thought, if we knew more about Kan Buyak's weapon—"

"That makes sense."

"You—you think so?"

"Have you learned anything useful from it?"

Tyn glanced down at the tattered cover, the torn bindings. She looked up again at Vehn. "It depends. But I think the Instruments represent our best chance of stopping him."

Vehn absorbed her answer.

"I've also spoken to Res Tahirah," she said. "The chances of us reaching the Architect's realm, much less stealing an Instrument, are low. Far too low." She ran her fingers over the raw, blood-smeared ring on her right wrist. "But I don't know what else to do. Before this, I believed . . ."

She stopped.

"If you had been in the Sanctum when he attacked, Kan Buyak would have killed you," said Tyn softly. "The others would still have died. Nothing else would have played out differently."

"But what if I could have protected them?" Vehn's voice was strained. "If I could have reacted before Kan Buyak breached the Sanctum?"

"Nothing would have changed."

"You don't understand—"

"I understand perfectly, First Spear. I saw what that sword could do." Tyn spoke low and clear, even though it felt like she was drowning. "Neither of us could have stopped him, because it wasn't about skill or speed or strength. He willed them dead, and they died."

Vehn seemed frozen.

"She's right."

Rion stood in the doorway. His arms were crossed. Tyn stiffened.

"I was at the infirmary," he continued. "When I heard the shouting, I jumped out the window and ran. The Healers were trying to stop him from getting inside the building, but the sword screamed, and they fell. He barely even looked at them, he just . . ." he shrugged. "A Spear attacked him from behind. Out of nowhere. Buyak didn't turn around; he kept walking. But then the Spear was dead."

Tyn remembered the way Chitanda's spear had splintered in two before Buyak's face, the feeling of disbelief.

Rion grimaced and shook his head.

"I'm sorry," he said. "For earlier. I should never have said what I did."

Vehn's eyes widened slightly in surprise. She hesitated, then nodded.

"Apology accepted," she said.

A tiny fracture in the First Spear's self-possession cracked open, and through it Tyn could see the woman Vehn used to be. It wasn't much and it wouldn't last, but somehow it made the grief she carried a little lighter.

Chapter Twelve

Neither the 355th nor the 124th realm restricted access. Neither required permission to enter, neither asked for a tithe nor set criteria for who might be permitted inside. Channels into and out of the realms could be created by any ruler.

"It's not good news," Tyn told Rion.

They stood on the bridge before the Hollows. The sky threatened a storm, the air tense and humid. The d'wens twitched. They dragged their hooves over the stones.

Rion watched as Res Tahirah drew patterns in the mud with their feet. "Why?"

The demon crouched and drove one hand into the shallow water. They caught hold of something and drew the object to the surface with a sharp tug. A black root, specked with wriggling larvae.

"Because it probably indicates that the realms are predatory," said Vehn.

Res Tahirah split the root between their hands and scattered the flailing grubs over the ground. They dissolved with sharp hissing sounds, forming small milky pools against the wet, dark soil.

"Right," said Rion. "Do we know anything else about them?"

"No one enters an unrestricted realm if they can help it." Vehn favoured him with a hard look. "Speaking of which, it would be in your interest to return home."

He turned to Tyn. "Which one are we going to?"

The white pools trembled and then expanded, forming a single large disk. With a click like a key turning in a lock, the disk snapped from liquid to solid and uncoiled downwards, a spiralling stairway into the earth. Res Tahirah stepped backwards and beckoned to them.

"The 355th realm." Tyn walked forward. "Its ruler is lower ranked. Our chances of survival are better."

"Good. That seems good."

Pax growled when Tyn tried to lead her closer to the channel, swinging her head from side to side in distress. The other d'wens followed suit; even faithful Indebe hissed when Vehn tried to pull him forward.

"If you'd prefer, your animals may remain here," said Res Tahirah. "I do not think they will enter Kan Sefune's territory willingly."

"That bodes well," said Rion.

Tyn murmured to Pax soothingly, stroking the tense muscles of her massive shoulders. She unstrapped her spear. "Will you care for them in our absence?"

"They will be waiting for your return."

She nodded, and briefly pressed her face against the soft feathers at the curve of Pax's neck. Her d'wen made an anxious sound, almost a whine.

"It's all right, silly girl," Tyn said. "Be good."

Pax pecked her shoulder, not hard, and Tyn pushed away her beak.

"We value the hospitality of the 213th realm," said Vehn.

The demon sketched a bow. "Let us see whether the High heed the warning. Take care, dwellers of Res Lfae. You are welcome back here."

Vehn squared her shoulders and waded through the mud to reach the stairs. Rion, muttering to himself, followed. But when Tyn walked forward, Pax yipped and took a few steps after her. The d'wen stopped again, nervously stepping from foot to foot.

"No, Pax," said Tyn. "You wait here, okay?"

Res Tahirah placed a hand on Pax's flank, and she grew calmer.

"Fortune favour you, Second Spear," they said.

She nodded. "Thank you."

Pax trembled and yipped again, quieter this time.

The stairs dripped with a glossy white paste, each step slick with it. Tyn walked with care, keeping her spear close to her body. A cold wind rose from below. Rion slowed and allowed her to catch up to him.

"Are you sure about this?" he whispered.

She smiled. "Are you?"

"No, I think it's insanity. But when it's over, I hope you'll feel obliged to take me back to Ahri."

She clapped him on the shoulder. "Impressive optimism."

The stairs grew darker as the clouded sky of the 213th realm faded overhead. Around and around, they descended the dripping spiral. The sound of their footfalls and the irregular trickling of the white liquid echoed in the tight space.

An ashen grey light emanated from the lower depths. Vehn, a little further ahead, was outlined in silver.

"What you did yesterday was kind," said Tyn, pitching her voice low.

Rion started.

"I think what you said helped," she added. "And even if it

hadn't, it was brave of you."

He snorted dismissively. But he also looked a little embarrassed, and maybe pleased.

The white liquid formed a small pool at the base of the staircase. Vehn left a trail of ghostly boot prints in her wake. Pale words, the letters curling and wet, were scrawled over the grey soil.

> *The way in is the way out.*
> *You may not go back.*
> *Kan Sefune waits at the centre.*

"Centre of what?" asked Rion. "What kind of rules are those?"

Vehn stood over the message, studying it. She rubbed her chin.

"The kind we follow very carefully," she said.

Beyond the base of the stairs, the landscape was buried in swirling fog. The looming angles of buildings shaded the scene with deeper greys; blurred patches of darkness that shifted with the mists. Closer, heaped piles of white stones marked the roadside; cairns left by long-gone travellers.

Tyn adjusted her grip on her spear. She joined Vehn at the message. The letters looked newly painted.

"No option to retrace our steps," she said. "That could be a problem."

"At least the rules are clear," Vehn looked over her shoulder at the staircase. In the gloom, her pupils almost eclipsed her irises. "Take the lead; I'll guard your back. Rion, stay between us."

The cairns marked the way, irregular heaps of rough painted

rocks as high as Tyn's waist. After the humid warmth of the 213th realm, this place felt cold. She strained her ears for any sound of movement. All she heard was the muffled echoes of their footfalls and their breathing.

"I don't like it here," said Rion.

"And yet I warned you against coming with us," said Vehn. "It's too late for fear; we can only move forward now."

He hunched his shoulders against the chill.

"You realise," he said, "that if we are attacked from the front, we can't run."

"I imagine that's the point."

Tyn came to a crossroads and stopped. To her right, the cairns led a zigzagging route down an easy slope, before vanishing into the fog. To her left, the buildings—almost but not quite visible. She squinted, but the fog seemed to grow thicker the longer she looked at it.

"I'm more concerned about hitting a dead end," she said. "I think we should keep to open ground if possible."

"Agreed," said Vehn.

Tyn stared at the mist.

"Second Spear?"

"It makes sense for us to move in stages," she said reluctantly. "One person scouts ahead, makes sure the path is secure, and shouts for the others. Because then if there is an impasse, only one of us is stuck. It's the logical way of progressing."

"No," said Vehn.

"But—"

"We stay together. That's an order."

Although it felt like a bad idea, Tyn was relieved. "Understood."

The cairns grew less frequent, but taller; islands in an ocean of mist. Tyn moved cautiously. The ground softened, the barren soil darkening and shifting like sand. When she looked back, the previous cairns seemed much further away than she remembered. Rion and Vehn's faces were shadowed, their features blurred.

Like Fanieq's realm, she thought, with a pang of unease. *Mist and silence, until the ghosts start screaming for blood.*

Something rubbed against her calf.

There was a half-second when she almost disobeyed the rules of the realm, when she nearly jumped backwards. Her thoughts caught up to her instincts; she managed to lunge sideways instead, an awkward motion that jarred her ankles.

"What's wrong?" demanded Rion.

The cat was a cool shade of grey, with large yellow eyes. It sat on the ground beside the cairn. Its tail slowly waved from side to side, and it watched Tyn with unblinking interest.

"There's a cat," she said.

It mewed.

Rion hurried closer, Vehn right behind him. The cat looked at them, then returned its amber gaze to Tyn. It licked its lips.

"It's just a cat," she said, and laughed. Adrenaline coursed through her and left her lightheaded and buzzing. She had been so close to jumping backwards. "Sorry. It caught me by surprise."

Rion eyed the animal. "What cat would live in a place like this? Maybe you should kill it."

"Ruler's mercy, Rion!"

He shook his head. "Why would it be out here? Why didn't you see it?"

"We are not murdering the cat."

The animal got up and arched its spine, claws extending into the soil. Then it wandered away into the mist. Its tail swayed with its steps. Rion scowled.

"Some kind of spy," he muttered.

"Let's keep moving," said Vehn.

They reached the end of the slope, and the land began to rise again. Tyn's damp clothes stuck to her skin and beads of moisture collected in her hair. Ahead, the twisted trunks of dead trees reared from the ground. The bark was scratched and peeling away, the wood beneath scored with traceries of white veins. At their bases, smooth black nodes peeked out of the ground. Some kind of root, but they struck Tyn as too hard and shiny, like the shells of beetles or the coils of a snake. She tapped one with the point of her spear. It flinched, and sank below the surface of the soil.

The light remained constant; a uniform grey twilight stretched across the whole realm. They walked. Although Tyn tried to stay alert, she found her thoughts wandering, her steps slowing until she almost came to a halt before snapping awake again. Once, she glanced over her shoulder and saw Vehn standing dead still, twenty feet behind Rion. The First Spear's head was tilted upwards, her eyes unfocussed and her spear hanging from nerveless fingers. But before Tyn could say anything, she blinked and continued walking. As if nothing had happened.

The fog had seeped through Tyn's skin. They could have been walking for mere minutes, and yet hunger gnawed at her stomach. Her feet ached.

"There's something up there," said Rion.

Tyn raised her head. Sure enough, beyond the trees she could see the murky shape of a slender tower. It rose high in the air; the summit enveloped by low clouds.

"Could that be the centre?" he asked.

Vehn drew alongside him, tracking his line of sight. "Perhaps."

But Tyn shook her head.

"No," she said. The word rang hollow in her ears. "That's the stairway from Res Tahirah's realm. We're back where we started."

Chapter Thirteen

The dripping stairs looped up into the sky. All around, the fog. The silhouettes of buildings. The white cairns.

> *The way in is the way out.*
> *You may not go back.*
> *Kan Sefune waits at the centre.*

And below it, a single line, a lone white streak in the dirt. All the writing appeared freshly painted.

"Our path must have curved," said Vehn.

Tyn crouched and wrapped her arms over her knees. Her nails had turned blue with the cold. She had led them in a circle, and for nothing. How long? How much time had she wasted?

"We followed the trail." Rion stood beside the stairwell. His black hair was glued flat against his forehead. "Whoever set it, they meant to deceive us."

Vehn scanned the mists ahead.

"We rest, then we continue," she said.

"That's it? We just keep going?"

Vehn nodded. She set her bag on the ground. "I'll keep first watch."

Tyn raised her head. "No, I should—"

"A couple of hours to recuperate, and then we move on."

Vehn sat down, leaning against her pack. She scraped loose strands of hair back from her face. "This is a setback, but we'll recover from it."

Tyn shrugged off her own bag, and lay down beside it.

"Wake me in an hour," she said. "I'll take over."

"Do not presume to tell me what to do," replied Vehn icily.

"You need rest too."

"And you overstep."

"In that case, I respectfully *suggest* that you need rest too."

Rion snorted. Vehn looked away.

"Do I need to beg before you listen, Upstart?" she asked, her voice like winter. "Would you derive satisfaction from that?"

A pause.

"My apologies," muttered Tyn.

"Your apologies mean nothing to me," said Vehn. She placed her spear across her knees. "You are ever and always a disappointment."

A great empty feeling opened up inside Tyn, a hollow space that expanded to crush her lungs and press against her airways. *I'm sorry,* she wanted to say, over and over until Vehn heard her and understood that she meant it. *I'm sorry. I'm sorry.*

But she said nothing at all. Instead, she rolled onto her side and curled her legs into her chest. Vehn shifted, settling into her watch.

After a minute, Tyn heard quiet footfalls. Rion lay down beside her, not touching, but close enough that she could hear his breathing.

"It's okay," he muttered. "She didn't mean it."

Tyn closed her eyes. The weight of her exhaustion bore down on her, although it was too cold for sleep. She edged sideways so that her back touched Rion's. He stiffened.

"Keep warm," she mumbled.

"I'm not cold."

"Then keep me warm."

Tiny pebbles dug into her side. With unexpected intensity, she missed Matir and her friends and her home and her ruler. She tried to keep her breathing smooth, but Rion must have heard the catch in her throat because he pressed his back closer to hers, then reached over and patted her on the shoulder. It was sweet and uncomfortable, and it might even have been funny if the gesture wasn't also so sincere. Tyn gently pushed his hand away.

She could not remember falling asleep, but it seemed only minutes later that Vehn was shaking her arm and telling her to get moving. Rion jolted awake as she sat up. He stared around in confusion until his memories caught up with him.

"Nothing but fog and silence," said Vehn. Her bag was already on her back, ready to go. "It's too easy to grow complacent."

Tyn rubbed her eyes. The realm looked the same as before, and she felt no less tired. When she got up, her muscles were stiff and slow. She rubbed her hands together to ward off the numbness.

"I'll be more careful," she said.

Vehn ignored her and started walking.

The path between the cairns ran straight as far as Tyn could see. She kept her mind rigidly focussed on the road ahead, her spear poised. Rion, in front of her, walked with his hands tucked into his armpits to keep them warm.

Vehn came to the crossroads, and this time turned towards the buildings. The misgivings Tyn harboured grew, but she kept her thoughts to herself. She could not afford to question

Vehn's authority, not now. And besides, her own route had led them in a circle. Who was she to object?

The buildings were tall, unstable constructs that grew stalk-like from the bare soil. They moaned and tilted as if under pressure from a great wind, although the realm was still. Most were only a few feet wide, just enough room for someone to stand inside, but no doors, no windows, all pieced together from warped planks of worm-riddled wood. Through the cracks between the boards, Tyn thought that she glimpsed occasional flashes of red light.

"Who built these?" asked Rion. "What are they meant to be?"

"Probably remnants from an earlier ruler's reign." Tyn moved a little quicker to catch up with him.

"But what are they for?"

She shrugged. "Whatever their purpose, they look abandoned now. What does it matter?"

Rion frowned as he studied one of the towers. "I don't know."

Vehn, a few feet ahead of them, cast an impatient glance over her shoulder. Tyn lowered her gaze and kept walking.

The buildings grew more closely packed. Some had toppled and lay across the path, half-sunken into the earth. A pale glint amidst the ruins caught Tyn's eye. She stooped to look closer. A scrap of tawny yellow fur. Cat hair. She rubbed the strands between her fingers, then scattered them over the ground.

Vehn came to the end of a tangled avenue of buildings and stopped. Tyn could see that the path ahead led down a set of rough-cut stairs. Beyond, there were no more towers.

"Is something wrong?" she asked.

"No," said Vehn and descended the stairs.

They came to a flat plain marked by the now-familiar white cairns. The fog roiled like a living thing, denser and more cold.

"Stay close." Vehn's voice sounded distant. She moved quicker than before, her braid swinging from side to side. The mist hid her legs. "Don't lose sight of—"

Tyn heard her breathe in sharply.

"First Spear?" Her stomach lurched. "What is it?"

Vehn failed to respond, so Tyn hurried forward. The First Spear stood stock still. A grey cat wound around her ankles, nuzzling her calves. It paused as Tyn approached, yellow slitted eyes wide and expressionless. It licked its lips.

Then it butted Vehn's ankle and slunk away towards the nearest cairn.

"It's the same one," said Rion. "It's the same cat we saw last time."

"Clearly it lives in the area," said Vehn.

"How?" Rion gestured at the empty plain. "There's nothing here; you must see that."

Vehn turned. "Keep moving."

Rion looked to Tyn for help. She only shook her head. Vehn stalked across the plain like she was possessed. The fog threatened to swallow her; if they did not hurry, she would vanish entirely.

The land sloped upwards, the cairns grew more sparse, and then they were amongst the dead trees once more. Tyn half-ran to catch up with Vehn.

"First Spear—" she began.

"Res Lfae is relying on us," said Vehn. Her eyes were ringed with shadows; even in the gloom, Tyn could see that she was paler than usual. "I will not let them down again, even if it means we have to walk through this place for the rest of our lives."

One of the black nodes growing up through the earth caught on her foot and she stumbled. Tyn caught her arm, but Vehn jerked away like she had been burned.

"Don't touch me," she snapped.

They continued in silence, none of them wanting to voice the obvious. Still, when the stairs to Res Tahirah's realm drifted out of the mist once more, Vehn seemed to collapse on herself, as if a wave had broken inside her and swept away the hope that she had been clinging to.

Below the message, a second line. A tally. Vehn kicked dirt over it, smearing the wet writing.

"I'll take first watch," said Tyn.

Vehn breathed heavily. With a curse, she threw down her spear. Her shout echoed out into the realm; the spearhead sank a foot into the ground.

"And then we carry on," said Tyn.

The next time, they turned away from the towers, away from the cairns, trying to forge a new path across the plains. The journey led them inexorably back to the stairway. After her outburst, Vehn withdrew into herself and barely spoke at all. She rested, rose again, kept walking. The following loop took them back through the city. Of the cat, they saw nothing further.

"Maybe it was trying to tell us something," said Rion, as he lay next to Tyn.

She had no answer. They were all exhausted and leaden with helplessness. Although they still had water, they had run out of food by the end of the fourth cycle.

"I think the loops are getting shorter," he said. "I counted my steps from here to the crossroads. I don't think we're going in a circle." He gazed at the stairs as they rose up into the sky.

"I think we're moving in a spiral."

Tyn shook her head and sat up. Vehn was hunched over her bag, eyes fixed on the misted road ahead.

"Get some sleep, Rion," she said.

Vehn did not respond to the sound of Tyn's approach. She was shivering, her coat sodden and heavy over her shoulders.

"May I take over?" Tyn asked.

The First Spear cast her a venomous glare. But she moved off anyway, wrapping her coat tighter around her body and propping her bag beneath her head as a pillow. She never slept close to Tyn or Rion, never complained about the cold or the ever-present dampness. Tyn took up her position. Vehn hardly rested at all, and when she did it was always with an air of seething resentment. Of the three of them, she took the most watches. She ate the least. Drank only when prompted. By now, she appeared to be fuelled by rage alone, and nothing Tyn said or did seemed able to reach her.

Air whistled up the stairway. Tyn leaned back, surveying the road. Her thoughts were slow, sluggish. She drew a spiral in the dirt, then scuffed it away and took *God Instruments and Their Makers* out of her pack. She flipped through a few by-now-familiar pages, but even the book couldn't hold her attention. How long had it been? They might walk forever, lost in the pale, chilled sea of fog. It would be easier just to stay here. Why bother repeating the motions when the result was the same anyway? Her eyes drifted closed.

When she woke, her calf stung. The others slept on. Peeling away the wet fabric of her trousers, she found four small puncture marks just above her ankle. The blood around the cuts had clotted already, but the size and distance between them suggested a small set of sharp teeth: two larger canines, two smaller. The right size for a cat.

She quickly pulled the fabric down. Her heart beat fast, and a cold nausea roiled in her stomach. The camp around her was quiet; there was no sign that anyone had trespassed.

Why hadn't she woken up? She should never have fallen asleep, but to be bitten deep enough to draw blood, surely she should have felt that? She closed her hand over her ankle. Phantoms of cats prowled the fog and dissolved.

"Time to move," she said loudly.

This time she counted the steps from the stairs to the crossroads. One hundred and sixty-seven. Vehn had taken the lead, and again they turned down the stairs and out onto the plain. Ninety-eight stairs. Rion could have imagined the change, but maybe he was right. The distances felt shorter, less tiring.

The cat sat at the base of the cairn. In spite of the dampness, its fur remained glossy and smooth. It held very still, apart from its tail, which drifted from side to side. When Vehn drew near, it rose and stretched.

"I really, really hate this cat," said Rion.

"It is not a cat," said Vehn. She allowed the animal to sidle up to her, to butt against her legs. She did not move. "But I suspect trying to harm it would be a mistake."

Tyn's ankle burned. The cat turned to look at her. When it licked its lips, she saw blood on its teeth. She shuddered.

"We should follow it," said Vehn.

The creature mewed, as if it might have understood her. Then it lazily sauntered around the cairn.

This is a bad idea, Tyn thought. Rion stooped to pick up a white rock. His expression was grim. But Vehn only hefted her spear across her shoulders and followed the animal.

It meandered from one cairn to the next, unhurried. From time to time, it looked backwards as if to confirm that they were keeping up. Its paws made no sound on the loose soil. For an absurd moment, Tyn could imagine what they would look like from an outsider's perspective: three hollow-eyed, starving people trailing after a small cat. But nothing about the situation was funny; she could only summon a deep sense of dread.

It almost came as a relief when she saw the dead trees. The cat paused at the first stump and raked its claws across the bark to sharpen them.

"We're back here again," said Rion.

"Your capacity for stating the obvious is profound," said Vehn. She scanned the fog.

The cat purred and padded forward.

"Maybe it *is* just a cat?" Rion said doubtfully.

Vehn hesitated. Then she started after the animal once more. "We keep following it, at least until we are through this grove."

A faint sound—or maybe the sense of being watched—made the hairs on Tyn's neck rise. She looked back at the cairn-strewn plain. At first, there appeared to be nothing out of the ordinary. Then the yellow eyes caught the light. She inhaled sharply. Three sets of eyes watched her from the shadows of the rocks, unmoving and unblinking.

"There are more of them," she said.

No one responded. Tyn turned back to the dead grove, only to find that Rion and Vehn had vanished. When she looked again, the cats were gone too.

"Damn it," she muttered.

She moved quickly amongst the leafless, curled stumps, and

stifled the rising tide of her anxiety. They could not be far ahead, and once they noticed her absence they would wait for her. Or else they would meet her at the stairwell.

"Rion? First Spear?" she called. The words vanished into the distance. She raised her voice. "Vehn!"

The silence mocked her. Tyn controlled her breathing. She would not panic. She was the Second Spear of Res Lfae, Ruler of the 194th Realm. She was good in a crisis. She had stood against gods and testified to the High, and even if she could not win every fight, she was stubborn enough to try.

The mist thinned and she glimpsed the stairway ahead. This time she was certain Rion was right; the journey was shorter. She broke into a run.

The black node, smooth and insidious, caught on the tip of her left foot. Her momentum sent her sprawling and she landed hard. Her spear rolled out of reach.

She had not even seen it. Tyn groaned. Nothing felt broken, but she was winded. She pushed herself back onto all fours and began to rise.

Something latched onto her ankle. Tyn looked around in time to see the root wrapping around her calf and a crevasse opening in the earth behind it. Then she was yanked backwards and down below the surface, into the earth. The light disappeared.

Chapter Fourteen

She could not breathe. The dirt choked her. Blind and crushed, she was pulled down, down, down through the rough, crumbling earth. She struggled, tried to raise her arms, to catch hold of anything. The darkness constricted around her; there was mud in her mouth, she was battered, cut by stones and roots, and there was no air, she was suffocating, sparks shot over her vision and her ears were full of roaring. She could taste blood.

Then the pressure released, and Tyn gasped. Her eyes flew open. Everything was dark, but she wasn't in the ground anymore. Wooden walls hemmed her in on all sides; her arms were crammed against her torso and she could not move. She spat a mouthful of dirt. Her lip was split, she could feel hot blood trickling down her chin.

"Help me," she croaked.

Her body shuddered uncontrollably. She tried to free her arms, but the space was too small. Between the planks above her head, she could see a sliver of light.

"Someone!"

Her voice was scratchy, little more than a wheeze. Clumps of earth clotted in her hair; the smell of the soil was everywhere. Tyn pushed her body against the planks as hard as she could. The walls held firm.

She breathed heavily. From above, she heard a faint scratching sound. The skittering of small claws against wood.

"Vehn!" she shouted, then coughed. She shoved her shoulder against the rough wall. Splinters dug into her skin. "Vehn, please!"

Her efforts had no effect. She cried out in frustration. There again, the soft crunching. The light above her head dimmed for a second, as if something had passed over it. Tyn strained, her shoulders aching from the effort. She managed to slip one arm upwards, so that she could stand more easily inside the tight confines of the prison. The crack of light was just out of reach; her fingers scrabbled against the wall, gouging at the wooden surface.

The cat purred.

"Rion was right," Tyn hissed. "We should have skinned you when we had the chance."

Soft paws padded somewhere above her head. Tyn punched the wall just below the crack. It creaked. She hit it again.

From behind the wall, she heard running footsteps. A hard object thumped against the outer surface.

"Tyn, is that you?"

Her legs turned weak with relief at the sound of Vehn's voice.

"Please help me," she whispered. "Please."

"Hold on." The First Spear grunted with exertion and a moment later another crack of light appeared near Tyn's waist.

"She's inside?" Rion exclaimed. "How is that possible?"

Vehn levered her spear deeper into the gap between the wooden boards and pushed down sharply. The plank split away. She set her spear to the next.

"Is she okay?"

Vehn ignored him and continued to ply away the board. It

snapped off and more light flooded in. Tyn threw her weight against the wall again, loosening the ancient, rough-hewn joints. Dust spiralled through the air. She coughed.

"Easy," murmured Vehn. With brute force, she ripped off a third board, and the gap was finally large enough for Tyn to fit through. She staggered out of the tower and dropped to her knees, panting.

"Tyn!" Rion sounded alarmed.

"Give her space." The First Spear peered up into the recess above the broken boards.

"Why are you covered in mud?" He stood a few feet back, and his skin was flushed and shining. He had been running. "Where did you go?"

She wanted to answer him, but the words tangled inside her mouth. Her hands were streaked with soil and caked blood, her nails turned ragged and black with dirt. The shock of her descent through the earth still reverberated inside her; the terrible grinding vibrations as she sank.

"Are you injured?" asked Vehn.

Tyn shook her head.

The First Spear reached into her bag and drew out her canteen. She offered it to Tyn.

"Drink," she said.

Tyn took the flask. She held it with both hands, trembling so violently that she almost spilled the water.

"How did you find me?" she croaked.

"I heard you calling."

Vehn must have covered the distance from the grove to the crossroads in mere minutes. Must have sprinted. Reckless of her, and she was lucky that Rion had managed to keep up. Tyn drank from the canteen and her heart slowed.

"Sorry," she said. "I fell behind. Lost my spear."

Vehn's expression was inscrutable. Tyn wiped dirt from her face. She spat again, but the taste lingered on her tongue.

"How did you get inside?" Vehn pointed at the tower with her spear.

"I—I don't know. There were more cats, before the grove. I tripped and the trees . . . swallowed me. I was underground and then I was here." She tried to hand the canteen back. "I'm sorry."

Vehn turned away. "Can you walk?"

"Really?" said Rion. "You won't even let her catch her breath?"

Tyn struggled to her feet. "I can walk."

"Vehn, this is cruel."

"Then I'm cruel. And it's 'First Spear' to you."

Rion glared daggers at her back. "Don't you care at all?"

"The Second Spear is not a child. If she says she is uninjured, if she says that she can walk, then she will walk." Vehn started down the road. "Or would you have me carry her?"

"She's right." Tyn motioned for Rion to follow after Vehn. "I'm fine."

He shook his head.

"No, you take the middle," he said. "I'm going to watch your back."

Tyn's legs carried her forward though the sprawl of towers. She could feel the press of the walls around her, the darkness suffocating her. What if Vehn had not found her? What if she had been left inside, alone, trapped and waiting for the silken whisper of lithe paws, the needle teeth?

Rion could not see it, or understand, but Tyn would have done anything for the First Spear in that moment.

They descended the stairs to the plain. The fog formed a grey wall, obscuring all but the closest cairn. Vehn raised her hand and paused.

In the distance, a rumbling sound—rocks rolling over one another.

"We need to stay together," said Vehn under her breath. The shadows under her eyes were dark purple, but her gaze was clear. "Within arm's reach. Any sign of danger, grab each other and run. If one of us goes missing, leave them. Do not even think of going back. Remember the rules."

Tyn nodded. Closer by, another patter of stones. Rion tensed.

"Let's go," said Vehn.

The mist was thicker and darker than before. Tyn shivered. Her clothes were torn, her coat and pack both lost. She picked up a rock, rolled it around her palm. Better than nothing.

Vehn moved steadily from one cairn to the next. Focus was written into her features and the taut lines of her legs; she crossed the plain on the balls of her feet. Her spear cut unconscious figure eights through the air, a clean, natural extension of her body.

Something soft brushed Tyn's leg. Lightning quick, she kicked. Her foot cut through empty space.

Vehn looked back in question.

"Cat," said Tyn. "It's fast."

Rion mumbled something derogatory and stepped closer to her.

Vehn returned her gaze to the path ahead. "It's toying with us."

Without warning, she thrust her spear forward. A blur of white flashed across the ground and disappeared with a hiss.

Vehn drew her spear back and examined the tip. A few strands of pale hair stuck to the blade. Round yellow eyes gleamed in the fog.

Tyn counted her steps. Thirty-five since the stairs, ten since the last cairn. Rion hovered at her side. Occasionally, he brushed her hand with his own, as if to confirm she was really there. Fifty steps.

"We've reached the trees," said Vehn quietly. "Watch your step."

The nodes, previously little more than glints in the soil, now protruded from the ground in fat, shining loops. Tyn faltered at the sight of them.

"This is madness," muttered Rion.

Vehn cautiously picked her way around the roots. Tyn clenched the rock within her fist. More than anything, she wanted to turn back, to never cross the grove again. But instead she took one step and then another, following Vehn's trail. The nodes shifted fractionally, sensing the vibrations of her footfalls. Behind her, Rion's breathing was shallow.

Without taking her eyes off the ground, she held out her hand for him. He took it. His skin was frozen.

"I won't let go," she said.

He did not reply.

She could see the place where she had fallen; the earth was rutted and gouged. The crevasse yawned wide at the base of a dead tree, and two furrows marked where she had dragged her hands through the dirt, trying to grip the surface. Her spear lay to one side.

Vehn paused, then diverted her path towards the turned earth.

"Don't—" Tyn started.

"Quiet."

Tyn held her breath. The roots along Vehn's path stirred; there was the one that had tripped her, there was the one that had dragged her under. With light fingers, Vehn crouched and picked up the spear. Rion's grip on Tyn's hand tightened. The First Spear slowly straightened; poised to jump at the slightest sign of trouble. With soundless, careful movements, she moved away from the furrowed soil.

Tyn exhaled. Vehn tossed the spear to her. She caught it in one hand. The weapon was familiar and solid in her grasp.

"Don't lose it again."

Tyn nodded.

They pressed on, and the mist ahead thinned. Tyn longed to run the final distance, to race towards the towering stairs. But she held her nerve. Eighty steps since the end of the plain. Her hands were slick. One hundred and ten. They passed the final tree and were out of the grove.

With a shiver, Rion let go of her hand. Her skin gleamed bone white where he had held it. She tried to offer a smile— *we're still here*—but could not summon the energy. She started up the hill.

Vehn had almost reached the stairway when Rion spoke.

"The end of a spiral is the centre," he said.

She paused.

"We can't be more than one more rotation from the end." His voice was strained. "I think you know that too. But we won't all make it around again."

"What are you suggesting?"

"I'm suggesting that this might be the last time that we'll have a choice."

She turned. "The Spears are not cowards."

"And I'm not a Spear, so I need to be the one who says this." He took a step closer to her. "Tyn will follow you if it kills her. Right now, it just might. I've only survived this long because you have both shielded me, and even you aren't invincible, First Spear. One wrong step and it's over."

"Then I won't misstep."

"Vehn, do you really want to find out what lies at the centre of this spiral?"

Her eyes narrowed.

"Do you think this god is going to grant you passage to the 12th realm? Do you believe that?" Rion sounded exhausted. "You don't. You can't possibly, after what we've seen so far."

"Res Lfae needs—"

"Your ruler needs you to survive. If they cared for you at all, they would tell you to leave this place. If Res Lfae expects you to die here, then I'm sorry, but they aren't worth serving."

"Watch your tongue!"

He flinched but did not yield. "It's not too late. We can still cross to the 124th realm and seek passage from there. But if you and Tyn are swallowed up by this forsaken place, Kan Buyak is one step closer to destroying your home. Your deaths will mean nothing. You will have killed Tyn for nothing."

Vehn shook with anger. She spun on heel and strode forward.

"If you pass those stairs, it's over," said Rion. "You won't be able to go back."

"Then leave me!"

"No," said Tyn.

Vehn stopped again.

"He's right," said Tyn, her words heavy. "Whatever you decide, whichever way you go, I will stay with you."

Vehn balled her fists.

"I am the Second Spear. You are my leader." Tyn stared at the ground. "And I know my duty."

Something inside Vehn caved. All the rage emptied out of her; her shoulders slumped.

"And I know mine," she said.

She placed her hand on the balustrade, the last of her resistance crumbling like a wall into the sea. With great weariness, Vehn began to climb. Mutely, Rion and Tyn followed.

Tyn only looked back once. Just beyond the stairs, where the message had been written, she glimpsed the edges of something dark and glittering. The mist shrouded it, but it reminded her of a giant mouth—a maw open and waiting for prey to walk inside.

Chapter Fifteen

Clear air and the warmth of sunlight on her skin, the bright chirps of birds and the gentle rustling of the living trees, the smell of flowers and wet grass, the dense sprawl of colour and shadow and light—Tyn absorbed it all. The rush of sensation was almost too much to stand, too intense, too potent after the dreary grey hell of the 355th realm. Early afternoon. A pair of yellow-winged cranes dipped their beaks into the dark waters, wading amongst bulrushes and lilies.

The bridge to the Hollows was newly overgrown with black spores, forming a dense, soft carpet underfoot. Tyn raised her head, relishing the sight of the canopy, the fluting birdsong. Bulbous fungi drooped from the high branches, teardrop-shaped mushrooms with violet frills.

"It's so bright," said Rion.

A water-stained sheet of parchment was weighed down by a stone on the balustrade of the bridge. Vehn picked it up.

"The High have been alerted to Kan Buyak's attack on the 194th realm," she read aloud. "I seek other allies, but Kan Buyak has gained word of my efforts against him. Time is short—I have named my successor. Follow the spores if you would travel to the 124th realm. Go well, dwellers of Res Lfae, Wielder of the Machete, Marquis of the Spinelight, Commander of the Demonic Concord."

Tyn shivered. If Res Tahirah had named a successor already,

the situation was dire. Vehn folded the letter and replaced it on the balustrade.

"The Second Spear and I will head to the 124th realm immediately." She traced the line of black spores with her eyes, following them into the wall of foliage. "Rion, I'd suggest that you remain here."

He scowled. "And what happens if the two of you never return? I'm stuck in this place forever?"

"No." She started walking. "You can await the return of Res Tahirah or the summons of Kan Buyak. If we fail, then, one way or another, you will be returned to the 194th realm."

"Why would I listen to Kan Buyak?"

"Because if he kills Res Lfae, you will not have a choice. So I suggest you pray that Res Lfae survives. While they grant us independence, Kan Buyak's rulership will chain us to his every command."

"Rulership?" he exclaimed.

Vehn gave him a flat look. "Yes. If Res Lfae is defeated, their realm can be claimed by the conqueror. That is the way of things. Kan Buyak would control us from the moment he takes the 194th realm, no matter where we are."

"We would end up as his *puppets*?"

Tyn touched his shoulder. "We're going to stop him."

"So if Kan Buyak kills Res Lfae, that's it? We're all dead?"

"It will be the more distinguished of Res Lfae's dwellers who draw the god's ire," said Vehn. "If you evade his attention, you are likely to survive."

"But you and Tyn? You'd be killed?"

"If we're fortunate."

"What does that mean?"

"Rion—" Tyn began.

"It means we're likely to be tortured to insanity," said Vehn without a hint of feeling. "Kan Buyak has a reputation for his treatment of insubordinate dwellers. The leaders of Res Lfae's tribes will be obvious targets."

Rion fell silent. Vehn pushed forward through the undergrowth, following the trail of spores.

"I'll stay with you," he said, after a pause. "Maybe I can do something to help."

The First Spear glanced back. It seemed that she almost smiled.

"If that's what you want," she said.

The cliff face, draped with velvet moss and feathery creepers, loomed above them. The trail of spores ended in a lush pool of furry black at its base. Water dripped and echoed off the rocks; somewhere in the trees, a bird whistled shrilly. It was cold in the shade.

Vehn grazed her blunt fingernails over the limestone wall. Flecks of quartz glittered in the shifting light of the trees. She closed her eyes and listened, forehead creased in concentration as she sensed her way to the channel. Then she nodded to herself. Opening her eyes, she tapped the largest of the quartz crystals, a chunk of pale yellow as wide as her thumb.

It rang, clear as a bell. As they watched, the stone grew dull and then liquefied, flowing away like melting ice. The hole it left behind was the size of a coin, but it grew wider as the rock around it silently dissolved. Through the channel, Tyn could hear singing.

"We find Kan Meiralle," said Vehn. "We get the permission we need."

She climbed into the crawlspace. Rion exchanged a look with Tyn.

"Are you sure you want to come?" she asked.

He opened his mouth, then shook his head.

"Tortured to insanity," he muttered. "Why didn't you say anything?"

"Better not to think about it."

"Are you afraid?"

"Of course. But other things scare me more."

"Such as?"

"Losing Res Lfae. Losing any more of my friends. The realm falling." She shrugged uncomfortably. "Oh, and heights. I'm not great with heights."

"You shouldn't joke about this." He placed his hand on the ledge of the tunnel.

"Forget about it, all right? For me?"

It seemed like he wanted to say something else, but stopped himself. Instead he climbed into the crawlspace.

Tyn took one more lingering look at Res Tahirah's forest, then clambered into the gap after him.

The singing grew louder, a sweet, slightly off-key alto floating down the crawlspace. Not a language Tyn recognised, but cheerful and mindless. The smell of flowers drifted out of the tunnel ahead, and beyond the tangle of Rion's limbs, she caught flashes of warm daylight. The singing broke off suddenly as Vehn exited the channel.

"Guests!" Someone exclaimed.

Rion manoeuvred his legs around and stepped down. Through the gap, Tyn saw pale green grass, sunflowers sprouting wild across the rolling slope of a hill. Daylight streamed over the field.

"We are representatives of Res Lfae, Marquis of the Spinelight, Wielder of the Machete, and Ruler of the 194th Realm,"

Vehn was saying. "We humbly seek an audience with Kan Meiralle on their behalf."

Tyn stepped down from the tunnel. The channel was set into a lone waystone in the middle of a sea of green. The grasslands undulated like ocean waves on a calm day; the rise of hills and fall of valleys stretching to the edges of her sight.

A tall, strikingly attractive man stood knee-deep in the grass. He wore a long brown shift, and his skin was rich and very dark, his eyes bright green. A circlet of bone blossoms grew from his skull, white blooms as fine as moulded porcelain. Between the flowers, black hair curled in careless ringlets. He beamed.

"Welcome to the 124th realm," he said. "I'm Oshe, Shepherd of the Desayven Green. The hospitality of Kan Meiralle is yours."

"We are grateful for your ruler's kindness, but our business is urgent," said Vehn. "Will Kan Meiralle hear us?"

"Of course," Oshe's smile faded. "It's been so long since we've seen outsiders, but I'm sure she would be eager to help you. Dwellers of Res Lfae, you said? And yet this channel belongs to Res Tahirah."

"Our errand took us via their realm."

"I see. The channel is new, and I had wondered . . . but anyway." He pressed his hands together. "As per Kan Meiralle's rules, you must partake of the offered bounty of the realm. I offer it to you."

Tyn frowned. "Bounty of the realm?"

"It just means you have to share a meal with us," Oshe said, a little apologetically. "Kan Meiralle feels it sets a positive tone for diplomatic relations. Can't move onto business before you've broken bread. She'll hear your request afterwards."

Vehn studied him for a few seconds. She gestured acknowledgement. "Very well."

He brightened. "I'll take you to Emethas then; the village is this way."

He kept up a stream of enthusiastic chatter as he followed a winding footpath down to reach the wider road. Large, slow-moving animals chomped at the grass in the fields on either side, their tufted ears twitching at insects, and their long, auburn fur hanging over their black snouts.

"We don't trust him, right?" muttered Rion.

"Not for a second," Tyn replied under her breath.

The road curved, revealing a string of small painted houses set between spreading oaks. Enormous silken nets hung between the tree branches, each rope twined with garlands of flowers and hanging baskets of fruit. People waved as they approached; even from a distance Tyn could see that their heads were also crowned with bone flowers.

"This is Emethas," said Oshe. "I know it's not as showy as most rulers' heartlands, but it has a certain charm."

Other dwellers were staring. They were all green-eyed and youthful, pretty and dressed in simple, muted clothing.

"The preparations for the feast will take a few hours, but I'm sure the delay will be worthwhile." He beckoned to a heavy-set woman. "Fessi, look, we have guests!"

"A feast is too much," Vehn interjected. "We are only emissaries. There's no need."

Oshe humour deflated. "Oh. It's—it's just the rule though. It applies to everyone, regardless of their status."

Vehn visibly restrained herself.

"Well, if it's the rule of your realm," she said.

"Worthwhile. I promise."

The woman he had called approached shyly, her hands tucked behind her back.

"This is Fessi, she'll help you to get ready." Oshe smiled at Tyn. "Meaning no disrespect, but would you like to bathe? You're quite . . . muddy."

She plastered a smile over her face. "I tripped."

"Down a sinkhole?" He chortled. "We have hot water to spare; please, feel free to make use of it. There are also clothes you are welcome to borrow."

"Thank you."

"It's only a pleasure."

Speaking in a timorous voice, Fessi guided them to the bathhouse. She kept darting furtive glances at Rion and tugging at a loose thread in her homespun shirt. There was something doe-like about her; her leaf-bright eyes wide and innocent and darting, her black hair silken and shining. Vehn regarded her with obvious impatience.

"We appreciate your assistance," she said at last, interrupting Fessi's mumbled explanation about hair oils. "You've been very helpful."

Fessi turned red. "If you need anything else—"

"We will be sure to ask," said Vehn, and drew the door closed.

The room was dark-panelled and humid. A misted window near the top of the far wall looked up into the trees, hazy and shadowed through the glass. Reed-woven screens divided the pools, allowing for some privacy.

Rion sat down on the bench beside the door. "They seem nice, so I assume they are planning to murder us?"

"We're significantly outnumbered." Vehn peered through the window. "If they wanted to kill us, I suspect they would have tried it already."

"Comforting. What do they want then?"

"Maybe they are being genuine," said Tyn. Rion and Vehn looked at her. She shrugged. "It's possible they are just isolated and eccentric. Without border restrictions, it's true that they would have very few visitors. In trying to be friendly to other rulers, Kan Meiralle's openness might have instead driven away potential allies."

"You mean she has no restrictions because she wants to . . . make friends?" Rion's eyebrows vanished under his hair.

"It's possible, but not likely," said Vehn. She laid down her spear and set her pack on the ground. "I expect you to remain vigilant, Upstart."

"Of course."

"Frustrating though the delay is, we may as well take the opportunity to recover." She pulled her vest over her head.

Rion jumped.

"I, um, I'll wait outside," he said.

"You are not equipped to protect yourself!" said Vehn, but he was already out the door. Her expression soured.

"It seems that he's shy," said Tyn.

"He's a liability." She knelt and unlaced her boots. "And I can scarcely afford more of those."

"But he might make a good Spear. In time."

"If we survive long enough for him to outgrow being a burden, then I will consider myself fortunate." Every inch of Vehn's skin was marked by old injuries, her chest and shoulders crisscrossed with pale welts, the years of her service written in scars. She stepped into one of the pools. "However, he does not deserve you making excuses for him."

Tyn put down her own spear—within reach—and

stripped. "He is trying."

Vehn made an irritated sound. "Stop recognising yourself in him. I see what you're doing, and it's stupid." She scooped water and rubbed her neck and arms clean. "You only want him to prove himself in order to believe that you could be worthy too."

Tyn swallowed her reply and stepped down into the adjoining pool. A screen separated her from the First Spear. The water scalded her, but she slid deeper, letting it rise up to her collarbone. The steam and the smell of gardenia made her head spin.

"I meant to say thank you," she said. "For finding me in Kan Sefune's realm."

"I don't require thanks."

"Still. I am grateful."

"You are my subordinate and responsibility." Vehn was quiet for a moment, and there was no sound but the lapping of water on stone. "Did you think I'd abandon you?"

Yes.

"Res Lfae comes first," Tyn said. "If I had been lost, I understand that you would have had no choice but to go on without me."

"No choice, huh?"

"No real choice." Tyn loosened her hair and let it spread through the water around her.

"In that case, would you have abandoned me?"

The question startled her. She took too long in answering it—there seemed no right way to respond. No, of course not, she would never be so heartless. Yes, that was what duty required and the course of action Vehn herself would take. Except she hadn't.

"Well?" said Vehn, half a challenge and half a threat.

Vehn, who despised her. Who suggested before the whole tribe that Tyn had slept her way to her rank. Who punished her for failing to meet her expectations, and chastised her for trying, and made sure that she never forgot the vast difference between their abilities. Who, whenever Tyn scraped through with some kind of success, either assumed foul play or demanded yet more from her. Vehn, for whom she would always and ever be a disappointment.

"No," she said. "I wouldn't have abandoned you."

The mud turned the pool murky.

"You're the worst kind of hypocrite," said Vehn.

"It's not the same thing."

"Oh yes it is. But you're the better person, the hero of the tribe, so it goes without saying that you would help *me*."

"That's not it. It's because . . ." she fumbled. "It's because you're more important than I am. I'm dispensable in a way that you are not."

"Spare me," Vehn scoffed.

"It's the truth."

"If Rion had gotten lost, would you have left him behind?"

She could not answer.

"So don't lie to me," said Vehn bitterly. "And keep your thanks. They're worthless."

Tyn wanted to keep arguing, to explain herself better, but Vehn's tone made it clear that the discussion was over. She ran her fingers through the knotted strands of her hair, combing out the grime. And maybe the First Spear was right, maybe those had been her assumptions. A small, defiant voice in her head suggested that she could hardly be blamed for thinking that way—Vehn usually treated her like dead weight. Besides, it shouldn't be an attack on her honour to *thank* her.

"I'm going to find out if the feast preparations are complete." Vehn stood abruptly; Tyn heard the splash of her movements. "Watch over Rion. The sooner we can leave, the better."

Tyn bunched her hair into a knot. "I'll come with you."

"There's no need." Vehn climbed out of the pool and crossed to her crumpled pile of clothing.

"You are the one who said we should stay together."

"And now I say otherwise." She jerked her shirt over her head. "Is that too difficult for you to understand? I can speak slower."

Tyn stood up.

Vehn glanced at her and then shook her head in disgust. "Do you want to make some kind of point? Spit it out, or stay out of my way."

"Six years."

"What?"

Tyn's heart raced. "Six years. For six years, I have done everything to please you, to earn even a scrap of your approval. I never spoke against you. I defended you to the others. I put up with every insinuation, every insult, everything, because that was my duty and you were my leader. I *idolised* you. And it was pointless, because you still treat me like I'm nothing." She reached out and picked up her spear. "But I earned my place."

"What are you doing?"

Tyn flipped the weapon over and sliced the blade across her forearm. Her voice was tight with anger.

"After we stop Kan Buyak," she said, using two fingers to smear her blood over her lips, "I challenge you to an ascension duel for the role of First Spear. Heed me or forfeit your place."

Vehn was mute.

"Well?" Tyn demanded. "Is that enough of a point for you?"

The First Spear stood frozen, eyes wide and her mouth slightly open. She made a small movement with her hand, as if she wanted to brush water from her face, then stilled.

"I heed you," she said slowly. She bent, picked up her own spear, and walked out the door.

Chapter Sixteen

Fessi had left a neat pile of clothing in the bathhouse, all woven from the same homespun brown wool. It chafed on Tyn's skin, but her own clothing was beyond repair—ripped almost to ribbons, and stained with soil and blood. The borrowed dress felt too long and tight; it hugged her thighs and ended past her knees.

Awkward to run in, she thought grimly.

Her head ached from clenching her jaw, and she felt miserable. What had she done? An ascendency duel? Of all the stupid things to propose. And yet it was Vehn's expression that remained fixed in her memory; the disbelief etched onto the First Spear's face. For once not cold, not sneering, not blank.

"Damn her," Tyn muttered.

Rion had been waiting outside, sitting with his back against the exterior wall of the bathhouse. He got up when she emerged.

"What happened?" he asked.

"I thanked the First Spear for finding me in Kan Sefune's realm."

"Right, of course. Storming off on your own seems like a rational response to that. How foolish of me to even ask."

She shook her head and walked down the path. He hurried after her.

"Hey, are you okay? Did she say something?"

"We have more important matters to worry about."

"That wasn't what I asked."

"Because I'm so desperate for Vehn's approval, aren't I?" She shook her head. "Leave it be."

A burbling stream ran behind the bathhouse, where a cluster of willow trees hung over the water. Dwellers stood in the shallow water, their skirts hitched up to the waist, and dredged out dark orange weeds and swollen bulbs. Fessi was amongst them. When she saw Rion, she went bright pink and immediately pulled down her skirt, soaking the fabric and dropping her basket in the process.

"Ah, there you are."

Tyn turned to see Oshe walking towards them from the direction of the village square. He rubbed his hands together.

"You look quite refreshed, my dear," he said. His eyes travelled over her in an appreciative way. "Like a whole new person. I trust the baths were to your satisfaction?"

"Thank you for your hospitality," she replied evenly. Beside her, Rion had bristled at *my dear*. "My leader was looking for you."

"To ask about the feast, that's right." Oshe smiled. "I told her that Kan Meiralle will grace us with her presence tonight. Our ruler tends to keep to herself, but comes to the villages when there are guests."

"She must be an unusual goddess to take such an interest in ordinary dwellers like us."

"You shouldn't speak so low of yourself, but yes. Kan Meiralle is special." There was a light of reverence on Oshe's face. It made Tyn uneasy; the way his features seemed to glow at even the mention of his ruler's name. Not with love, necessarily, but with something far hungrier.

Fanatic, she thought.

"Where is the First Spear now?" asked Rion.

"I invited her to wait at my house. I could take you there, if you'd like?"

As they walked around the bathhouse, Tyn noticed that the shrubs beneath the rear window had been crushed. As if someone had been standing there recently, and peering inside.

Oshe's cottage was small and tidy, a two-room stonewall building a little way upstream from the village. Flowering bougainvillea climbed the walls, and beans and tomatoes snaked up leaning trellises in the tiny plot adjoining the house. Bees meandered over the blossoms.

Oshe snatched a handful of sugar snaps on his way past, and popped the bright green pods into his mouth.

"After you, after you." He gestured at the entrance, still chewing. While bringing up the rear, he put his hand on the small of Tyn's back to usher her inside. The gesture struck her as far too personal, but she tolerated it.

The inside of the house was unremarkable, if cramped. The kitchen took up most of the front room, and a couch sat below the window. Hunks of cured meat hung from the rafters. It smelled predominantly of wood smoke, but the scent was laced with something strangely sharp and chemical. Wildflowers drooped in a glass on the windowsill. Tyn noticed Vehn's pack propped up against the wall, although there was no sign of the First Spear herself. Oshe followed her gaze.

"Wherever your friend has wandered off to, I trust she'll return soon," he said breezily. "Make yourselves comfortable; there's bread in the cupboard if you're hungry. The door at the back leads to the porch; sit outside if you like. I'm afraid I must go help with the preparations for tonight, but if you need anything I'm not too far away."

"Thanks," she said.

When the front door closed, Rion sank down at the kitchen table and rested his head on his arms. Tyn watched Oshe through the window as he strolled back toward Emethas.

"Do you think we're in danger?" asked Rion without raising his head.

Oshe never once looked back. There was a spring in his step, and he walked with his hands in his pockets.

"We might be," she said.

"Should we run for it?"

"Without breaking the rules of the realm, I don't know if that's possible. We have to stay for the feast. Accept the bounty of the realm and all that."

"Which means we also have to meet their special, reclusive goddess. By the way, what *is* the difference between a god and a demon? I've been meaning to ask."

"Demons ascend to rulership via conquest, gods inherit via succession."

"So all demons are murderers?"

Tyn pressed her lips together. She stared out the window a little longer.

"So are most gods," she said at last. "There are no clean hands in Mkalis. But I don't think the dwellers here will harm us, not yet. They want something. Until they have it . . . I don't know, but I'm sure Vehn's reached the same conclusion. She must be trying to find out what they're after."

Rion breathed out heavily.

"If she hasn't returned in an hour, then we'll look for her." She turned around. "For now, try and get some rest. You're exhausted."

"As are you." He lifted his head. "Do we fight about who is on watch? That seems to be a Spear custom."

"The thing about the Kisdja tribe is that your superiors always win the argument." She briefly rested her hand on his arm. "It's okay, take the couch. I'll wake you if anything happens."

A smile tugged at the corner of Rion's mouth. Half-mocking, he pressed his fists together in acknowledgment.

The back garden opened out into the woods. The stream gurgled somewhere to Tyn's left and the sounds of the village drifted through the trees: voices, strains of music, the rumbling of carts. She settled down on the porch. Removed from the bustle, it was peaceful here. Drowsy chickens pecked about their coop.

Six years!

Tyn groaned and rubbed her temples. She must have sounded like a child.

After a few minutes, she sighed and reached for *God Instruments and Their Makers*. Better to take her mind off of things; there was nothing to be done except wait for Vehn anyway. The book welcomed her like an old friend. She smoothed the old pages under her hands, careful and gentle, and returned to the chapter on God Locks.

Res Paseca, a low-ranking ruler of great ambition, gained considerable notoriety after she forged the first Lock. Exhibiting great cunning, she made use of the Instrument to seal her adversaries within cracks between realms.

Thrust into the wild chaos of the rift and without hope of reprieve, the stranded rulers were thus offered an end to their suffering, should they abandon pride and comply in selecting her as their

Successor. Those that accepted her bargain, she granted the mercy of death. Those who refused, she bled into the Forging of further Locks.

Thus did Paseca the Avaricious claim one realm after another, rising in power and status. Eventually she met her match in Res Ketlebo of the 88th Realm, Sower of Starlight who smote her before she could drive him into her well-worn trap. Res Ketlebo, an avowed abolitionist of the Instruments—

"You shouldn't have that book."

Tyn blinked and looked up. The light had fallen over the hills; the sun blazed in the west and turned the rolling landscape bronze. She experienced a moment of complete disorientation, the sense of time having slid out from underneath her. When she started reading, it had scarcely been midday. Now Vehn stood on the porch, her arms crossed and her face stony.

"I, um . . ." Tyn swallowed. "I had permission from the library—"

"No, I meant that it should not be in your possession any longer. You lost your pack in Kan Sefune's realm. So how do you still have the book?"

Like a disturbed colony of ants spreading from their nest, Tyn's skin prickled.

"I must have put it in one of the other packs," she said slowly.

"Do you believe that Rion or I would carry it for you? Without noticing? You did no such thing." Vehn held out her hand. "Give it to me."

"First Spear—"

"Think," she interrupted. "Why would you have taken it with you in the first place? It's unnecessary weight—you could easily have left it in Res Tahirah's realm before we departed for Kan Sefune's. That would have given you more room for food."

"I thought it might be useful."

"You're lying. You didn't think at all. I've seen you reading it, and it's as if you enter a trance. The way you hold it, like it's . . . like it's a child. Something precious. That's not normal."

Tyn scowled. "I want to prepare for the conflict with Kan Buyak."

"Even the way you're speaking right now." Vehn stepped closer, her hand still outstretched. "This is not how you usually address me, Second Spear."

Tyn's mouth hardened. "Then tell me how you would prefer to be addressed."

Vehn's composure did not waver; she was cold and implacable.

"Give the book to me," she said. "That's an order, not a request."

For a second, Tyn almost refused. She wanted to hug *God Instruments and Their Makers* to her chest, to hide it away. It contained the answers they needed, she was sure of it; and had a comforting, familiar weight in her hands.

The moment passed. She held the book out and Vehn took it from her. As it left her fingers, she felt a slight twinge in her chest, like something unravelling.

"Forgive me," she said.

Vehn grimaced. She gave the cover a look of distaste.

"All I expect is that you fulfil your role," she said. "The rest is irrelevant."

"About earlier . . ."

"That is also irrelevant. As you said, Res Lfae comes first. You can have your ascendancy duel afterwards, if we're still alive." She flipped open the book and scanned the contents. A faint line creased her forehead. "You said you found this in the Tedassa library?"

"Yes."

"Why would Res Lfae ..." She shook her head. "Never mind. Where is Rion?"

"He's sleeping inside."

"Good. At least one of us will be well-rested." She tucked the book under her arm. Her eyes swept the hillside and she dropped her voice. "The feast is almost ready; I expect they'll summon us soon. Remain on your guard tonight."

"Do you know what they're after?"

Vehn shook her head. "No. But I saw them draining all the pools in the bathhouse."

"What?"

"At first, I thought it might be some compunction about cleanliness; outsiders soiling their space. Strange behaviour, but not that remarkable. But then they started carrying wooden boxes inside. At least a dozen, and by the way the dwellers held them, whatever they contained was valuable. And heavy."

"But you don't know what was inside?"

"No. And perhaps it doesn't matter." The fading light silhouetted her in red. "Whatever they want, they've waited this long. They must mean to bargain."

"Which suggests we still have some power."

Vehn nodded.

"Follow my lead tonight," she said.

Through the house, a loud rapping rang out.

"Honoured guests?" Oshe called from the front door. "Come on! The festivities are about to begin!"

Chapter Seventeen

Kan Meiralle's dwellers had drawn great sheets of waxy fronds over the cobbles of the village square, and strung incense burners from the nets in the trees. There was jubilance in the air, a raw vein of excitement that showed itself in the quick smiles and bursts of laughter. The dwellers draped themselves in coloured scarves, and hung tinkling golden charms from their bone flowers.

"Everyone is trying to impress," said Oshe, with a conspiratorial wink. He himself had shining rings dangling from the elegant spurs at the edge of his hairline.

"Impress us or your ruler?" asked Rion sourly.

"Oh, that depends. For some, it's both." His teeth shone brilliantly white.

"Sorry I asked," muttered Rion.

Dwellers laid out plates of pale brown bean paste, chillies roasted and stuffed with yellow seeds, slivers of shaved pumpkin wrapped around tiny fish, bowls of fermented milk laced with fruit and crushed spices. They set each dish down with reverence, and snatched hopeful glances at Vehn, Tyn, and Rion's faces, obviously anxious for their approval.

"Sit!" encouraged Oshe. "Here, quickly, Kan Meiralle is coming."

Tyn knelt where Oshe indicated. The smell of the food made her mouth water. The other dwellers had also gathered around the tables, and now gazed in the direction of the river.

A breeze stirred through the village, carrying the scent of wildflowers, and then Kan Meiralle emerged from the trees. For all the apprehension Tyn felt, the goddess's appearance was far from monstrous. Twice the height of her dwellers and willowy, Meiralle's thick hair cascaded in a red cloak over her shoulders. Her white skin was painted with brown stripes across her cheekbones and neck, and bone flowers flowed from her head and arms. More bones twined around her waist in a fragile belt, others dressed her long fingers in ivory rings. Simple clothes, leather shoes. Dozens of tiny gold hoops looped the lobes of her ears. She wore a half-smile, as if delight were only a breath away, waiting to be shared.

"Kan Meiralle, Quiet of the Woods, Beloved of Multitudes, and Ruler of the 124th Realm," said Oshe. "May her reign be eternal."

Kan Meiralle regarded him fondly. She drew up to the table, inclined her head to everyone, and took a seat. Her hair billowed like cotton cloth in the wind.

"By her favour and rule, please eat," said Oshe.

Tyn pressed her fists together respectfully, using the pause to verify which plates the dwellers took food from. She picked up an orange chilli, and Rion copied her. Although she was starving, she forced herself to exercise restraint and ate slowly.

"Thank you for your generosity, your Reverence," said Vehn. "We are unworthy, but will tell our ruler of your kindness. I am First Spear Vehn of the Kisdja tribe, dweller of Res Lfae."

Kan Meiralle tilted her head towards Vehn. Her eyes, luminously green, possessed a keen, intelligent light.

"My ruler prefers not to speak directly," said Oshe. "With your permission, I might serve as her voice?"

"Of course."

Oshe's eyes glazed and his shoulders loosened. Something about his expression altered. When he next spoke the cadence of his voice was completely different.

"I'm happy that you are here," said Kan Meiralle through his mouth. "Please, be at ease."

"Under the circumstances, that is difficult." Vehn folded her hands in her lap and sat up straighter. "Our realm is under threat. We have come to ask permission to use your Reverence's channel to the 12th realm."

"The Architect's domain?" Kan Meiralle looked thoughtful. "How unusual. But it is not yet time to discuss business. You seem weary and hungry, and I would offer you the care of my realm."

"But—"

"Eat." Oshe smiled gently. "You don't need to fear—I shall aid you. But for now you must rest. Surely you can spare a little time?"

Vehn nodded, tight-lipped.

The food tasted good. Tyn's borrowed clothing itched. She glanced at Rion. He had relaxed; the sharpest edges of his suspicions blunted. Fessi, on his left, stammered as she suggested he try the fish. Vehn picked at her food unhappily. She caught Tyn's eye and made a slight gesture with her hand, a Spear signal disguised in the motion of reaching for her drink. *Retreat as soon as possible.*

Tyn pretended not to see.

"Could you tell us about the Architect, your Reverence?" she asked. "As a matter of interest, rather than business?"

The goddess turned her attention to Tyn for the first time.

"You are also a dweller of Res Lfae?" she asked.

"Tyn and Rion are both my subordinates," Vehn said quickly, while glaring at Tyn. "They are only present to assist me."

"Yours must be a realm devoted to its own hierarchies." Meiralle smiled, and Oshe mirrored her. "However, there's no need for such rigid formality here. I can share some of what I know regarding the Architect, although there might not be all that much to say. My channel to the 12th realm was constructed by my predecessor almost three thousand years ago."

"And yet it still stands?"

"It does. As we are quite isolated, I guard the old paths carefully. The Architect, in grace and wisdom, still values our alliance."

"Do they ever come here?"

"Oh no. That would be unthinkable. The ruler of the 12th realm is . . ." Meiralle seemed slightly at a loss, and Oshe's mouth hung open and slack while she considered. "The ruler of the 12th realm is not altogether."

Tyn waited, and then asked uncertainly: "Not altogether what?"

"Just not altogether. The Architect confounds language. I would speak more clearly, but that might provide a false impression of the ruler's nature."

"Do they have emissaries then, if they themselves do not leave the 12th realm?"

"No one leaves the 12th realm anymore, I don't think. The dwellers . . ." Again, she struggled. "The dwellers are shaped—integrated—in such a way that makes movement unlikely. Other entities live within the realm; these have been known to travel, although they have not done so for many centuries."

Tyn frowned. "I'm not sure I understand."

"I suspected you would not. Tell me instead of Res Lfae. I have heard a little of them, although news moves slowly around here." Kan Meiralle leaned forward in perfect unison with Oshe. "They overthrew Kan Temairin, is that right?"

"Eight hundred years ago."

"That long already? How strange; it felt like yesterday. And now they too are in danger of losing their realm."

Without even turning her head, Tyn could feel Vehn tense beside her.

"We won't allow that to happen," Tyn said evenly.

"That is good. I find the tides of bloodshed and conquest saddening. So, are you here on their orders?"

"Not on their orders, no, but always in their interest."

"What a peculiar answer." Kan Meiralle gave Tyn a knowing look. "You are cautious, I see. Honest, but cautious. Those are valuable traits."

Flattery will get you nowhere. Tyn bowed her head.

"I am honoured by your esteem," she said.

"Your ruler must value it too, enabling you to travel so widely. You have the free use of their channels?"

"I—"

"I serve as the sole Bequeather of Res Lfae's channels," Vehn interrupted. "My subordinates travel under my authority only."

"Is that so?" The hoops in Meiralle's ears jingled as she turned back to the First Spear.

The conversation drifted, and the rest of the meal was passed in polite, stilted small talk. Tyn remained tense. Something was wrong here, but she could not put her finger on it. Vehn had grown quieter and more distant as the time passed, but Rion seemed to have forgotten caution. He was animated and smiling, nodding as Fessi spoke.

At some point, the masquerade had to end. Tyn just could not see what Kan Meiralle was waiting for—they had been defenceless from the start. An attack felt too long coming.

The goddess made a small gesture and Oshe stood up.

"Thank you, everyone," he said, as himself. "Kan Meiralle will retire to the House of Silk now, where she will discuss the guests' business with our realm." There were a few muted sounds of disappointment. "Our visitors are tired; we should not delay them any longer."

Kan Meiralle gracefully rose to her feet. She towered above Oshe. Over the course of the meal, she had not eaten, nor spoken a single word from her own mouth. She curled the fingers of her left hand and beckoned to Vehn.

"She will negotiate with you now," said Oshe. "Alone."

"Why?" asked Tyn quickly, then realised that might have sounded impudent. "I would prefer to accompany her," she added.

"She is your leader, is she not? Kan Meiralle can negotiate with her directly. You and your friend may retire to Fessi's house for now."

Tyn shook her head. "I would prefer to accompany her, as would Rion."

Kan Meiralle regarded her with an expression of sadness.

"Our ruler will speak to her, and her alone," said Oshe. "There is no cause for distress."

"I'm not distressed, I'm—"

"Quiet, Upstart," Vehn muttered as she got up. She bowed to Kan Meiralle. "Very well. Let's talk."

Tyn watched as Vehn accompanied Kan Meiralle down the street, Oshe leading the way and chatting easily. Was she overreacting? Rion frowned as they disappeared, but then Fessi drew him back into conversation. Other dwellers had begun to clean up the plates and cups; someone played a flute and a couple swayed to the tune. No one had shown the slightest trace of aggression; they had been nothing but kind and generous. But still, something was not right. Vehn had not been happy to leave them; that had been clear from her face. She was acting out of desperation.

"The negotiations could take some time," said Fessi. "Would you like to come with me?"

What do we have to negotiate?

But Tyn trailed after Rion anyway. This was wrong. She should have insisted on staying together; they were stronger as a team, they were tribemates. If she had not argued with Vehn earlier, then maybe the situation would have turned out differently. Now the First Spear had no one to watch her back.

Fessi's cottage sat on a wide plot of land outside Emethas. The long-haired herbivores grazed in the field outside, and small moths fluttered over the pale grass. Crooked trees hung heavy with large yellow fruit, and rows of herbs—sage, sorrel, calamint—grew in their shade. While Fessi fumbled around her kitchen, brewing tea, finding cups, adjusting a vase of flowers, Tyn sat on the porch outside.

"This place doesn't seem that bad," said Rion, leaning against the balustrade. He gazed at the twilight field. "All things considered."

"Given up on Ahri already?"

He made a face. "No. But maybe we misjudged them."

Tyn returned to watching the road.

"What?"

"Nothing," she said. "I worry about your naivety, that's all."

He snorted and walked towards the back door. "You're only

jealous the goddess wanted to speak to Vehn instead of you."

She did not bother to reply. The door closed behind him.

The sun sank across the sky and vanished into the fold of the hills. It remained warm, even as the light faded. The animals clustered together and, shoulder to shoulder, they lowed to one another in melodious, rumbling warbles; each note vibrating in Tyn's chest.

The stars had just begun to appear overhead when she saw someone walking down the road from the direction of the village. Oshe. Tyn picked up her spear and strode out to meet him.

"Where is Vehn?"

He looked startled by her aggression, but recovered. "I'm sorry, you must have been anxious. Everything is fine."

—*rything is fine.*

Tyn shook her head. "Where is she?"

"Your friend made an agreement with Kan Meiralle, and has crossed into the 12th realm. She asked me to pass her orders to you."

Tyn blinked. "She crossed without us?"

"I received the impression that she was in a hurry."

"But she wouldn't—"

"She wants you to remain here until she returns, and expects that she might be gone for a day or two." Oshe peered at her. "Are you all right, my dear? You look a little unsteady."

"I don't believe you," she said.

"I didn't mean to upset you, but that's the message she gave me. I assure you, your friend is perfectly fine."

"Let me see her."

"As I've explained, she is no longer here."

Tyn clenched her fist around her spear and took a step towards Oshe. He raised his hands in alarm.

"I'm not going to play this game," she said. "You will tell me where you've taken Vehn, or I will force the answer out of you."

"Tyn, what are you doing?"

Rion hurried down the road, Fessi behind him. He was flushed and his hair was mussed.

"Stay out of this, Rion."

"What's going on?" He caught up to her and tried to take her arm. She jerked away from him.

"I was explaining that your leader has crossed to the 12th realm," said Oshe. "Tyn took the news somewhat personally."

"Vehn got permission?" Rion sounded uncertain. He looked from Oshe to Tyn. "But that's good, isn't it?"

—good, isn't it?

"She would have told us. She would have taken me with her." Tyn rubbed her forehead. She was sweating, but felt cold. "It's a lie."

"Are you okay? I think you should sit down."

"Rion, I need you to trust me." His face swam in her vision. "This is wrong. Vehn is in trouble."

"She's very pale," said Fessi. "Maybe our food . . . ?"

"But I ate everything she did and I'm fine."

"Listen to me!" Tyn gritted her teeth. She had been an idiot; she should have taken Rion and ran right after the feast.

"Maybe it's shock," said Oshe. "Your realm has close-bound ties between members of the same tribe, doesn't it?"

"Well, yeah," said Rion uncertainly. "But Vehn and Tyn hate each other."

Tyn reached out, wanting to shake him, wanting to tell him to wake up, none of this felt normal or right, realms without border restrictions were avoided for a reason, and she could not keep him safe if he did not believe her. Her spear slipped from her fingers. He caught her by the arms.

"Whatever the reason, she seems to be taking it quite hard," said Oshe. "I'm sorry. I had no idea this would happen."

"Tyn?" Rion struggled to pull her arm around his neck to prop her up. "Hey, talk to me. You're burning hot."

"We've got to find Vehn," she groaned.

The last thing she felt before falling into darkness was a sharp pain at the base of her neck.

Chapter Eighteen

She was forgetting something. It felt important, but danced out of her reach every time she thought about it too hard. Her bare feet dangled in the stream and the cool water kissed her ankles. Rion and Fessi lay on the grass on the opposite bank, talking, very close together, hands touching. Occasionally, Fessi giggled as she fed Rion slices of red fruit. Rays of sunlight warmed Tyn's shoulders.

Something bad had happened. But surely it could not be so terrible, if she couldn't remember it? Res Lfae, it was something to do with them. A jolt of fear ran through her mind, and with it an awful sense of loss. Confusion. Where was she?

Vehn—

"Something the matter, my dear?" asked Oshe, startling her out of her reverie. He dropped down next to her.

"I'm not sure," she said, then tried to smile. "No, probably not."

"That's good." He brushed her hair away from her face and leaned in to kiss her. "I'd hate to see you sad."

His lips were soft and his tongue slipped smoothly into her mouth. For a split second, she felt a deep revulsion. Then she relaxed and returned the kiss. Across the water, Rion laughed.

"I don't know what's wrong with me," she said.

"I'm going to suggest," Oshe drew away, lounging backwards, "that nothing could possibly be wrong with you."

"You're revolting."

"You bring out the worst in me."

They headed upstream to swim beneath the falls, and dove for freshwater pearls, cracking apart oysters with rocks, laughing. Tyn felt deliriously happy, and at the same time, terribly, chillingly afraid. She wanted to be alone, but Oshe or Fessi were always there, cajoling her to swim deeper or run faster, and Rion was there too, but he seemed . . . inaccessible. Their eyes met from time to time, and Tyn thought he looked scared. But then they were swept up in another current of bliss, and she forgot her doubts.

They returned to Fessi's cottage as the moon rose over the hills, all of them dripping wet from the river and exhausted. Everything was silvery and beautiful; Fessi talked of hidden glades beyond the forest, midnight ventures to the dance halls the next village over. Her crown of bone blossoms entranced Tyn, so delicate and lovely, and she hardly heard a word of what was said.

There were other gaps in her memory, absences that loomed like sea caves, and dark churning waters below.

"Come back to bed," said Oshe, snaking his fingers between hers. "You'll get cold."

She stood in the middle of Fessi's kitchen. There was a knife in her hand and she could not remember picking it up. The blade caught the moonlight, a white curve. Then it was gone.

"I'll be there in a minute," she said, smiling. "I'm a little thirsty, that's all."

"Don't be too long." He raised her hand, placed kisses upon each of her knuckles. His green eyes glowed in the dark. "Or *I'll* get cold."

"We can't have that."

He chuckled and withdrew up the stairs. Why was her heart beating so fast? She felt sick. With unsteady hands, she pumped water into a cup. Through the window, the trees looked ghostly and unreal, the leaves bright as metal. She swallowed too quickly and spluttered. Oshe was waiting; she should return to bed.

Beneath the trees, a flash of movement. Tyn leaned over the counter, straining to see through the darkness. There was someone there.

—*back to bed.*

Tyn quietly unlocked the back door. The shadows of the porch formed dense blocks of darkness; she could remain unseen. The knife was in her hand again; she moved on the balls of her feet. Invisible and silent. She held her breath and crept forward.

There again, a movement at the base of the trees, closer this time. They were good, almost as quiet as she was and equally cautious. Their silhouette merged with the tree trunk behind them.

A spike of pain shot through Tyn's abdomen, and she could not stop a small gasp of surprise from escaping her mouth. The shadow in the trees froze. For a moment, they were both silent.

"Tyn?" said the shadow, their voice barely louder than her breath.

—*back to bed.*

—*back to bed.*

—*back to bed.*

After a second of hesitation, the shadow muttered a curse and stepped out from beneath the trees. A tall man, brown-skinned, with black hair bound in a short ponytail and silver rings in his ears. A vivid white scar cut across his throat.

"Tyn, I know you're there," he whispered.

Another flash of pain. She pressed her hand to her mouth to stop herself from making a sound. A light came on upstairs.

"I promise I'll come back for you," the man said quickly. "But I can't afford for them to discover me."

"My dear?" Oshe's voice floated out of the house.

"Go," she said, her throat locked. She felt light-headed again, and her mind was filled with echoing.

The man nodded once.

"Wait for me," he said.

She could hear Oshe's swift footsteps on the stairs. The man melted back into the shadows of the trees. She closed her eyes for a second—*fix him in your memory, he was here, this was real*—and then the door creaked.

"Why are you outside?" asked Oshe. "Is something wrong?"

Her thoughts grew clouded and slow. She turned. Oshe stood in the entrance, his eyes wide with concern, his curling hair tousled around his face. He held a candlestick in one hand.

"The moon was so beautiful," she said. "I could not help myself."

For a second, she saw his eyes narrow in suspicion and dart past her to the dark field. Then, quick as mercury, his expression cleared.

"Not as beautiful as you," he replied. He crossed the porch and slid one arm around her waist. "My huntress. You look so lost and lonely, it could break my heart."

"Flatterer."

"Don't be so heartless." He ran a lock of her hair through his fingers. "Won't you come inside now?"

"Then I'll miss the moon." She drew back from his embrace.

"We could stay out here, couldn't we? Look at how everything shines. Isn't it lovely?"

He smiled. "You strange creature. Of course, if that's what you want. But maybe a blanket?"

"If you insist."

He kissed her cheek. "I do."

They sat side by side, covered in a blanket woven from the wool of Fessi's animals, and Oshe whispered poetry to her as the moon travelled from one horizon to the other. Her eyelids grew heavy.

When she woke, she found herself in bed, with dawn bruising the sky and Fessi's sweet singing ringing out from the kitchen. The smell of wood-roasted meat drifted up the stairs. Tyn rolled out from beneath the covers.

"You're awake," said Oshe. He was already dressed, a green tunic beaded with pearls along the shoulders. "Hurry up and get ready; we're going to the East Forest today. It's a long walk."

She feigned distress and then dissolved into laughter. Her body felt light and strong, her whole being suffused with joy. Oshe shook his head in fond exasperation.

She was forgetting something, but it felt unimportant.

The East Forest lay almost at the border of the next province, and Oshe suggested they could visit some friends of his, maybe spend the night in Dremeral. Fessi walked behind Rion with her arms draped over his shoulders. He kept trying to shrug her off, but she only giggled and returned, murmuring into his ear. He blushed at something she said, and for some reason Tyn found his expression hilarious. He was so naïve, so helpless.

He looked at her then, and she stopped laughing.

"Tyn?" he said. She heard him like there was a gulf between

them; a great, empty distance. "Tyn, I think . . ."

"A game!" Oshe declared. He took Tyn's hand and spun her around like a dancer. "Enough walking, I'm bored. Let's play a game."

"What kind of a game?"

"Hm." He raised his eyes in abstraction. "Something with prizes, I think. You know of anything fun, my dear?"

"I . . ." A brief wave of disorientation. She caught sight of Rion's face, but he looked eager and excited now. Waiting for her to answer. "Do you know Seekers?"

Oshe grinned. "That's perfect. You hide, and I'll count?"

"But you'll only hunt her," Fessi complained. "What about us?"

"No, I'll play fair. You can hide too." He winked at Tyn. "Although there's only one prize I'm after."

"You have to find me first."

"My heart will lead me straight to you, my dear."

"That's the most nauseating thing I've ever heard."

Oshe clutched his chest, still grinning, then turned around sharply and covered his eyes with one arm.

"Ninety-nine," he said. "Ninety-eight."

Tyn shoved him playfully, then took off in the opposite direction, running down the road and into the undergrowth. Rion and Fessi headed up another path, the latter pulling Rion by the hand. The leaves whispered in the breeze. Tyn's pulse thrummed. She needed to run, needed to hide, to find a place where no one would ever find her. Her dress was awkward; she hitched it up to free her legs. Dresses, she never wore dresses, or flimsy beaded sandals, or her hair loose and hanging around her shoulders. Her head spun. Of course, she wore dresses. Why shouldn't she?

She paused, bracing herself against a tree.

"Seventy-two, seventy-one . . ."

Had to hide, that was the game; she was having so much fun. She cast around, then moved towards the thicker undergrowth at the base of the slope. If Oshe wanted to find her, he would need to work for it. She had played this game hundreds of times; it was a Spear training exercise for new initiates. Vehn had noticed her skill and complimented her, years ago; she had told Tyn that her potential outstripped any other initiate in the last decade.

Vehn.

Her vision darkened and she stumbled. A hand closed over her mouth.

For an instant, all Tyn felt was shock. Then instinct moved her. She grasped the assailant's wrist, twisted, and when they turned she swept their legs out from beneath them. They fell onto their back. A heartbeat later and she had them pinned.

"It's me, it's me." The man grimaced in pain. "Tyn, stop it."

She bared her teeth in a snarl. "I don't know you."

"This is my real body." He struggled to throw her off. "You only ever saw the surrogate in Mkalis. It's me, Vasethe."

The name gave her pause. She wavered. There was something about his face, too . . . In the distance, Oshe continued counting down. The man tried to work free of her grasp. She tightened her hold on his wrists. She was stronger than him.

"You once said that you trusted me without knowing why," Vasethe gasped. "You are the Second Spear of Res Lfae, Ruler of the 194th Realm. You're afraid of heights. You have a d'wen named Pax, and you ride her like a maniac, and you broke your arm trying to stop Fanieq from hurting your ruler."

"I don't—I don't remember—"

"Look at me," he pressed. "Look at me, Tyn. This isn't you. None of it is real."

"Vasethe?" The name sounded strange coming from her mouth. "You're—why are you—"

"I'm here to get you out of this realm."

The noise in her mind suddenly became deafening. She shook her head, unable to speak. No, he could not make her leave, Oshe needed to find her, she was supposed to hide. Pain coiled inside her gut and she shuddered.

"Come on, Tyn," he said.

"No," she managed. Struggled for a moment. "There's something wrong with me."

"I can fix it, but we need to go *now*." He worked his right arm free. Her grip had grown slack.

"I'm sorry." She slid off him and the world went black for a second. "I'll lead them in another direction. Get out of here. Don't come back."

"Thirty. Twenty-nine. Twenty-eight," counted Oshe loudly.

Vasethe straightened. He reached out and gripped her shoulders. Steady, deft hands, achingly familiar, the ghost of another life. The pain in her abdomen grew worse and her breathing came out harsh. She remembered.

"Oh no," she said.

"Hey. Just focus on me, all right?" he said gently. "We survived the Realm of Ghosts. This is nothing."

"I left you behind in the Realm of Ghosts."

"Because I begged you to."

"Twenty-two. Twenty-one."

"We're going to do this together," he said. "Even if I have to drag you out of here kicking and screaming."

She tried to laugh, and choked on it. "Vasethe—"

He pulled her to her feet. "Less kicking would be good though. Can you run?"

She steadied herself against him. "I don't know."

"I can guide you." He took her wrist. "The alternative is to carry you, but I think that will be too slow."

"Fourteen. Thirteen."

Vasethe led her through the trees and she stumbled after him. The echoes in her head howled ever louder, but she could still hear the countdown. Seven. Six. Oshe's cheerful voice rang through the forest. Her legs dragged; she was clumsy and half-blind.

"Vasethe." The pain flared and she clasped her midriff.

"Stay with me." Although Vasethe sounded calm, she could hear fear beneath the surface. Fear, and an undercurrent of anger.

"If he catches up—"

"The channel to Res Tahirah's realm is just outside the village. We can make it."

"One. Zero." Oshe raised his voice louder. "The hunt begins!"

She gasped and doubled over. Vasethe shifted his grasp to her shoulder, supporting her. He rested his forehead against hers for a second. Memory prickled across her skin; she knew this gesture, she had been this close to him before.

"You need to do this," he said.

She breathed in through her nose, out her mouth. The echoes told her to run, to kill him, to scream.

"My dear, where have you wandered off to?" Oshe called in a singsong tone. Tyn turned towards his voice—she should return, he would worry, how cruel of her to run away—but Vasethe tightened his grip. She faltered.

"Focus on me," he said.

She nodded.

They shambled along a near-invisible trail. Vasethe moved silently, but Tyn knew she was making too much noise. Behind them, Oshe narrated his search, loudly wondering where she might have gone. Every step felt impossible. Vasethe pulled her arm over his shoulder to support her better. For a few seconds, she lost track of time. The world veered and rolled, and he was all that kept her attached to the ground. She could feel his heart beating.

"My dear, I give up!" called Oshe. "Come back to me."

Her heart burned, she felt a hot rush of excitement at the prospect of seeing Oshe again. When she tried to turn around, Vasethe restrained her.

"Come on, we're so close."

"But he's waiting," she said. Vasethe did not understand; it was imperative that Oshe found her as soon as possible. She refused to be a disappointment, not again, not to him, not when he had treated her so kindly.

"Listen to me," said Vasethe. "Tyn, *listen*. I swear that I can fix you, but I don't have the power here."

—*come back to me.*

"You should go," she said faintly. "He's going to be very angry."

Vasethe ignored her and kept moving, dragging her along with him. Ahead, the sunlight grew brighter. They had reached the edge of the forest.

"I miss you!" Oshe sounded closer and more urgent. "Why won't you come?"

Tyn bit down hard on her tongue. Blood flooded her mouth, and the sharpness cut through the tumult of sound and violence inside her head. A tall stone pillar stood just inside a field; beyond, a cosy village nestled into the trees.

"They guard the entrances, but not the exits," Vasethe murmured. "People are expected to stay of their own accord."

He held her close to his side for a second, listening. Then he nodded.

"We're going to run," he said. "Keep going. Even if I'm stopped, you won't break any rules by leaving. Ready?"

She moved her head once, stiffly. He gripped her hand.

The rest was a blur of fear and pain and brightness. The distance from the trees to the pillar was about thirty feet, but it felt far further, an indeterminable space that shifted and morphed beneath her. The channel opened to Vasethe's touch and he shoved her into the crawlspace. She wanted to object—he should go first—but it was too late. She dragged herself forward, arms scraped raw on the hard, crystalline walls of the tunnel.

—*come back to me.*

—*come back to me.*

—*come back to me.*

She whimpered as agony jack-knifed across her torso. This was too much. Vasethe was speaking, urging her onwards. He was right behind her, she had come so far, just a little further and they would be safe. Trust him. He knew he had failed her before, but not this time. It was his turn to save her. Trust him.

She crawled the last few feet and fell through the channel into Res Tahirah's realm.

Chapter Nineteen

A stretch of her memory, empty. Brief snatches of lucidity, a few seconds when the pain and the noise receded enough for her to make sense of the world. The colour and birdsong of Res Tahi-rah's realm, Vasethe talking to her while she panicked—where is Oshe? where am I?—a channel, the smell of home, the plains be-low Tahmais and the taste of the dust in the air, dusk dropping into darkness, and then finally a small, shadowed room.

"Can you hear me?" Vasethe asked.

She lay on her back on a hard floor; a lantern hung from the ceiling above her. Through the open door, she could see an endless white expanse, bright in the moonlight. Two spears lay on the floor beneath the window, Vehn's and her own.

She groaned. "Oshe . . ."

"He's not here." Vasethe knelt at her side. His hair had come undone and there was a bruise forming on his jaw. "It's just us."

Her mouth was dry. "Where am I?"

"Eris' house, although she isn't around at the moment."

"My chest hurts."

"I know." He rested his hand on her shoulder. He looked worried. "I'm going to try to stop it, but I've never done this before. You'll need to be still."

The pain churned in her midriff and echoes gathered like stormclouds inside her head. "I'll try."

"No, that wasn't . . ." He grimaced. "This isn't going to make sense right now, but I can stop you from moving. I'm asking your permission for that."

She nodded. "Do it."

He squeezed her shoulder. She noticed that there was blood on his lips.

"Be still," he murmured.

She breathed in sharply as her limbs went slack. The muscles of her arms and legs stopped responding to her.

"Vasethe," she whispered.

"Don't be scared."

"How did you do that?"

His skin shone in the lantern light, he was perspiring. "Eris taught me a few things. It doesn't matter right now."

That was . . . he spoke through blood. That's a ruler's *binding.* Vasethe shifted and moved his hand to her stomach, pressing lightly as if testing something.

"What are you doing?"

"Trying to work out where it is."

Tyn winced as the pain spiked. Vasethe caught her expression and withdrew his hand immediately.

"No," she said. "Whatever is inside me, get it out."

He hesitated.

"Please." She squeezed her eyes shut. "I don't care, just get it out."

He took her hand with his left, muttered something she did not catch, and then pressed the fingers of his right hand to the hollow below her sternum. They sunk through the fabric of her dress and into her flesh. She gasped.

"I'm sorry," he said.

There was no pain. She opened her eyes. No wound either,

but Vasethe's wrist ended where it met her chest like his hand was submerged in water. She could sense it, a feeling of obstruction, like something lodged in her throat. Her breathing grew quicker. She tried to speak, but only produced a wordless sound of horror. Vasethe moved, and his hand seemed to pass through her without really touching her at all, and yet she could *feel* it.

"Please don't be afraid," he said.

"How?" she whispered. It felt deeply wrong, and her body rebelled against it. If not for the binding, she would have thrashed, but it held her secure.

Vasethe's gaze had gone distant. The whites of his eyes darkened to coal-black, and his breathing emerged haggard. Pain twisted his face. He grew still.

Abruptly, his hand closed into a fist; he grasped hold of something. Agony blossomed in the space between Tyn's ribs. She cried out. A deep wrenching sensation ripped through her chest, then there was a snap.

Vasethe pulled a red, squirming worm out from between her ribs. It squealed in distress as it flailed in his grasp. Easily the length of his forearm and as wide as his thumb, it had hundreds of tiny black abscesses along its back. They adhered to Vasethe's skin like suckers.

"Got it," he said. His eyes returned to normal and he sagged.

Tyn heaved for air. She wanted to throw up. The creature continued to wail.

"Unbind me," she rasped.

"You may move," he said, and her body was her own again. She rolled onto her side, wrapping her arms across her chest.

"I'm so sorry, Tyn," he said.

A cloud had lifted from her mind, and everything around

her had a terrible clarity; the room, the windows, her own skin, all of it felt too close and sharp. She pushed herself onto her knees.

"Give it to me," she said.

Vasethe did not ask, he just held out the parasite. It tried to latch onto his wrist, but she tore it away. In her hand, the creature felt slick and cold. Its touch stung her. She crawled across the room and picked up her spear. The worm's squealing became frantic as she dragged herself through the front door and out into the yard.

Tyn pried the suckers off her palm and dropped the creature onto the ground. It writhed. On her knees, she raised the spear.

"Lightless take you," she breathed, and drove the blade down.

The worm sprayed blood over her arms. With vicious force, she twisted the weapon through the creature and into the ground. It curled around the blade, agonised. Then it went still.

Neither of them spoke. Vasethe had his right hand cradled to his chest, and he was breathing heavily. Tyn let go of her spear, let it clatter onto the ground.

"How long?" she asked.

The silence grew deeper.

"Probably six days," he said. "When I first realised you were in trouble, I think you had just been ensnared."

She covered her eyes.

"Tyn, I—"

"I need you to answer the next question honestly," she said. "Because I can't remember everything."

The words got trapped in her mouth. Vasethe was frozen.

"About Oshe," she said. Stopped. "I can't remember if I—if he . . ."

"No."

She lowered her hand.

"He only kissed you once." Vasethe's expression was neutral, tightly controlled. "By the river. He might have tried more, the night you saw me in the trees, but you insisted on staying outside. Nothing happened."

She looked away from him. She remembered the river.

"If there was any chance he—" Vasethe broke off. He gathered himself again. "I would have intervened, no matter the result. I only waited so long because if I was caught—if I had to eat their food—there would be no one left to help you."

"Bounty of the realm," she said quietly.

"If they offered, I would have been forced to accept."

"I understand." She looked up. "You swear that was all?"

"Yes. I swear."

The weight bearing down on her lifted, a little. The nausea remained. "Rion?"

"I stayed with you, and I lost track of him a few times. But I don't think so." Vasethe stared down at his hands. "Those dwellers, they weren't really interested in either of you; they just wanted to keep you distracted while the parasites developed. Your friend kept rejecting the woman's advances, and she seemed to realise it was the wrong tactic."

"And . . ." Tyn's mouth was dry. "And Vehn?"

A long silence.

"She's alive," said Vasethe.

There was a sour taste on the back of Tyn's tongue. She felt cold.

"I have to go back," she said.

He nodded. "I know."

"If I get ensnared again—"

"Then I will get you out again."

"You were lucky to manage it once." She smiled weakly. "Don't take the risk a second time. I need you to ask the border keeper for help; Res Lfae is in trouble."

Vasethe looked worried. "I know about Buyak. Eris is just . . . where she's gone, I can't reach her. She was supposed to have returned by now."

A small part of Tyn felt relieved. The border keeper had not abandoned Lfae after all—she simply didn't know that they were in danger. Vehn had been wrong.

"When she returns, then," she said. "If it isn't too late."

Vasethe nodded. "Of course."

With effort, Tyn stood. "And then, after this is over, could we talk? There's a lot I want to ask you. Like when you became a ruler."

He also got to his feet. It clearly taxed him. "I'm not, exactly. But things have . . . happened. It's complicated."

"The border keeper told me that you did something stupid."

"Just the one thing?" He reached beneath his shirt and pulled out a golden dial on a chain. "Here. You should take this."

Her heart beat quicker.

"Fanieq's God Compass," she said.

"Eris had locked it away, but I managed to get through her wards. I used it to sneak into the 124th realm without the dwellers noticing. And it helped me to keep an eye on you." The Instrument swung gently back and forth. "With this, they won't even realise that you left, and if you run into trouble, you can cross out of the realm."

She took it from him. The metal was freezing cold. Just like last time. It fit into her palm snugly, like it had been waiting to return to her.

She looked up at Vasethe, really looked at him for the first time, and her chest ached. He was right; before now she had only seen his surrogate body, but she knew his real face, knew how to read him, and how he smiled, and the sound of his laughter. She could not remember being Raisha, but she knew him all the same. Somehow, that made things better.

"Thank you," she said.

He shrugged, a little embarrassed. "You would have done the same."

She hesitated. Then she stepped closer and hugged him. His shoulders stiffened for a second, before he sighed and relaxed. He wrapped his arms around her.

"I'll wait for you in Res Tahirah's realm," he said. "I can't promise that I won't come after you though."

She shook her head slightly. "I'll be careful."

"I wish you didn't have to go back."

She drew away from him and picked up her spear, wiping off the parasite's blood. The reflection of the saltpan gleamed luminously white on the blade.

"Don't worry." She held the weapon tighter. "I can handle this."

Chapter Twenty

Tyn approached Fessi's cottage from the direction of the forest. It was night, drawing towards early morning, and clouds hung dense and pendulous over the moon. She left her spear hidden in the grass. If matters unfolded as planned, she would be able to retrieve it later. Rion came first.

The animals in the field watched her steal closer to the house, unblinking and unmoving. In the darkness, they struck her as menacing; their heavy bodies denser blots of shadow in the landscape. They breathed in unison as they stared at her, deep and slow. She gave them a wide berth.

Light spilled out of the kitchen and across the porch. Through the open windows, Tyn caught the strains of an argument.

". . . fool. Now my receiver is anxious, and I can't settle him." Fessi's voice was no longer simpering and shy; she spoke with cutting severity. Tyn could see the dweller's shadow outlined against the pantry door, the intricate curves of her bone blossoms reduced to a single, hard-edged mass.

"She'll return," said Oshe. "I have this under control."

"Hah! Is that so? When Kan Meiralle emerges from the Persuasion—"

"Look, I'm calling the stupid woman back. What else do you want from me?"

"I want you to fix this. Frankly, I should have taken her off your hands after she tried to stab you with the kitchen knife."

Tyn crouched in the herb bed. She tore a handful of leaves from the calamint bush, crushed them between her fingers, and then rubbed her eyes. The mint burned, and she blinked rapidly as water formed along her eyelashes. She wiped her hands clean and stood up.

"Oshe!" she cried. "Oshe, where are you?"

Instantly, the kitchen fell silent. Tyn staggered towards the back door; a second later it flew open. Through her stinging, tear-stained vision, she saw Oshe run out, his face haggard. Fessi appeared behind him.

"Oshe!"

He opened his arms and she stumbled into his embrace. It took steel not to recoil from his touch—his hot breath, his slack, forceless body, the faintly chemical smell of him—but she kept her reactions in check.

"It's okay now, my dear," he whispered, stroking her back. "You're safe."

Tyn sobbed. "I was all alone."

"Why did you run off, my huntress? Where were you?"

"You told me to hide." She spoke into his shoulder. Her throat hitched. "I thought you'd find me."

"I'm sorry." He let her go, studied her face with concern, took in her wet, bloodshot eyes. "But everything is fine now; we won't play that game again. You don't need to cry anymore."

"We were very worried about you," said Fessi.

Oshe patted Tyn's shoulder. She longed to crush his arm inside her grip; she wanted so badly to hurt him. But not yet.

"I'm tired," she said. "Let me go to bed."

"Aren't you hungry?" he asked. "You must be, after wandering for so long."

Tyn fought to hide her fear. *A question, not an offer.*

"I just want to lie down." She wiped her eyes. "Oshe, you said that you would find me, and then you didn't. You said that your heart—"

"I know, I know, my poor lost lamb." Was that a hint of irritation in his voice? He slipped his hand down to her waist and she barely concealed her disgust. The idea that she could have welcomed his touch made her skin crawl. "I am truly wretched."

"I thought that you had forgotten me."

"How could I?" He steered her into the house. Tyn saw a look pass between him and Fessi. Victory? Relief?

Rion hunched over on the window seat, asleep. His head rested on his chest at an uncomfortable angle, and his eyebrows were drawn together in a frown. His eyelids twitched, some fraught dream playing out behind them.

"I need to talk to Fessi, and then I'll be right up," said Oshe. "Go on."

Tyn looked away from Rion. A deep anger seethed in the pit of her stomach. Something of her feelings must have shown on her face, because Oshe's placid smile slipped.

"Go on," he repeated, with greater emphasis.

She climbed the stairs. Behind her, Fessi made a comment, too quiet to decipher. The dwellers' low voices faded to a murmur.

The bedroom was a mess. Tyn paused in the doorway. The time she had spent here was lost; she could recall fragments, sweet nothings and a nameless, looming fear, but the rest was blank. Clothes and plates were strewn over the floor, the bed left unmade. The window that opened out over the hillside stood ajar, a breeze ruffling the curtain. She closed it and sat down on the bed.

The Compass hung heavy beneath her dress, equal parts unnerving and reassuring. She touched it and breathed out slowly. Rion came first, then Vehn.

In that case, would you have abandoned me?

"Never," she muttered.

There, the slight squeak of the floorboards and the quick fall of Oshe's feet. Tyn inhaled and lay down. Closed her eyes, even as it went against her every instinct. The door creaked.

"I'm here," he said. "You must have worn yourself out, trying to find your way back home."

She nodded.

"You're still angry, aren't you? I can tell."

She sighed, rolled onto her side. Exposed her back to him.

"I'm just tired," she said.

He crossed the room. She felt the bed dip under his weight.

"My dear, you mustn't stay angry. It hurts me. Forget about today."

"Hm."

"Tomorrow, you won't remember your sadness. You'll see." He draped an arm across her and tucked himself into the curve of her back. Tyn could not repress a shiver, but Oshe seemed to misinterpret her feelings.

"Such delights," he whispered into her ear. "You cannot imagine. I shall show you tomorrow."

"Tomorrow is too long a wait."

He laughed. "Oh?"

She turned over to face him. The corners of his sick, fever-green eyes creased in amusement.

"My impatient huntress," he said. He extended a hand, cupped it around the back her neck. "You are full of surprises."

She swung her leg over him and let him draw her towards a kiss. He shut his eyes, lips parted. Tyn ran her fingers over his cheek.

Then, swift as a viper, she clamped her hand over his mouth and drove her shiv up through the base of his ribcage.

Oshe's eyes flew wide. He made a small, shocked sound. Tyn held firmly onto the blade and twisted it into his heart. Blood bubbled around her hand, hot and gushing.

"Looks like you bring out the worst in me too," she whispered.

He tried to cough. She crushed his mouth beneath her palm. There was shock in his eyes; an edge of indignation, as if he could not quite believe that she would dare to kill him. Then fear. A spasm of pain.

Tyn did not blink, not until the final death rattle had emptied from his lungs and his heart came to a stop. Then she pulled out the knife. Blood rushed from the wound. She drew away from the corpse. The torrent of feeling she had held at bay hit her all at once, and she leaned over the side of the bed and vomited.

Glassy-eyed, Oshe stared at the ceiling. The impression of her fingers marked his cheeks. She had seen death before, had killed before, and it was always ugly, but she had never stood so close to the violence. It had never felt so personal. Oshe lay as lifeless as the crown of bone ringing his scalp.

She wiped her hands clean on her dress, then peeled it off and bunched the coarse woollen fabric into a wad. She shoved it into the bed beside Oshe and threw the coverlet over him.

There were more clothes in the wardrobe, and she changed quickly. Although events had worked out in her favour so far, the smallest mistake could bring everything crashing down.

She strained her ears for any noise from downstairs. If she drew Kan Meiralle's attention, if Fessi raised an alert, then her task would become next to impossible. She flicked open the catch on the God Instrument.

"Where is Rion?" she whispered.

The lid of the casing misted. The engraved golden surface dulled and grew translucent, and an image of Rion curled up on his side appeared on the metal. In the background, she could see a window and the moon. The compass needle swung to the left.

"And Fessi?"

The needle moved a fraction further left. Fessi was in the kitchen, busy soaking slices of meat in a dark yellow oil. The dweller's mouth moved; she was talking to herself. Or to the food. Tyn peered closer. It might have been a trick of the light, but the meat appeared to be moving too.

Tyn closed the Compass.

The moon had risen high above the tree branches before Fessi finally climbed the stairs. The dweller's steps were soft and careful, as if she was trying to avoid disturbing the peace of the cottage. Tyn held her breath. Fessi paused outside the door.

Keep going. There's nothing to see here.

The dweller mumbled something to herself—something like "absolute disaster"—and then the floorboards creaked as she carried on down the landing. Tyn counted to two hundred, then consulted the Compass again. Fessi was in bed. Rion remained downstairs.

She eased open the bedroom door. The air on the landing was cooler and fresh; she had grown accustomed to the iron tang of Oshe's blood and the sour smell of her vomit. Fessi had left a lamp burning in the kitchen, and it cut a yellow wedge across the ground.

Tyn moved on the balls of her feet; slow steps, transferring her weight an inch at a time. Sweat rolled down her neck. One stair. Pause. Another. She *could* kill Fessi, there was no doubt in her mind about that, but the memory of the shiv sliding through Oshe's chest was still in her hands. She shrank before the idea of killing a woman in her sleep. Vehn would have done it, but Tyn could not bear to.

She reached the ground floor. Across the room, she could see Rion curled up on the window seat, dreaming fitfully. He murmured to himself. She crept across the room.

"Rion?" she said.

He did not wake.

She crouched beside him. Ready to clamp her hand over his mouth in case he spooked, she touched his arm.

His eyes opened blearily.

"Hey." She pressed a finger to her lips. "It's me."

"Tyn?" He sat. His skin had a waxy, wan quality and his pupils grew massive in the dark. He looked around in confusion. "Where's Fessi?"

"We're going to play a game in the woods," she whispered. "Fessi's gone ahead."

He squinted. "But she said that she wanted me to sleep."

"Not anymore." Tyn took hold of his wrist. It felt thinner in her hand. "You have to be as quiet as you can, all right?"

"Because we're playing . . . a game? I don't know if I want to."

"She's waiting," Tyn coaxed.

He got up reluctantly. She tried not to flinch as the floorboards groaned beneath him.

The back door was unlocked. The night tasted sweet and

cold; perspiration chilled on Tyn's skin. She guided Rion to the road. He struck her as distracted and puzzled, but not in immediate pain. The parasite, whatever it was, knew no more than its host—so long as Rion could be convinced, it would lie dormant. Just as well; Tyn doubted she could drag him the distance if he was fighting her, certainly not while remaining quiet.

The animals in Fessi's field stood still, watching her with their candle-bright eyes.

Unnatural creatures, she thought.

"I feel strange," said Rion.

She tightened her grip on his wrist and started towards the trees where she had left her spear. "Don't worry. You'll be back to normal soon."

Chapter Twenty-One

For most of the journey, Tyn managed to stave off Rion's doubts. The distance was shorter, somehow, than she remembered—hadn't it taken almost a day in Oshe's company? But time had flowed differently in the dweller's presence; she had moved through a languid foreverland, distracted constantly, flitting from one empty moment to the next. The stickiness of his blood lingered under her fingernails.

Alone with Rion, she moved much faster, and paused only to reassure him. But by the time they reached the far side of the woods—the lights of Dremeral glinting up ahead—she had begun to lose him.

"Fessi isn't here," he said. "You've been lying to me."

"No," she said, keeping her voice even and reasonable. "We're almost there, and she's going to be so happy to see you."

He resisted her. "Why would she be out here in the middle of the night? This feels like a trick."

Tyn steadied herself. She turned around.

"Rion, you trust me, don't you?"

A shadow crossed his face. He grimaced.

"I think you do." She squeezed his hand. "I want you to think about nothing at all. I want you to hold my hand and follow, and I want you to know that Fessi is at the end of this path. Can you do that?"

"Fessi is at the end of this path," he repeated.

"Yes, she is." Tyn turned and kept walking. "Everything is going to be fine."

She heard his breathing grow ragged, and knew the pain he was feeling.

The waystone reared out of the field. Tyn stopped at the edge of the forest and studied it for a minute. Apart from the rustle of the breeze and the occasional buzzing of an insect, she could detect no movement. Behind her, Rion moaned.

"Tyn..."

"You're doing so well," she said. "Fessi will be proud of you."

"I don't care," he said, pressing his hands to his stomach. "About her. Tell me *you* are proud."

She looked at him in surprise. In the moonlight, his face shone with sweat. His eyes were burning.

"Of course I'm proud of you," she said.

He nodded and produced the faintest of smiles.

"All right, then," he said.

The waystone opened to her touch. Rion, gasping, crawled through the passage first. She followed after him and flinched with each of his muffled whimpers. On the far side, Vasethe helped Rion out of the channel.

"You took longer than I expected," he said.

"Had to wait for someone to go to bed." Tyn lowered herself from the passage.

"Are you okay?"

She nodded. Vasethe's self-restraint soothed her and helped her to focus. She put her hand on Rion's back. He trembled.

"Fessi..." he said.

"Vasethe's going to take you to her, all right?"

Rion looked at her with wide, imploring eyes. "I need to go back."

She rubbed his shoulder gently.

"Tyn, it hurts."

"I know. I do. But if you can hold on a little longer—"

She stopped abruptly and pushed Rion towards the cliff wall behind her. The undergrowth rustled.

"Dwellers of Res Lfae," said Res Tahirah. They emerged from the screen of dark foliage. "And a friend? Who might you be, I wonder, to have accessed my realm."

Since Tyn had last seen them, Res Tahirah's physiognomy had changed. They had grown more compact and colourful; splays of scarlet moss grew across their ribs and their legs were dashed with short orange fronds. The demon looked more aggressive, less delicate. They strode forward. Tyn lowered her spear, although she felt unsure, suddenly, of the ruler's intentions. Vasethe glanced at her.

"I am relieved to see you are alive, Second Spear," said Res Tahirah. "Although it seems you have suffered in following my advice."

"We knew what we were getting into."

Res Tahirah beckoned to Rion. Tyn moved aside to let him pass. The demon placed a long-fingered, fungi-speckled hand on Rion's chest and shut their eyes.

"I see," they said. "So that is the nature of the 124th realm."

Without warning Rion slumped; his knees buckled and his head lolled sideways. Tyn lunged to catch him, but Res Tahirah supported his body before he could hit the ground.

"Be at ease; I have only put him to sleep for a while," he said. "The creature inside cannot hurt him now."

Tyn nodded stiffly. The surge of adrenaline subsided; for an awful moment, she had thought Res Tahirah meant to kill Rion.

"Is the First Spear still within the 124th realm?" They laid Rion upon the velvet carpet of moss.

"I'm going back for her."

"I see. A difficult task." They clicked their tongue. From the path through the forest, Tyn heard the clip of hooves. "And perhaps not a wise one."

Pax emerged from the trees first. She yipped, and made straight for Tyn. Her feathers and fur had a glossy sheen, her eyes sharp and inquisitive. Tyn hugged her around the neck, breathing in her familiar smell. Pax nipped her, and then tried to chew on the loose tresses of her hair.

"You silly creature," Tyn muttered. Vasethe heard her and smiled. The other d'wens had followed Pax out of the forest; Hermoz sniffed at Rion's prone form.

"Res Lfae managed to make contact with me," said Res Tahirah.

Tyn snapped back to attention. "Are they safe?"

"For now, yes. I told them what you are attempting. They do not condone the course of action."

"But they aren't hurt? They are out of Kan Buyak's reach?"

Res Tahirah made a placating gesture. "They are well, if angry."

Angry was fine, so long as her ruler was unharmed. Tyn almost felt like crying. If Res Lfae remained secure, then there was still hope for the realm. She pushed away Pax's beak.

"Vasethe, take care of Rion," she said. "Hermoz can carry him; it'll be faster."

They heaved Rion onto the d'wen's back. He hung like a ragdoll in the saddle, his nerveless fingertips knocking Hermoz's foreleg.

"Tyn," Vasethe muttered.

"Yes?"

"If you are planning to do what I think you plan to do . . ." He brushed her hand in a way that might have looked accidental. "Don't."

"Worst case scenario only." She offered him a boost, and he swung himself into the saddle behind Rion. "I promise."

He steered Hermoz with his heels, turning her around. "I'll be waiting for you."

"Go."

Hermoz sprang forward. The other d'wens looked up at the sudden movement. Pax tilted her head to one side and chirped quizzically. Tyn stroked her neck and watched Vasethe disappear into the forest.

"You called him Vasethe. That would make him the border keeper's friend?" asked Res Tahirah.

"Yes."

"He has a strange smell. And the free use of Res Lfae's channels. An interesting figure."

Tyn shrugged. The demon walked towards the cliff face. They ran their hand over the rocks, pensive.

"I have something for you," they said. "It was difficult to obtain, so keep it close."

They turned and held out a flat red disk. Tyn took it. Around the size of a large button, the edges were serrated and sharp.

"It is a key," they said. "It should lead you to the God Instruments in the 12th realm."

"How did you get this?"

They huffed. "I will only say that the Concord still had some resources at their disposal."

Tyn turned it over in her hand, then shook her head. "Since I'm returning to the 124th realm, you should not give this to me. If I fail to make it out—"

"How pessimistic, Second Spear." They smiled. "But it would be no better for me to keep it, as I am coming with you."

"What?"

"A debt is owed." They touched Pax's beak. The d'wen nuzzled their hand. "Res Lfae has done much for the Concord. You made that observation yourself. You also asked whether all demons have been reduced to cowards."

She cringed. "That was unfair of me."

"But my answer is no. Not me, not yet." They lowered their hand. "For Res Lfae, we will take back the First Spear from Kan Meiralle."

They gestured and the cliff face split open with a crack like thunder. The channel gaped.

"Will you allow me to ride with you, Second Spear?" they asked.

She swallowed.

"It would be an honour, your Reverence," she said.

They nodded. "Then may fortune favour us both."

Pax burst through the channel and into the 124th realm. Tyn crouched low in the saddle and Res Tahirah held onto her waist. The demon was curiously light, as if they might be hollow beneath their skin, but their grip was firm and strong. The crystal passage gave way to sweeping grass.

Tyn thrust out the shaft of her spear and knocked down the dweller guarding the waypoint, throwing the woman flat on her back. Pax kept running. Dawn lay poised at the eastern horizon, and the clouds bloomed in spectacular crimson and apricot and amber.

They flew down the road; the darkened hills on either side nothing but rippling impressions of wind and shade. Pax barked joyfully as she tore across the hard-packed dirt, and the lights of the village grew larger. The trees were still strung with lanterns.

"Kan Meiralle stirs." Res Tahirah's voice was not loud, but it sounded clear despite the rush.

Tyn nodded. She had expected no less.

They reached the first of the buildings; Tyn reined in Pax's charge, swinging a wide arc around the square. Res Tahirah leapt down and landed lightly on the cobbles.

"Can you buy me some time?" Tyn asked.

"I will." Mushrooms blossomed in a ring around the demon, swelling yellow and poisonous, growing as large as Tyn's head, larger still, and spreading outwards on the ground. "If nothing else, what I have in mind will be distracting."

Tyn nodded again and spurred Pax onwards.

The God Compass led her past the square and toward the bathhouse. She could hear voices now, shouts of alarm. Lamps flared to life behind windows, and doors slammed. As they drew up to the riverside building, she dug her feet into Pax's sides to slow the d'wen, then jumped to the ground.

The front door wouldn't open; Tyn slammed the end of her spear against the lock. Once, twice, and the wood splintered inward. The door popped open.

The steamy heat of the bathhouse had evaporated and the pools glittered darkly. Not with water. All across the ground, worms crawled and twitched. They retreated from the light that filtered through the open door, squirming like newborns. There had to be thousands, each half the size of the one Vasethe had pulled out of her chest.

Tyn strode inside. The parasites squealed as she crushed them underfoot. She blinked, letting her eyes adjust to the gloom.

Chains ran from the ceiling to a cushioned pedestal against the far wall. A dense grey mesh—fuzzy, thick-stranded—covered the platform and gathered into a long tube at its centre. The chains led into the weave, the mesh swallowing the links.

"Ruler's blood," Tyn whispered.

The Compass pointed straight to the podium.

She rushed over and tore at the cocoon with her bare hands. The strands stuck to her skin like spider webs.

"Vehn?" she said. "Can you hear me?"

The worms began to squeak. A few tried to climb up her legs. Tyn kicked them off and stomped down hard. She ripped open a gash in the cocoon, and through it she could see the First Spear's bloodless arm.

"Hold on, hold on," she muttered. She picked up her spear and sliced upwards along the tear. "I'm here, I'm getting you out."

Vehn breathed in harshly. Livid red marks covered her skin, and her hair coiled around her face and shoulders like slick black kelp. Her lips had turned blue; with each inhalation, she shuddered. Tyn cleared the mesh from her face and neck, and pulled her upwards. The First Spear's eyelids flickered.

"I won't give you permission," she breathed. "I won't let you invade my home."

"Vehn, it's me."

The First Spear seemed not to recognise her. She shrank from Tyn's touch. "Please stop. Please. You can't use the channels. I won't let you."

"I'm not going to hurt you."

"I was meant to protect them, but I've ruined everything," she whispered. "Unforgiveable. I can't do it again. They're going to kill me."

"No one is going to kill you." Tyn freed Vehn's arms and waist, and leaned the First Spear against her own body, forcing her to sit upright. Vehn was trembling. Manacles clinked at her wrists; there could be no breaking her free, not without hurting her. Besides, what hope did they have of ever reaching the channel like this?

That left one option.

"Vehn, listen." Tyn took off the Compass and hung it around the First Spear's neck. The coldness of the metal must have shocked her; Vehn's eyes focussed for a second. "You need to save Res Lfae, all right? No matter what it takes."

The First Spear flinched at her ruler's name. Tyn pulled Res Tahirah's key from her pocket and pressed it between her leader's cold fingers.

"Survive. They need you." Tyn turned the dials on the Compass. She pictured a small dark room in Ahri. "And tell Vasethe I'm sorry."

She snapped the case closed before she could change her mind. Vehn vanished. The manacles clanged onto the stone pedestal, empty.

No easy escape for her, no emergency failsafe. Somewhere in the distance, a cry of pure rage split the air. Tyn held her spear tighter.

The village had transformed; the streets bulged with crushing, expanding walls of cauliflower-shaped fungi. The mushrooms snapped the branches off trees as they climbed, and the trunks groaned and creaked. Dwellers burst from their houses, staring in horror and bafflement at the advancing ring of white.

A lantern, knocked from the trees, had set the roof of a building alight, and the fire spread greedily across the thatch.

Pax hissed at the fungi; feathers splayed out in aggression, head angled low. Tyn swung into the saddle.

Another inhuman shriek, closer this time.

Tyn wheeled Pax around. Setting her fingers to her lips, she whistled, shrill and piercing. Pax danced back and forth, her head swinging in agitation.

The wall of fungi ballooned outwards, but a hollow appeared in the centre of it; a small space that grew wider as Tyn watched. Res Tahirah emerged from the gap. She clasped their wrist and pulled them onto Pax's back.

"The First Spear?" they enquired, unflustered.

"She's gone. Safe."

The demon did not question this. For a third time, a scream cut through the tumult.

"It seems we have angered Kan Meiralle," they said mildly.

Tyn pressed her heels to Pax's ribs. The d'wen needed no further encouragement; her powerful body surged forward across the road and down the slope to the river. Water sprayed around her hooves, plants whipped past her, and Tyn had to duck to avoid being hit by low-hanging branches. Then they were up the bank and weaving through long grass and purple flowers, across a field that glistened with early morning dew.

Tyn's eyes teared up in the cold wind. Res Tahirah's arms around her waist felt amorphous; they seemed to change from one second to the next, growing and shrinking; thin, root-like tubers budding and then smoothing away from the surface of their skin. Despite the detachment of their voice, the demon's presence felt feral—unfathomable in a way that Res Lfae never had been. Close to them, the world corroded, overlapped by a burgeoning film of unreality. Luminous beads of gold lichen burst from the earth beneath Pax's hooves.

The field ended and they were back on the road once more, heading east towards the channel. Tyn wiped her eyes. At the tree line, she could see an uneven row of dark masses, eyes catching the orange sunrise.

"Trouble," she said, and the wind whipped the word out of her mouth.

The great, green-eyed animals advanced towards them in a terrible lumbering gait; boulders gaining speed as they crashed down a mountain. The ground shook. Pax veered left, off the road and over a gully in a single leap.

"They mean to herd us back to their mistress," said Res Tahirah.

The animals trampled the ground, closer and closer. So much faster than Tyn would have expected; across a straight distance, they might rival Pax.

"Gah!" She gritted her teeth and turned her d'wen to face the herd. Pax barked a challenge, all bravado, although her feathers lay flat with fear. The animals bore down on them, fifty feet, forty; Tyn tucked her spear in close, lay flat against Pax's neck and whispered to her, be brave, be brave, then she pushed the d'wen to run.

Meiralle's beasts might be fast in a straight line, but they had none of Pax's agility. The d'wen flew straight towards the leader of the herd, then swerved, cutting around the animal's flank. Tyn felt hot fur brush the side of her leg, but the beast could not stop, could not turn quickly enough.

Pax broke left again, and Tyn leaned hard in the saddle, forcing the d'wen to keep straight, to head for the forest where the beasts would be unable to catch them. Pax lunged to the right and past another beast.

"Come on!" cried Tyn.

The rest of the herd was closing in, but their charge was broken, momentum lost. They had not expected their quarry to turn and face them. Pax summoned a final burst of speed and shot across the field. Then they were clear. The road ahead snaked into the woods and they raced to meet it.

Tyn raised her head and shouted in exaltation. She felt giddy with victory. Pax barked back at her, and slowed, sides heaving. The animals huffed and snorted in the field behind them; Tyn heard the rumble of hooves as they turned to give chase once more.

For the first time, escape felt possible. The whole realm stood against them now, every dweller, every living thing, but they could *run*. They were not beaten yet. Between Res Tahirah's powers and Pax's stamina, maybe, somehow, they could pull through. The forest grew darker as Pax loped deeper into the trees, and the beasts fell behind, unable to keep pace.

A spark of hope flared inside Tyn's chest. She had saved Vehn and that was what mattered, but maybe, after so many failures and dead ends, she could have this victory too.

They were close to Dremeral when Pax's energy finally began to fade. Tyn coaxed her along.

"We're nearly there," she said. "Come on, girl."

The d'wen crooned and tried to break into a run, but after a few strides she slowed again. Sweat drenched her fur. Between the trees, the sunrise drew long shadows across the ground.

Res Tahirah sighed. "Ah."

Tyn drew Pax to a stop.

"What is it?" she asked.

The demon let go of her waist and climbed down from the d'wen. Their body had grown stable once more; this time blue and coral orange frills branched across their chest. The fungal filaments fluttered as they breathed.

"Kan Meiralle waits," they said. "My channel is obstructed; the way is barred."

A cold hand smothered the light inside of Tyn. Her body felt heavy. Res Tahirah saw that she understood and spread their hands, a gesture of apology.

"I regret that it is so," they said.

"As do I, your Reverence." Her own voice sounded distant. She looked towards the curve of the road. "It has been an honour. I'll try to cut you a path, if I am able. If you escape, will you . . . will you tell Res Lfae about this? About me?"

"I will."

"Thank you." She leaned forward to hug Pax. It was stupid that the d'wen would be trapped here, especially after she had been so brave and loyal. Pax stamped her hooves and ruffled her feathers when Tyn squeezed her too tightly.

"Sorry, girl," she muttered. She straightened in the saddle and gathered herself. Better like this. Better to meet the end on her terms. Her mind would stay her own.

Something soft and cool brushed the back of her neck. She twisted around, but the road behind her was empty. The wind? She had been sure she felt . . .

When she looked ahead again, Res Tahirah was gone.

"Your Reverence?"

Tyn walked Pax forward. The birds and insects had fallen silent; the demon had vanished. Her skin prickled. She unclipped her spear from the saddle.

Then, ringing through the trees, she heard Fessi's voice.

"I offer you the bounty of the realm, Res Tahirah of the 213th Realm, Bright of the Faded, Speaker of the Demo—" Abruptly her voice cut off.

Tyn snarled and rushed forward.

Kan Meiralle was standing in the field beside the waystone pillar, Fessi at her side. The dweller clutched her throat, gagging; she choked as grey and white mushrooms cascaded out of her mouth. With every second, more sprouted, so that she could not draw breath or speak. She dropped to her knees.

Res Tahirah stood a few feet from the goddess, hands behind their back. They watched dispassionately.

"I will accept the bounty of your realm," they said. "As that is your rule."

Kan Meiralle looked down at Fessi, an expression of mild annoyance on her face. Then she leaned over, grasped the crown of bone blossoms on the dweller's head, and crushed her skull.

Tyn jerked in horror. Fessi's limp body fell to the ground. Kan Meiralle wiped her hand on her dress.

"You do not love them, then," said Res Tahirah. "What manner of ruler are you, I wonder?"

The earth around the pillar erupted with silver spines, each as tall as Pax, and bristling with thin needles. Kan Meiralle staggered backwards to avoid being impaled on the spears of fungi, and rage shone in her eyes. Res Tahirah took a step toward her, and more spears pierced the ground, driving the goddess away from the waystone. A needle touched her skin and she whipped her arm away, burned.

"I have no further interest in your realm," said Res Tahirah. "I hope that you have not misunderstood the situation: I did not come here to conquer you. I will eat your poison if I must, but then allow me to depart. You will find I do not digest easily, goddess."

Kan Meiralle's jaw opened. Instead of a tongue, thick black parasites roiled within the toothless cavern of her mouth. They stretched their oily bodies toward the light.

"You will be mine!" she hissed, the words emerging from the depths of her throat. "You and your realm, they will be *mine.*"

Res Tahirah glanced to the left sharply. A wave of spines collapsed. They fell like shattered ice, and from the ground below more parasites emerged, but these were much larger, more like snakes than worms. Pax growled. The demon jumped backwards, and the fungi parted around them like arms, sheltering them. The earth rippled with the parasites' hideous flesh. More spines broke apart.

"So you would see this through?" said Res Tahirah. They sounded tired, resigned. "Very well."

They gestured and the waystone split open. The channel gleamed, crystalline and dark. Simultaneously, a ribbon of gold lichen unspooled over the worms, running from the channel to Pax's hooves. Beneath it, the creatures withered and dissolved into paste. Kan Meiralle shrieked again. She advanced towards the demon.

"Go, Second Spear," said Res Tahirah, not loudly, but their voice seemed to emanate from right beside her. "Your ruler needs you, and this fight is mine."

"Your Reverence—"

"Not all demons have been reduced to cowards. Run."

Tyn bit back a curse and urged Pax forward. The lichen glittered. It stuck to the d'wen's hooves, scattering through the air like clumps of wet sand.

Kan Meiralle glanced towards the noise. Her gaze settled on Tyn for a moment, recognising her, coldly evaluating, but then Res Tahirah tilted their chest backwards and paper-thin orange protrusions flew from their fluted skin. The barbs sliced into the goddess's body like sickles. She howled in pain.

"Your reign ends today, goddess," said the demon.

Incandescent with rage, Kan Meiralle fell upon them. With her bone-clad fist balled, she drove her hand into Res Tahirah's ribs. The blow crushed the delicate blue folds of their skin; the fretwork of ripples and swirls crumpled. An instant later legions of parasites swarmed over the demon's body. They burrowed into the ruler's torso.

"No!" shouted Tyn.

Kan Meiralle recoiled suddenly. She twitched and then scratched at her arm, the same place where the needle had cut her earlier. A layer of foam formed at the corners of her mouth. Her eyes widened.

Res Tahirah shambled away from the goddess as she began to convulse.

"Aim true, Second Spear," they said, voice faint as a whisper.

"No!"

They pointed to the centre of their chest, skin shifting with power and the parasites eating through them. Then, trembling, they spread their arms wide.

With a cry of anger and grief, Tyn threw her spear.

The blade sank into Res Tahirah's chest. They staggered and fell. Soft grey fungi cushioned the earth beneath them. The demon breathed in once, unsure and pained, and then their body unravelled in a shower of brilliant, shining spores.

A flurry of air lifted the particles across the field; they danced in the sunlight. Tyn breathed raggedly. A few spores landed on Kan Meiralle as the goddess heaved and seized. The skin they touched melted like wax.

Tyn spurred Pax toward the channel as the goddess's screaming grew louder. The spores touched the grass and the parasites, each glowing spark a final, hungry weapon. All around Tyn now, the particles swirled and consumed, and the parasites bled into a foul, decaying slurry. Blackcap mushrooms and featherweed sprang from the gore.

A few more steps, a last bark of defiance, and Pax leapt through the cracked stone and out of the dying realm.

Chapter Twenty-Two

The Ahri night was quiet. Nothing lived beside the saltpan, and not even the wind stirred. The whole world possessed a frozen, pristine quality, as if Tyn might have been the first to see these stars, this desert, this great, long stretch of the shadowline. As if she might be the last.

Vasethe sat in the doorway of the house, exhausted, his eyes half-closed. The last few hours had passed in a blur. He had been waiting for her in Res Tahirah's realm as promised, in the forest below the dark cliffs. They had travelled back to the 194th realm together, where Tyn gave Pax and the other d'wens over to the care of the Midplain stables. From there, Vasethe had showed her to a hidden channel out on the plain below Tahmais. A channel to Ahri, a channel that should not exist.

Vehn and Rion lay sleeping in the room behind him. Tyn leaned against the wall under the awning outside, her arms crossed.

"Will you claim Res Tahirah's realm?" asked Vasethe.

A thousand stars raining over Kan Meiralle's realm, bright and yellow. Her spear sinking into their chest.

"No," muttered Tyn. "Even the thought . . . they had named a successor. It would be an insult to their memory for me to undermine that choice."

"Do you know who they selected?"

She shook her head. She knew so little about Res Tahirah. They had only been one of her own ruler's eccentric friends, one of the demons mentioned in passing at parties, one of the ones best left to their own devices. A ruler of secrets. It did not make sense that they should have died like they did.

They had been kind. And brave.

"I couldn't claim their realm," she said. "Even if it would help me to protect Res Lfae. I can't do it."

"I understand."

Tyn uncrossed her arms and let them drop to her sides. "Besides, me as a ruler?"

A faint, tired smile. "You would make a Demon Empress to be reckoned with."

"Don't be ridiculous."

Vasethe sighed. The silence gathered around them, impossible and vast. Tyn wet her lips and tasted salt.

"So which are you, then?" she asked. "God or demon?"

Vasethe grimaced.

"What?"

"That's the problem. I'm not . . . either, exactly."

"What does that mean?"

"Eris has forbidden me from talking about it." He rubbed his forehead. "It's . . . I made a mistake. As a result, I have *some* rulership powers."

"Which realm?"

Vasethe shifted, and his head dropped lower toward his chest. He looked so deeply exhausted, like he had not slept in weeks.

"This one," he said quietly. "Ahri. Surely you had worked that out by now? Ahri, the first of all realms."

Tyn did not reply.

"Lfae knows." Vasethe spoke to the ground at his feet. "Buyak might as well. Eris is trying to fix it, but she's been gone for far too long. I can't find her, even with the Compass."

Tyn's voice was hushed. "I did not know Ahri *could* be claimed."

He shrugged, not looking up.

After a moment, Tyn took a seat next to him. He shuffled sideways to make more room for her. His movements had a laboured quality, as if a deep-rooted pain weighed on him.

"Is there anything I can do?" she asked.

He shook his head. "You have enough to worry about."

"Vasethe—"

"I'm fine. Tired, that's all."

She glanced at him sidelong. He was cradling his arm, the one he had used to pull the parasites from Rion and Vehn. Although she could see no injury, his pain was obvious. She looked away again.

"Should I address you as 'your Reverence?'" she asked.

He snorted. "I'd really prefer if you didn't do that. Ever."

Behind them, Rion murmured in his sleep. He had curled up on his side; his fists clenched and drawn in toward his chest. Vehn lay beyond him, still as a corpse, flat on her back. Tyn found it hard to even look at the First Spear; deathly pale and bruised and thin. Her appearance was like an accusation. Whatever Kan Meiralle had done to her, Vehn had not broken. She had safeguarded the realm through it all, defenceless and alone.

"I should have reached her sooner," said Tyn. Her nails dug into the palms of her hands. "But I was so . . . I should never have let them separate us."

Vasethe made a soft sound of reprove. "It wasn't your fault."

But look at her. Tyn remembered Vehn's tortured breathing and her own chest ached. Six wasted days lost in a fantasy, while the First Spear suffered on her own. It was too hideous to think about.

"You risked everything to get her out of there," said Vasethe. "You can't blame yourself for this."

"Hm." She picked at a thread in her shirt. The clothes belonged to the border keeper, but fit comfortably despite their difference in height. The weathered cotton felt cool on her skin.

"She will recover," Vasethe insisted. "They both will. There was nothing else you could have done."

With effort, Tyn nodded. She did not believe him, but what was there to say? It was done now. Three dead parasites lay in the sand at the far end of the border keeper's yard; their oozing bodies drying in the hot, arid air. She could have impaled a thousand more, and it still wouldn't be enough.

"I need to ask you a favour," she said, her voice low.

"Go ahead."

Strung along the fence of the border keeper's yard, panes of stained glass gleamed in the starlight, bright and sharp-edged.

"Will you give me the God Compass again?"

Without hesitation, Vasethe reached into his pocket, pulled out the Instrument, and pressed it into Tyn's hand. When he touched her, his skin felt feverishly warm. For an instant, she experienced the same dizzying sense of dislocation as she had felt when he had gripped her shoulders in Kan Meiralle's realm—as if, for a moment, she had stepped into someone else's life. She *knew* him, but she could not remember how. A similar confusion passed over Vasethe's face. He withdrew his hand.

Tyn quickly looked away, with a strange sort of guilt. "You don't have any questions?"

"If you say you need it, I believe you. And . . ." She heard him swallow. "And it might help to keep you safe. Give you an escape, if you need it. I want you to have that option."

She gripped the Compass inside her fist. Her mouth was dry.

"Do you know what we're up against?" she asked.

"I think so."

She looked at him again. "Have you spoken to Res Lfae?"

"No. I know where they are, but I haven't attempted to reach them. I . . . I think that I'm being watched. I can't risk exposing your ruler."

She frowned. "Are you sure?"

"I don't know. Maybe I'm wrong, but it seems like Buyak knows far more than he should. I think he must have a spy."

The hairs on the back of Tyn's neck rose, and the shadows of the house suddenly seemed thicker. She shivered, then flicked open the catch on the Compass. The metal disks shone in the moonlight.

"I find that a lot about Kan Buyak doesn't make sense," she said. "Ever since the Tribunal of the High. At the time, I believed he must have found a loophole in the rules of Kan Helquas' realm, something that allowed him to evade censure. But maybe he didn't need to."

"What do you mean?"

Her heart beat faster. She spoke to the Compass. "Where is Kan Helquas?"

The Instrument responded to her, easy and natural as breathing. The needle spun and pointed towards the desert. Away from the shadowline, the saltpan, and Mkalis. In the misted surface of the lid, a dark-skinned infant lay sleeping in a shadowed cradle.

"Kan Buyak never needed a loophole." Tyn's voice sounded far-off and flat. "He could lie all he wanted, because he set the rules himself."

Vasethe stared down at the Compass.

"Kan Helquas is dead," she continued. "She was dead before the Tribunal even began. Buyak is the ruler of the 5th realm."

The words hung between them, heavy and dark. The stillness of the air felt suffocating.

"That can't—how?" Vasethe spoke hoarsely. "How can that be?"

"He had the God Sword all along."

"But he didn't! Fanieq intended to use Eris' blood to forge it; she told me that was Buyak's goal." He sounded desperate. "There has to be some mistake; this can't be right."

Tyn closed the Compass. "He could never have touched Kan Helquas without the Sword."

"But he didn't have—"

"What does it matter?" Her patience frayed. "By whatever means, Kan Buyak has the Sword now, along with the might of the 5th realm. He fooled everyone. And once he finds Res Lfae, he will . . ."

She paused. Buyak's voice echoed in her mind.

Find your ruler and tell them to cooperate with me.

What could possibly require Lfae's *cooperation*? Why wouldn't Buyak just kill the demon, seize control of the 194th realm, and take whatever he pleased? He had all the power.

What if this had nothing to do with revenge?

"Vasethe," Tyn said unsteadily, "is your channel to the 194th realm life-bonded?"

He frowned, taken aback by the question. "Yes, to Lfae. They said it would be safer. They said that, if they die, the channel would fall apart—"

She buried her face in her hands. Vasethe stopped talking. The night was entirely silent; nothing to be heard but the pounding of blood inside Tyn's own head.

"The channel," said Vasethe at last. "Buyak wants to cross to Ahri."

He needs Lfae alive. He needs their consent. "Collapse it."

"I can't. Eris might know a way, but—Tyn, no one else was even supposed to know it exists. It's hidden." Vasethe shook his head, and then struggled to his feet, using the doorframe for support. "It doesn't matter. I'll go to Lfae and tell them to give Buyak what he wants."

"No."

"There's no other way."

"No," she repeated. It felt as though walls were closing in on all sides. "You have no defence against him; if Kan Buyak reaches Ahri, he will kill you, and then he will kill the border keeper. So, no, you will not tell my ruler to *surrender*."

She got up, brushing past him as she walked into the house. On the floor, Rion mumbled in his sleep. The room felt oppressive; the air too close.

"He can't be allowed to conquer your realm," said Vasethe fiercely. "Do you expect me to do nothing? I've seen what he does to his dwellers."

Tyn crouched beside Vehn. As gently as she could, she prised open the First Spear's clenched fist. The vault key had cut into her palm, forming a circle of ugly puckered sores. It would hurt her to hold a weapon.

"Will you take them back to the Sanctum?" she asked.

"Tyn—"

"There will be another way to fix this." She slipped the key into her pocket, walked to the window, and picked up Vehn's spear. Then she lifted the Compass, and turned the dial on the side of the Instrument. "I'm asking you to wait. You said you wanted me to be safe—and I want the same for you."

Before he could respond, she snapped the Compass shut and the room dissolved around her.

Chapter Twenty-Three

Cold air bit into Tyn's skin, and her breath emerged in white gusts. She stepped out onto the ledge of a small alcove. Overhead, the sky gaped with black rents—huge holes worn through a silver blanket, gouges torn from a metal sheet, so dark and empty that they seemed to suck in the shallow light of the realm. From her vantage point, she could see an endless sea of dense, purple-leaved hedges, rising twice her height from the dark earth.

The smell of tar and crushed pine needles drifted over the branches. It tasted of fear.

The watchtower from which she had emerged stood fifty feet tall, white like a strut of bone and covered in deep red striations. Her alcove was set two-thirds of the way up, and a lazy spiral of stairs led around the exterior of the building. Water trickled from the mouths of weathered faces carved into the walls. Faces of dwellers or rulers, and every expression frozen in a rictus of gaping ecstasy. Whispering flowed out with the water, never pausing and without a hint of feeling.

"... in the curve of the wing the shadow of the dog and the falling of the bodies into lines that diverge and bloom that smear and rend and are drawn into newness and burst as the rotten fruit under the bodies that fall into lines that crack the bone and open wide the flesh and crawl inside the fallow womb where they will beat the curve of the wing where the swollen lines that bend are lines that swallow . . ."

The droning made Tyn's skin crawl. She tried to block it out, but it wormed inside her brain, echoing and falling into new cadences, new patterns of meaning. It seemed to rise from deep below the tower, and drifted out into the cold air like vapour. If she listened too long, she began to feel oddly weightless—as if she could step off the stairs and into the air without any fear of falling.

So this was it. The Domain of the Architect, the 12th realm. No other titles, no names, no descriptors, and apparently only connected to Kan Sefune and Kan Meiralle. Only Kan Sefune now; Res Tahirah had made sure of that. Tyn could understand why other rulers wanted nothing to do with this place. In the distance, there were more towers, fifteen, maybe twenty.

"Where is the Architect?" she whispered to the Compass.

The needle spun, paused, spun again. It could not settle on a direction, and the image in the lid was unclear; indecipherable shapes winnowing away and reforming. Tyn snapped the lid shut and looped the chain around her neck.

In the distance, a sawing shriek, metal scraped over stone. Animal grunting, closer by. Then nothing again. The torn sky revolved, the black rents circling eastwards. The rips slowly expanded and then pinched together, like bellows emptied of air.

Tyn hunched her shoulders against the bitter cold and descended the stairs. Her instincts urged her to leave this place; an unspeakable menace lurked just out of sight. Odd geometries stuck out to her; the line of the tower's shadow mirrored the thin channel of water gathered on its southern side, the angle of a hedge bent to reflect a hole in the sky. Or maybe it was the smell that disturbed her, the caustic stench that lingered over everything. Her nerves stretched thin.

When she reached the base of the tower, she took the vault key out of her pocket. The flat disk emitted a faint insect whine, and quivered at her touch. When she held it to her left, the sound grew louder.

"Find me the lock you'll fit," she murmured.

A stooping stone tunnel descended below the secretive wall of leaves. Holding Vehn's spear at the ready, Tyn ducked into the short passage. Water pooled on the ground and roots grew from the crumbling ceiling, stretching to catch her hair and clothes. Small creatures scratched around in the dark, skittering away when she drew closer. She climbed up on the far side.

The ground beyond was overrun with crawling grey weeds, feather-soft and whispering under her boots. A layer of silt gathered in the grooves between the flagstones, and an icy wind blew down the corridor of trees; it shifted desiccated old leaves with a sound like crumpling paper.

Tyn listened to the key, then moved down the western path. The watchtower's long shadow fell across the labyrinth. At the corner, the paths diverged again. Tyn paused, drew a cross in the silt, and continued.

It took her a while to notice the sound over the rustling wind through the hedges, but as the gentle padding grew louder, it became unmistakable. Footfalls. Something heavy, something with paws. The creature moved along the neighbouring corridors and kept pace with her. When she paused, it stopped. When she retraced her steps, it snuffled and turned, snapping a branch from the hedge.

Tyn held Vehn's spear so tightly that her hands ached. She could smell the creature, a sour musk, could hear it breathe. It was trying to be quiet.

She gritted her teeth. With a swift jerk of her wrist, she

slashed the spear through the hedge.

The creature jumped, claws scratching over stone. It grunted a few times.

Then it giggled.

Tyn breathed hard. On the other side of the hedge, the creature loped off, footsteps retreating back in the direction of the watchtower. When she reached the next corner, there was no sign of it.

Other entities, Kan Meiralle had said.

Tyn pressed on, moving quickly. The key's mosquito whine grew louder, and the disk thrummed like the wings of a trapped bird. At each intersection, she marked her passage, west and south, west and south, travelling ever deeper into the maze. Between one hedge and the next, the plants grew stranger. They warped in shape and colour, the spreading foliage shading from dark purple into mauve and then vermillion.

Towers loomed over the top of the hedges, pale and stark; some clustered close together, others only distant white lines. When Tyn looked back, she could no longer see the tower she had emerged from.

She came to a junction and paused. A rough-hewn sculpture stood on a raised plinth between the diverging paths. It might have been a horse, except that the creature's neck roped backwards and around its own body like the coils of a snake. The dark brown stone had worn smooth—the sharp edges of the animal's head reduced to soft ridges—but it appeared to be shrieking as it tore into the flesh of its own leg.

Looking at the statue made Tyn feel strange. A seeping numbness stole across her body, and she found herself following the lines of the animal's neck, over and over, around and around, as the rest of the world dissolved into an indistinct red haze.

She blinked and snapped to her senses. The statue was just a statue once more, but she had no idea how long she had been standing there. Her skin felt much colder, and moisture had dampened her clothing. The smell of tar had grown stronger.

Tyn set off down the left path, faster than before. This realm's nature was oblique and twisted; the longer she stayed, the worse it would become. One of the watchtowers stood only a few hundred feet away—from the top, she might gain a clearer sense of what lay ahead. She moved towards it and the weeds grew thicker, dead creepers snarling over one another and all but burying the flagstones.

What was the point of a maze in an unreachable realm? Who was supposed to use it? There was a claustrophobic madness to these endless, obsessive corridors; a sense that they had been carefully designed, fit for an inexplicable purpose.

A little way behind her, Tyn heard the careful tread of paws on stone. The creature had caught up with her once more.

She broke into a sprint to reach the watchtower's tunnel, and scrambled through the short passage. This tower looked less worn than the previous one; the faces in the walls stood out clearly, insane grins plastered over their mouths, murky water drooling from their lips and over their chins.

Tyn raced for the stairs and climbed. The creature, whatever it was, sounded large. If it followed her here, she might prove more agile on the narrow, curving steps. At the alcove she stopped, panting.

". . . within the secrets of the mill the means to grind and the turning that pulls closer to a point where the lines meet in the pool and the sinew that grows the trees and the bodies that fall into order as is their purpose as is their function all together and cloistered in the lines that grow wild and splinter white and spray..."

The labyrinth wavered in her vision. The lines of deep red hedges looked, for an instant, like the intricate veins of a colossal creature. Tyn scrubbed her eyes. The impression faded.

In the leafy corridor outside the watchtower, she caught a glimpse of movement.

The creature crept forward, head roving as it sniffed the air. It stood at least eight feet tall, and almost as long from snout to heel. From Tyn's distance, it resembled a terrible pastiche of bear and pig and man. Its fur ran from pale brown to white, and it moved on all fours, powerful and quiet. Its face was gruesome; a human mouth and teeth drawn into a permanent grin by the wide nostrils of a pig snout. Its glittering black eyes scoured the hedges. Looking for her.

Perhaps by chance, perhaps because it sensed her gaze, the creature glanced up at the tower. It gave a guilty start when it saw her, and took a few hasty steps backwards as if it wanted to hide. Then it stopped. Stared back at her. Very deliberately, it raised and lowered its great, bulging shoulders.

Oh well, it seemed to say. *I suppose you've spotted me now.*

Tyn returned its stare, unblinking. She held completely still.

With casual indifference, the creature turned and lumbered back into the labyrinth. It knew that she would have to come down from the tower. When she did, it would be lying in wait.

Once it was out of sight, Tyn exhaled. She leaned heavily against the wall behind her.

Even with the rest of her tribe, confronting that creature would be a challenge. On her own... She looked down at Vehn's spear, the black sandalwood worn smooth as water, the steel crossguard polished mirror-bright and gleaming. Not good odds. She needed to locate the vault before the creature found her again.

The Compass pressed against her chest like a disk of ice. She drew it out and consulted it once more, but the needle only spun aimlessly as it tried to point to the Architect.

"Where is Rion?" she murmured.

He sat at Vehn's bedside in the Sanctum barracks, scowling at the ceiling. The First Spear still appeared to be unconscious.

"Where is Vasethe?"

The saltpan stretched out behind him. He leaned on the fence of the yard and watched the desert. Waiting for the border keeper.

"Good," Tyn muttered, and closed the Compass.

The vault key hummed louder as she ran. She didn't bother to mark her way through the maze anymore. In places, the hedges had collapsed, ruptured by an unknown force, and she climbed straight through the gaps.

More statues, each stranger and more macabre than the last. The plants in this area no longer grew from sap, bark, and wood. They bunched close to each other, their branches entwined, and glistened with raw, oozing wetness. In unison, they swayed, they breathed. The leaves of the hedgerows shrank and paled to a soft, shiny pink, edged in a rim of white. Hundreds of thousands of fingernails. Tyn had an idea, now, of why the Compass failed to point to the Architect.

The creature was patiently waiting when she rounded the corner of the next corridor.

Up close, it seemed even larger. In a fluid, oddly graceful motion, it rose up on its hind legs, so that it stood taller than the bleeding, breathing hedges. It let out its hyena giggle again.

Tyn gritted her teeth and held her ground. No use running; she'd never get away—either she used the Compass or she fought. Vehn's spear felt heavy in her hands.

You'll be strong, but you'll never be the strongest, said the First Spear, from the dark recesses of her memory.

The creature's fur had peeled back on its belly, where mangy patches of brown skin were stitched up with twine. Its paws, each the size of Tyn's head, ended in curved, yellow claws. A single blow would kill her.

Which means you'll need to compensate. Vehn swung her spear overhead, effortless and clean. She had been younger, less hard. She watched Tyn imitate her. *You'll need to be faster, smarter, braver and more stubborn. You'll need to time your attacks better, use your opponent's strength against them.*

The creature dropped back onto all fours, and the flagstone path shook with its weight. Fingernails fell from the hedges, clicking as they hit the ground. Tyn adjusted her stance, slid one foot backwards, drew the shaft of the spear level, and bent her knees.

The truth is that you don't need to be the strongest, said Vehn. *I'm not. You just have to be good enough.*

The creature's eyes shone bright with bloodlust and intelligence. Its nostrils twitched and spittle flecked the wide fleshy curve of its lips. Then the muscles in its legs contracted; one bound, two, it surged down the path like a landslide.

And you are.

Tyn exhaled. The creature barreled toward her, twenty feet, then ten. She pivoted on her heel, pulled the spear backwards—it saw what she planned, jerked to the side, surprised by her recklessness—and then she threw, releasing the spear with a scream of defiance. The oncoming force of the creature's own momentum slammed into the blade, and the spear split its neck open. It staggered, shocked, not yet afraid or in pain, and Tyn lunged forward and grasped the shaft of the weapon. With the full weight of her body, she rammed the blade down its gullet.

The creature gagged and swiped at her. She jumped away, tripped, and then scrambled to her feet again. It clawed at the spear, tossing its head from side to side. Instead of blood, pale yellow pus sprayed from its mouth and neck. It could not grip the shaft, and the sandalwood held firm. With an awful, racking cough, its front legs buckled.

Tyn unsheathed her shiv. The creature had forgotten her, lost in its struggle to dislodge the spear. It flailed and kicked, tearing at the hedges, and cascades of fingernails fell from the trees. Tyn waited. When it turned, she strode toward it. Quick and unflinching, she plunged the knife into the hollow at the base of the creature's skull.

Every muscle in its massive body tensed. Then it slumped and crashed onto the flagstones. A last wet, guttural sigh left its mouth. It stilled.

Tyn tugged the shiv. The blade slipped free with a sucking sound. She wiped it clean on the creature's matted fur, and returned it to the thin scabbard strapped to her forearm. She set her foot to the creature's shoulder; through the sole of her boot, she could feel its heat. With a grunt, she pulled the spear free.

"Go well," she murmured to the dead creature.

The vault key fell silent at the end of the corridor. Ahead stood a stone pedestal with another monstrous statue atop it; this time a rearing, centipede-like animal with human hands growing from its belly, and too many mouths. On either side of the pedestal, the plants breathed ripples of cold air. Tyn's sweat froze on her skin, and her teeth chattered. She walked up to the statue, gripping Vehn's spear tightly.

With a final quiver, the key broke apart in her hand. The statue's innumerable fingers twitched. Tyn was transported back to Kan Meiralle's realm, the sea of parasites burrowing through Res Tahirah's skin. She swallowed.

The statue shivered again, then slithered forward on crooked lines of broken fingers, winding over the back of the pedestal and down below the hedge. In the recess where it had stood lay a single wafer-thin shard of gold.

Tyn picked it up. Cold as the air, heavier than it looked. The shard flickered in her hand, the metal shifting and settling as she held it. She carefully tucked the God Instrument into her pocket.

Then, with trembling hands, she fumbled open the Compass. In her mind, she held the image of home. A breeze stirred the fingernail leaves of the labyrinth, and she was gone.

Chapter Twenty-Four

The Sanctum looked the same. Smelled the same, the faintest trace of Lfae's fragrance lingering in the trees; the familiar mix of iron and star anise, carnation and copper. A cloudy day in Tahmais; the plains would see rain, and the sky above the mountain would run scarlet and gold in the evening. Tyn's heart ached. How could nothing have changed? How could it still be beautiful now?

The barracks stood open. She walked inside.

"Rion?" she called.

Her voice echoed through the empty rooms. Strange, how much larger the building felt without the bustle of the tribe.

"Rion, it's me."

"Tyn."

Vehn's voice floated down the stairs. Tyn frowned. The First Spear's tone had an odd edge to it, a restrained anxiety. Something was wrong.

"We're up here," said Vehn. "On the roof."

Tyn opened the Compass and whispered a question. The image in the lid resolved, clear and sharp. Her chest tightened. For a moment, she could not move.

"Tyn?"

"I'm coming," she said.

They were right at the edge. Rion was kneeling and Vehn stood beside him, her dagger against his windpipe. Her hair was loose and curling, her eyes bloodshot. She looked unsteady, but her hands did not waver.

"I had suspicions," said Tyn. She carefully set Vehn's spear on the ground. She unstrapped her shiv and scabbard. Laid them down. "Ever since the attack on the Sanctum, when I saw Kan Buyak use the Spinelight Gate."

"He was never supposed to get inside the Sanctum." Vehn's expression remained unreadable, but her words came out hoarse.

"Tyn?" whispered Rion.

"It's okay." She raised both empty hands. "Everything's going to be fine."

"This doesn't feel okay to me."

Vehn made a slight movement with her head, like she wanted to look away. Her pallid skin had a faint sheen, a fever yet to break.

"Just stay still," said Tyn. She cautiously took a step toward them. "She won't hurt you."

"I'm sorry. She woke up and—"

"Quiet," said Vehn. She pressed the edge of the dagger against his throat, just shy of breaking skin. Rion fell silent.

"You don't want to do this," said Tyn.

A faint tremor in Vehn's hand. The blade wavered and Rion closed his eyes.

"I know you don't want to do this." Tyn took another step forward. "Vehn, talk to me. Tell me what happened."

"Just give me the God Compass."

"I want to understand."

"What is there to understand? I gave Kan Buyak permission to enter the realm. I unbarred his channel. Jevin and Chitanda and Hale, all of the Healers, that was my fault." Her face contorted. "Everything that happened was my fault. And now I'm going to find Kan Buyak, and give him permission to use the Ahri channel too. If you are so smart, if you had this all worked out, then why did you never confront me?"

"Because I wanted to be wrong," said Tyn softly.

The muscles in Vehn's forearm twitched. Rion swallowed.

"I hate you," Vehn whispered. "More than anyone else, I hate you."

Tyn lowered her hands to her sides. She was only a few feet from the First Spear now. "You were deceived. Kan Buyak tricked you, didn't he?"

"Stay where you are."

Tyn stopped.

"You should have left me in Kan Meiralle's forsaken realm." Vehn's voice cracked. Her shoulders shook. "Left me to the worms and the voices in my head. You should have left me to die."

Tyn shook her head. "No."

"I deserved it!"

"No one deserved that, and least of all you." She took another step. "I'm sorry it took me so long to find you. I'm sorry I let you down."

"I said *stay where you are!*"

"If you let Kan Buyak into the realm, then I know you did it for a reason." Tyn managed a small smile. "Everyone knows that you would protect Res Lfae and the tribe at all costs. That's why you're the First Spear."

Vehn's eyes were wild. "Shut up!"

"You made a mistake. But that doesn't mean we can't fix it together." Tyn held out her hand for the dagger. "Let me help."

"You can't help me." Vehn pulled Rion backwards, her legs

right against the balustrade. "If Kan Buyak doesn't kill me, Res Lfae will. All I can do is try to set things right before one of them succeeds."

Tyn shook her head. "No matter what you've done, Res Lfae would never hurt you."

"Oh, what would you know?" Vehn burst out. Her face twisted with grief. "Of course you believe they would forgive anything, because they'd forgive *you*. You can sleep with Matir, you can start a war, you can do whatever you want, and they still love you."

Tyn froze and Vehn laughed bitterly.

"You thought I didn't know? Give me some credit, I'm not *that* stupid, Tyn. As if it even mattered anyway. None of it mattered." She swallowed. "Do you know what it's like to go from being their most trusted counsel to being a tool? To give your entire life to them without so much as a hint that they approve or care? I gave everything to try to please Lfae. Look at me! I sacrificed everything, but in the end you stole it all away, and they don't even give a damn."

"You're wrong," said Tyn fiercely. "Res Lfae would die for you. You've always been their favourite."

"They named you successor!"

The words hit her like a punch to the gut. Vehn's shoulders shook; she was crying and Tyn had never seen her cry, not once, but now it seemed like she could hardly breathe, her body wracked with sobs. She flung the knife down and shoved Rion away. He scrambled out of reach.

"Take it! Take the role of First Spear!" she said. "It's all yours, Tyn. I hate you. I hate you. I hate you."

Tyn closed the remaining distance between them and wrapped her arms around Vehn. As if the last of her strength had finally deserted her, Vehn slumped inside the embrace, still crying, her face pressed against Tyn's shoulder.

"We're going to fix this," Tyn whispered.

"It's all my fault."

Tyn held her tightly. Beyond the wall of the Sanctum, the evening lights of Tahmais flickered to life.

Chapter Twenty-Five

Vehn's room was austere and cold; a bed, a small desk and chair, a cupboard, and a basin in the corner. During the time that the Sanctum had stood abandoned, a thin layer of dust had formed on the windowsill. Tyn lit the lamp on her desk.

The First Spear hunched on the edge of her bed, a blanket wrapped around her shoulders. Tyn sat down on the desk chair, while Rion remained standing near the door.

Ready to flee, Tyn thought sadly. She could not really blame him.

Vehn kept her eyes on the floor.

"Do you know what Res Lfae and the border keeper were arguing about?" she asked.

Tyn shook her head.

"I wasn't supposed to find out either." Vehn's voice was low. She had grown thinner during the week in Kan Meiralle's domain, and her already angular face appeared almost skeletal. "It was the Ahri-dweller. He claimed a realm that was already taken."

"The argument was about Vasethe?"

Vehn nodded. "The border keeper should have called for his immediate impeachment to settle the matter. But she didn't, because it would have meant risking the possibility of him being sent to the Lightless. Instead, she wanted Res Lfae to set forward a Ruler's Decree."

Tyn shook her head. "A ruler's decree?"

The First Spear drew her blanket closer. "I had to search through half the historical documents in Tahmais to work out what that meant. It's an old custom. *Avse ja dmes*, in Old High. A Ruler's Decree is a formal, binding agreement. If at least half the rulers of Mkalis accept the Decree, it passes and alters the nature of all the realms."

"And if it fails?"

"The Aspirant—the ruler who first declares the Decree—is impeached. Their realm is seized by the High, and they fall to the Lightless." Her voice dropped. "The border keeper wanted Res Lfae to serve as the Aspirant."

A chill passed over Tyn.

"It would have been impossible to gather enough support to pass the Decree," said Vehn. "Res Lfae could see that, but they also knew that the border keeper was desperate. It tormented them. At the Tribunal, after the trial was lost to Kan Buyak, they finally agreed to go ahead with it."

Tyn shook her head slowly. "But I was with Res Lfae after the trial. We never met the border keeper."

"They spoke while you were still inside the Avowal." Vehn looked up at last. "I heard them. The border keeper planned to upend the foundations of Mkalis, and damn us all in the process. Res Lfae was going to help her do it."

"Then what would have happened to us?" asked Rion.

Vehn glanced at his face quickly, then lowered her gaze again. The sight of him seemed to hurt her.

"I don't know," she said. "The High would have decided our fate. But the realm as it stood, our home ... If we lost Res Lfae, we would lose it too. Kan Buyak left a message for me, as we were departing the 5th realm. He said that he could stop the border keeper."

Tyn leaned back in the chair, and closed her eyes briefly. She knew where this was going.

"He wanted to meet with me," said Vehn. "I didn't know who else to turn to, so I agreed to talk."

"He offered to kill Vasethe," said Tyn.

Vehn was quiet.

"You couldn't do it yourself, because Res Lfae granted him empane status."

"What is that?" asked Rion.

"It's a rule. It confers protection over a chosen guest to the realm, so that no dweller can wilfully harm that person without inflicting that same harm on Res Lfae." Tyn felt empty. "That was it, right? If you let him into the realm, Kan Buyak would kill Vasethe for you."

After a long pause, Vehn nodded.

"Res Lfae would have sacrificed themselves otherwise," she said. "I had to do something."

Tyn rubbed her eyes.

"I opened the channel to Kan Buyak's realm," said Vehn. "And I granted him access to the Spinelight Gate outside the Crux Fortress. Just that one Gate; I knew the Ahri-dweller's surrogate body was hidden there. But as soon as he had permission, Kan Buyak seized control of the whole system."

Tyn remembered the way the Gate outside the college had failed to heed her when she tried to cross to the Sanctum. "He removed everyone else's permissions."

"He should never have possessed the power for it, but . . ." Vehn stopped. Gathered herself. "The channel to Buyak's realm is all the way out on the Nteke Strait. The nearest Gate is at the Gulf. After he cut off my access, I was stranded. Indebe was already tired from the journey there. He could not run. I pushed him, but still, we couldn't get back to Tahmais fast enough."

The futile panic. The horror and helplessness and denial. Tyn could imagine Vehn racing across the plain, could feel the overwhelming dread as the alarms sounded and the pain grew across her shoulders, the disbelief when the deaths spiked cold and unmistakeable at the base of her neck. And ever since then she had carried the secret of her treachery alone. Tirelessly working to fix her mistake while knowing that the damage had already been done.

Tyn stood up and Vehn raised her head. The look on the First Spear's face was strange, not afraid exactly, but apprehensive. Like she awaited a blow.

"I know you care about the Ahri-dweller," she said.

For a moment, Tyn did not move or reply. Then she turned to Rion.

"I need to talk to the First Spear alone," she said. "It won't take long."

He nodded warily. "Of course."

Even after he left the room, Tyn did not immediately speak. She walked over to the window and watched the river outside, the water moving sedately through the Sanctum.

"You're the earliest memory I have of Mkalis," she said at last. "You, walking through Tahmais with me. Everything before that moment is hazy, but I remember you."

Vehn said nothing. Tyn turned to face her.

"I understand why you did it," she said. "Why you let Kan Buyak in. If the circumstances had been different, maybe I would have made the same choice. I don't ... I can't hold it against you."

"And if your friend had died?" Vehn's tone was flat, her grey eyes unreadable. "Would you still be so understanding then?"

"It's enough for me that he didn't."

"And Hale? Chitanda and Jevin? Do they not matter?"

Tyn looked down.

"I think you want me to blame you for their deaths," she said softly. "But that won't bring them back."

Silence. The lantern burned steadily on the desk, casting long shadows over the walls.

"You taught me how to hold a spear." Tyn's voice remained low. "You are the first person that I remember in Mkalis, and you made me believe I could belong here. I would have no other leader, Vehn. We will fix this together, but for now you need to rest. Please."

"I see them when I fall asleep," Vehn whispered. "And they tell me that I—"

She broke off. Tyn looked up and found Vehn's eyes.

"We will avenge them," she said. "Together."

Rion was waiting in the corridor outside, leaning against the wall with his arms crossed. Tyn was not sure how much of the conversation he had overheard, but he gave her a sceptical look when she closed the door.

"She did threaten to kill me," he muttered.

"She would never have done it. You know that."

He sighed. "Do I?"

Night had fallen and the trees outside the windows were black silhouettes. Tyn's feet dragged as she walked down the corridor. She had last slept in Kan Meiralle's realm, which felt impossibly long ago. Rion trailed after her.

"Are you all right?" he asked

"I'm worn out, that's all. And I'm sorry you were caught up in this."

He shrugged. "It's fine. I'm still breathing."

Tyn reached her own door. Briefly, she felt confused, as if a part of her had expected her old room to have vanished since she left the Sanctum. She touched the handle.

"Tyn?"

"Sorry." She turned to face him. "There's just a lot on my mind. Is something wrong?"

He rubbed his arm. "No, not exactly. But I wanted to say thank you."

"She regrets it, you know. Vehn never meant—"

"Not that." He paused. "Well, that as well. But I meant coming back for me in Kan Meiralle's realm."

"Oh." Tyn waved her hand. "Of course. Don't mention it."

"No, listen." He frowned. "When I woke up in Mkalis, I was . . . I don't think I was a good person, in my last life. When I found myself here, I felt that I deserved better. Like you were all beneath me. It made me angry." He shifted his weight to the other foot. "The first thing I tried to do was burn down this place."

"That was actually about the third thing you tried to do."

He scowled. Tyn laughed.

"Forget it," she said. "You've had possibly the worst ever initiation to the tribe. We can offer you some grace."

"But I want to be better." He uncrossed his arms. "When you were dragging me through that forest, I kept wondering why you came back. Because I knew that if I had escaped, I would have kept running."

"Rion—"

"It's true. But you came back for me."

"Because you're my friend."

"Then I want to be a better friend," he said. "I want you to be able to rely on me the way that I rely on you. So, could you— could you teach me? How to be a Spear?"

The open sincerity in his voice was new, she thought. It suited him. A pity that he could not see how far he had already come.

"I can do that," she said.

Rion's face broke into a smile.

Chapter Twenty-Six

Tyn slept, dreamless and deep, until the first rays of sunlight touched the shutters. Then she listened for a few minutes to the birdsong. Each second felt like a gift. She could almost pretend that none of it had happened, that the tribe was still here, that the nightmare would pass, that no one needed to die. But when she rose, she was ready.

Give this to Res Lfae, she wrote at the top of a sheet of paper. The God Compass caught a shaft of light and gleamed bright gold. Without its cold weight around her neck, she felt exposed, but she could not risk the Instrument falling into Buyak's hands. It would be worse than bequeathing him access to Ahri herself.

Below that, she had copied out a section of *God Instruments and Their Makers,* the greater part of the chapter on God Splinters.

The God Splinter, alternately the Key of Undoing or the Tool of Dissolution, was first forged by Res Kwasam, Weeper of Blood, Ruler of the 310th Realm, who sacrificed both her own life and some twenty thousand of her dwellers in the creation of the Instrument. Her efforts were ultimately futile in halting the conquest of Kan Imasu, Maker of the Profane, Ruler of the 67th Realm, who bore forth in striking down Kwasam's allies despite their possession of the Splinter.

Being amongst the most temperamental of all God Instruments, easily shattered and impossible to control, the Splinter is thus also considered amongst the least valuable. Its unique characteristic—its Mutability—enables the Splinter to alter form according to the presence of other Instruments in the Wielder's vicinity.

She had not been surprised to find the book lying on her bed the night before. It should have been lost to Kan Meiralle's realm, but then, it should also have been lost to Kan Sefune's. When Vehn took the book from her, the parting had felt temporary. It had wanted to return to her hands.

Tyn slipped out of her room and padded down the hallway to the stairs. She held her breath, listening for any sound of movement from Vehn's room.

While most Instruments bend to the will of their Wielders, and thus behave in ways that are predictable, the Splinter is observed to instead bend to the will of Opportunity. It is, in all capacities, a reactive Instrument. In the Wielder's hand, it may prove a hammer, or shield, or a useless bauble—the circumstances of its Wielding determine its form.

The Sanctum was dark and empty. Tyn whispered a word to the door of the barracks armoury and it unlocked. Racks of weaponry glinted in the half-light, daggers and knives, polearms and practise swords, and the spears of her tribe's namesake, rows upon rows of them. She chose a spear with a single band of red leather tied below the blade. Bloodroot shaft, a simple iron crossguard, an old Temairin steel head. Plain but strong; the weapon had a weight that suited her. It felt right.

The Splinter, encountering another Instrument, will exert a kind of magnetic attraction upon its fellow; bring the two into direct contact and the former will seek to Unmake the latter. For that is the Splinter's use—it serves no purpose other than to break down its own Kind.

As Res Tahirah had suspected, the High would not preserve a weapon. But the fact that they had chosen to save the Splinter made a peculiar kind of sense. The only Instrument they could agree to keep—an Instrument to wield against other Instruments.

She closed the armoury door behind her and headed towards the Sanctum gate. Rion and Vehn would still be sleeping. She imagined the moment they discovered her gone, and felt a twinge of regret. By then, it would be too late to change anything.

The gates opened to her touch. The city beyond looked curiously flat, its lustre lost during the time Lfae had been gone. She glanced back at the quiet gardens and the dark trees behind her.

"Goodbye," she murmured.

The Spinelight Gate took her to the sleepy Jorec District, where the forges still smouldered from the previous day's work. Baskets of fine-honed spearheads and bolts and shivs lay outside the doors—Tahmais was preparing for war. Tyn only stayed long enough to toss *God Instruments and Their Makers* into a burning furnace. The pages flapped like they were being riffled by a high wind, and then they caught and blazed.

The next Gate took her to the main entrance of the Tedassa College. She walked into the building, spear in hand, and approached the front desk.

"I need to speak to a scholar named Naamkis," she said.

After her business was concluded, one final Gate took her to the guardhouse beyond Tahmais, out on the mountain plateau. She walked quickly as the sun crested the eastern peaks, the warm air buoying her upwards along the path. She had last travelled this way with Res Lfae and Vehn on the way to the Tribunal. The plain stretched away on her left, a swath of dark blue. The tallest of the baobabs had just started to catch the light, their highest branches like fragments of amber drifting in the sea.

The channel to the 5th realm was overgrown with grass and wild flowers. It was closed to her now, but she had expected no less.

Tyn drew Buyak's egret feather out of her pocket. She pricked her finger against its point, and the quill hungrily drank her blood. It turned pink.

"How unexpected." Buyak's voice whispered on the breeze. The feather fluttered. "I had all but given up on you, Second Spear."

"I would speak with you," said Tyn. "Open the channel to the 5th realm."

A pause.

"The 5th realm, you say? That is also interesting." The stones rumbled and the smell of sulphur rose from the ground. "Very well. I will be waiting."

The earth cracked open to reveal the stairs down into the channel. A hot wind swept the loose strands of hair back from Tyn's face. She closed her eyes for a second. This was the right choice, the only choice.

It might have been her imagination, but as she took the first step into the channel, she thought she caught the scent of iron and star anise drifting over the mountainside.

The passage descended steeply, and the walls of the tunnel glowed with thousands of red gems, all radiating heat. Sweat gathered at the back of Tyn's neck; she rolled the shaft of the spear across her palm. Ahead, she could see the molten chrome walls of the Passage of Scarabs.

The beetles lay dead on their backs in the black dust, their shining wings faded. Tyn walked forward slowly, taking in the devastation. Their corpses rose in mounds and sloped up against the walls.

"Did you have to kill them?" she asked.

"Helquas' dwellers proved... recalcitrant." Buyak's voice echoed through the passage. "While I could subdue them by force, it hardly seemed worth the effort."

"You would prefer to live in a mausoleum?"

The scarabs' bodies crumbled into powder.

"Is this less offensive to your sensibilities?" he asked.

She could tell he was amused. With effort, she kept her expression neutral. Continued walking. She would not give him the satisfaction of a reaction, even as the wind rose and wreathed her in the dust of the dead dwellers' bodies.

The realm looked much the same as when she had last seen it, only the burning city now lay still—the fiery creatures had vanished, and the buildings no longer moved. The flames blazed and fell, but nothing lived down there, not anymore.

Without warning, Tyn's feet left the ground. She breathed in sharply.

"Allow me to assist," said Buyak.

She twisted instinctively, trying to work free of his binding. It had no effect. She rose through the air, and the city dropped away below her feet. Fear seized around her like a vice.

"I trust you like the view," he continued. "Fanieq mentioned that you had an aversion to heights in your previous life. Is that true?"

"Put me down," she said through gritted teeth. Her head pounded with blood, and she felt dizzy, sick to her stomach. The city below shimmered in her vision.

"Strange, isn't it, the things we carry from life to life? Do you suppose you will hold onto this phobia when you die again? Or will you simply fear me?"

A shadow fell across Tyn's back. She was now hundreds of feet above the entrance to the Passage of Scarabs, higher still above the city. She cradled her spear against her body.

Lfae. She held their face in her memory. Tried to block out everything but her purpose, but it wasn't enough. Terror choked her.

Then her path through the air shifted, and there was solid ground underneath her once more. She fell onto her knees. The binding evaporated.

"Welcome to my garden," said Buyak.

The island—or islands, she realised—hovered in the air. Tyn used her spear to stand up. The floating archipelago was joined together by short, trellis-covered bridges of quartz-flecked granite, and each small landmass bloomed with white, black, and cobalt blue flowers. Pale flames licked the edges of their petals.

The largest island lay directly ahead, where the ground rippled with thin ribbons of purple silk. At its centre, Buyak waited for her.

"It's been too long," he said.

He reclined on a white stone bench, one leg outstretched, the other hanging languidly over the side. Fire washed over his clothing and skin, but nothing burned. The God Sword rested beneath his left hand.

Tyn forced herself to walk forward, but she paused at the bridge. The abyss below her yawned. Legs shaking, she took a small step, then another.

Buyak laughed. A second later, an invisible force dragged

her across the remaining distance.

"Fanieq spoke the truth, it seems," he said.

Lfae. Vehn. Rion. Vasethe.

Tyn lifted her head. "The goddess knew me in my past life?"

"The goddess killed you in your past life." Buyak made a careless, throwaway gesture. "You were to drive Yett to the border keeper, and he was to drive the border keeper to Fanieq. Did no one see fit to explain this to you after you escaped the Realm of Ghosts?"

"Yett?"

"Oh, so you *have* been left in the dark." He laughed. "At the time, I thought the whole scheme was needlessly elaborate, but I suppose that it did ultimately work. And now here you are, a pawn until the very end. A small player in the game, but far more useful than I expected."

"Ever a tool of the gods," she said, hand wrapped tightly around her spear.

"One of many, but yes. Useful."

"You deceived Vehn."

"Your First Spear?" He raised one elegant eyebrow. "But she is the deceiver. Yett's surrogate body was not where she said it would be. Nor was the border keeper in the Sanctum."

"I was referring to the Tribunal." The silk ribbons brushed Tyn's ankles, moving like snakes. "The conversation Vehn overheard between Res Lfae and the border keeper. That was an illusion of yours, wasn't it?"

"What gave me away?"

"I've seen your work before; the concealed entrance to the 41st realm. I know what you are capable of." Tyn kept her gaze on the god, on his white-toothed smile. "Besides, the border keeper had already accepted Res Lfae's answer.

The matter was settled."

"And yet your poor lonely superior was so easy to fool. I gave her what she expected to hear and she ate it up."

Tyn pressed her nails into her palm, restraining her anger. "What are you trying to achieve?"

"That is not your concern, is it?" Still relaxed, Buyak lifted the Sword from the ground. "Where is Lfae now?"

Tyn smiled back at the god tightly.

"I have no idea," she said.

Buyak's good humour faded.

"Come now," he said. "Answer truthfully."

The binding compelled her to speak, and she obeyed.

"I have no idea," she repeated.

A flash of irritation crossed Buyak's face. "Do not try my patience. Have you been in contact with the border keeper?"

"I have not."

"Yett?"

"Are you talking about Vasethe?" Tyn let her smile grow wider. "As a matter of fact, I travelled to his realm yesterday."

That captured the god's attention.

"I could have told you where to find the channel," she continued. "That channel to Ahri that you so desperately wanted? I knew where the entrance was hidden. I could even have bequeathed you access to it, if you had asked me an hour ago."

Buyak sat up, laying the Sword across his legs. "Where is it? Answer now."

Tyn relished the words as they left her mouth. "I have no idea."

At first, Naamkis had been reluctant to help, but understood the situation once Tyn had explained it. The scholar had accompanied her to Restricted Experimentation. Together with the project's researchers, she had applied the College's controversial memory hex, excising any recollection of the Ahri channel from Tyn's mind. All that was left was a blank, impenetrable stretch of empty time.

"Then did you come here to die?" Buyak's tone was soft, dangerous. "Is that it?"

Tyn shrugged.

His body had not changed, but the god somehow seemed to occupy more space. Power rolled from his skin like waves, seething in the air around him.

"I could make that hurt," he said. "More so, once I have conquered your ruler and claimed you. I could make dying a *very* slow process."

"You could. But why not try it now?"

Buyak stood. The motion sent a shockwave of power out across the island. Tyn held her ground. Where the god stepped, fire blossomed. He turned the hilt of the sword within his hand.

"Why did you wish to speak to me? Did you come to beg for mercy? Did you want me to spare your friends?" His silver eyes bore into her. "Or did you think I would spare you?"

Tyn exhaled. The roaring in her ears grew louder with each step he took toward her.

"No," she said. "I came to break your Sword."

As Buyak moved to strike her, her spear rose to meet his screaming blade; the God Splinter tied to the shaft morphing like quicksilver. With fluid grace, it flowed from a thin sliver of gold into a line of dagger-sharp prongs. A sword breaker.

The Sword struck the Splinter with an unearthly shriek, inches from her face. The force drove her backwards, but it held; the breaker caught the blade.

Silence. Shock spread over Buyak's face.

Tyn twisted the spear with all the force she could muster. She heard a crack—

—and reality folded inwards. The sky and the ground beneath her fragmented into millions of tiny shards, hanging in the air like mirror glass. Buyak disappeared.

"Where am I?"

The voice seeped out of the ether, echoing and awful, a thousand words layered on top of each other, ranging from death rattle to laughter to howl. Blood dripped from Tyn's ears.

"Where am I?" Fanieq repeated.

He forged the Sword from her *lifeblood.*

Tyn struggled to move. Suddenly reality shifted again and she stood in the throne room of the 41st realm.

"I know you."

This time the goddess's voice was singular. A shadow sat upon the broken throne, the impression of moonlight and deep water.

"Yes, I know you," she said. "You were . . . you were the messenger."

Light flared from the ceiling and then subsided.

"Am I dead?" the goddess asked.

Tyn's mouth was parched. "I think so."

"Yes. Yes, I think I'm dead. I remember the border keeper, she came. She was kind. I think I remember that. I think that she killed me."

There was something scattered and distracted about the way the goddess spoke. The room flickered and then reformed; the hole in the ceiling vanished and the colours changed, changed again. Her voice grew clearer and faded.

"I am pulled apart," she said. "I am bleeding without blood, burning without skin. But just now, I feel like myself again."

"Buyak forged your soul into a God Sword."

"Buyak." A pause. Fanieq seemed to gain a grip on her consciousness. "Ambitious and weak and cruel, but necessary. I'm surprised he attempted the forging on his own. He was always more inclined to leech off the efforts of others. Your name is Tyn, isn't it? I remember now. Raisha."

"Yes."

"I broke your arm. I threw you from my window. And yet you refused to bow to me." The shadow grew larger, more dense. Tyn thought that she caught a glimpse of bone-white hair. "I might have admired that, once. That obstinacy. Is the border keeper still alive?"

"Yes."

"Good. I want you to make sure that she destroys Buyak. I want him to burn. I want him to suffer so that he begs for death." Her voice faded. "Make him pay for doing this to me."

The sense of a sigh, and then the world came undone again. Tyn breathed in and Buyak was before her.

". . . have you done?" he said. She saw fear in his silver eyes.

The God Sword shattered.

Tyn stumbled backwards. Razor-sharp metal shards exploded outwards; one sliced across her shin, another cut a bone-deep gash over her right forearm. Blood splattered across the flowers; it rushed bright and red down her wrist. She regained her balance and switched the spear to her left hand, raising it to an unsteady guard.

"Oh, you will pay for that," snarled Buyak. He dropped the useless hilt and raised his hands like he intended to rend her limb from limb, like he would rip her apart with brute force alone.

Across the ground, the broken pieces of the sword stirred.

Tyn's eyes strayed toward them, but Buyak was too consumed by anger to notice as the shards pivoted like iron filings before a magnet.

Then, in perfect unison, they flew towards the god and impaled him.

Buyak grunted and stopped. He looked down. Metal protruded from his arms, legs, and torso. A tremor ran through the length of his body.

"Leave me," he said.

The shards drew outwards. Then they plunged back into his flesh. Buyak screamed and the broken sword's voice joined his in a wild cacophony of howling. The metal bubbled and melted, fusing with his skin, sliding into his blood. He drew breath and tried to heal the damage, whispering rules, repeating them, but the sword melded itself further into him even as he closed the wounds. His body swelled and twisted; before Tyn's eyes, he began to change. He screamed again. Steel-coloured blisters burst across his right arm.

She ran. Her feet flew across the bridge and she was on the next island. Around her, the flowers shrivelled and died, their flames snuffed out.

"Come back here!" shouted Buyak.

She reached the edge and lurched to a stop. The burning city glowed far below. Nowhere to go, nowhere to run. Her heart pounded.

"Lfae," she whispered. "Vehn. Rión. Vasethe."

She turned around. Buyak dragged himself towards her. With each movement, his limbs shrieked with Fanieq's voice. His right hand had re-formed into a misshapen metal point, and loose, bloody rags of skin hung from his ribcage. Grotesque wounds healed and reopened, over and over.

"What have you done?" he rasped. His back arched and he made an awful choking sound. Tyn steeled herself and adjusted her grip; the spear was awkward in her left hand. Buyak glared at her with white-hot loathing. But amidst the rage and pain, there was also fear in his eyes.

"Kan Fanieq sends her regards," said Tyn.

The god surged forward. She dodged sideways, out of his path, but not quite fast enough. The edge of his disfigured arm clipped her hip, and pain blossomed up her side.

She tried to return the blow, aiming for his throat.

Buyak hardly flinched as he blocked her. There was no grace to his movements, he was only vicious and ceaseless; he drove her across the island one stride after the next. The dead flowers turned to ash. Tyn could not think, could not attack, could only stumble backwards until there was nowhere left to go.

With a vicious snarl, Buyak shoved her over the edge.

Her heart stopped. Tyn reached out, but there was nothing to grasp onto. The dawn sky filled her vision. Her body tipped backwards, and there was nothing, nothing, nothing but empty air.

She screamed.

A flash of light, and Rion appeared above her. He threw his arms around her shoulders, and then they were both falling.

The wind rushed past them. Tyn could not breathe. She clung to Rion; his body her only anchor, her mind blank with terror. The island soared away above them. He was warm. Something hard pressed against her throat; his hands fumbled around her neck. He shouted, and the roar snatched the words from his mouth.

Then she hit the ground.

She was inside the Sanctum, beneath the trees. Her arms

were empty, Rion was gone. The God Compass lay against her neck.

For a moment, she felt paralysed. Everything had happened so quickly, and she could still hear the rushing of the air in her ears. Could still feel Rion's arms.

"No," she whispered. "No, no, no."

She scrambled upright, and dropped her spear as she fumbled with the catch on the Compass. It opened.

"Where is Rion?" she demanded.

The needle paused, then spun north. In the lid, an unfamiliar room, an unfamiliar place.

Tyn cursed. The Compass could not fail now, she needed to reach him. She twisted the dial and pictured the 5th realm, the exit from the Passage of Scarabs. She clicked the lid shut.

Black dust swirled in the air and the city smouldered in the valley.

"Rion!" she yelled.

She staggered down the slope, sinking up to her knees in ash. She coughed; her lungs burned.

"Where is he?" she asked the Compass again, breathless.

The needle swung, pointed to nowhere. Tyn flung the Instrument away from her, not caring where it landed. Her arms and legs were stained black with soot; she half-ran, half-fell down the hillside. He had been right there. She had to reach him. Had to find him, that was her job, she was supposed to protect him.

"Rion!" She coughed again. "I'm coming!"

She could feel heat radiating from the valley, scalding even from afar. The city swam in Tyn's vision. She fell again, and got back to her feet. Her legs sank deeper and deeper into the dust.

Behind her, she heard someone approaching, but she did

not turn, she kept pushing forward. When they wrapped their arms around her, she struggled.

"Let me go!" she shouted.

"I'm so sorry, Tyn."

She struck out at Lfae and they let her, but their arms did not move. She could not get free.

"He needs me!" She struggled harder. "Get off me, I have to find him."

"Tyn—"

"You told me to take care of him!" Her voice cracked. "I have to take him back to Ahri. I promised him, I promised him. Let me *go*, Lfae!"

"He's gone," they said softly. "You felt it too."

"No!" She thrashed. "No! He's down there."

Lfae pressed their face to the top of her head, holding her close. They said nothing else, they just let her curse and hit them, until at last she was sobbing and begging them to fix it, to fix him, bring him back, please, please, not like this, not when he had tried so hard to be better, not when she had failed him right at the end. There were other people around them; she dimly heard the border keeper's voice, but she did not care.

Lfae carried her back up the slope and she wept in their arms.

Chapter Twenty-Seven

Buyak had fled, back to the 200th realm and his homelands. New rules festered and bred in his domain, forbidding breathing, forbidding speaking, forbidding violent thought. He was paranoid and hurt, and withdrew into his poisoned shell to tend his wounds, spitting out edicts to keep anyone from reaching him.

Tyn sat in the garden outside Lfae's conservatory, hollow-eyed, and listened as the border keeper explained the situation to her ruler.

"I could follow," said Eris. She studied the lid of the God Compass. "I'd need to break dozens of his rules, but I think I could kill him."

Lfae leaned against the wall. They looked weary. Tyn had ripped the collar of their shirt, and they had not yet mended the damage.

"The 5th realm's power lies behind the establishment of those rules," they said. "Even you would be obliterated."

"I never said I would survive. I just said I could kill him." Eris glanced up at Lfae. "Ask me and I'll do it."

"Is that really how you want to go, Midan? For the sake of a coward like Buyak?"

"For you, actually."

Lfae scoffed.

"He'll be weak, between his wounds and the way that he is

burning through his power."

"Which means that he'll need time to recover. We have evidence now; we can force the High to pay attention." They made a dismissive gesture. "No, leave the bastard to bleed. I'd sooner kill him myself anyway."

"As you wish." Eris closed the Compass. "With your permission?"

Lfae nodded. Eris walked across the grass and stopped beside Tyn's bench. With a sigh, she sat down. The God Compass hung from its chain between her fingers, and Tyn watched it sway from side to side. The Instrument shone in the sunlight, clean and bright. Not a trace of the soot and ash from the 5th realm remained. She raised her gaze to the border keeper's face, and her voice emerged low and ragged.

"Can you bring him back?"

Lfae quietly turned and walked away. Their shoulders were tight as they disappeared into their house.

"That's what the stories say." Tyn's throat hurt. "That you can resurrect the dead."

Eris shook her head.

"Under some rare circumstances, I've been able to divert a soul from Mkalis back to Ahri," she said gently. "But never the other way around. Here."

She held out the Compass. After a moment, Tyn took it.

"I tried it once." Eris leaned back a little. She watched the breeze stir the yellow leaves of the trees. "When I lost Yett. I remember thinking that if I was just strong and clever and determined enough, if I just sacrificed enough, I would be able to do it."

Tyn opened the Instrument with numb fingers. The now-familiar needles and dials slowly turned in the morning sun.

"I wish I could bring your friend back, Tyn," said Eris. "I would, if it was within my power."

"But he fell." Tyn swallowed. Took a breath. "He fell to save me."

Eris rested her hand on top of Tyn's. Her skin was cool.

"How do I—" The words were so difficult. "I was meant to protect him. What am I supposed to do now?"

The border keeper squeezed her hand.

"Live," she said simply. "Live and remember."

The needle turned to point north. In the lid, Tyn could see a woman seated below a window. She rocked slightly, and she was smiling. An infant lay in her arms.

"The ones we lose are not lost forever," whispered Eris. "Even if they slip out of reach."

Tyn touched the child's head with the tip of her fingernail. It was difficult to tell through the misted surface of the Compass, but she thought they had mismatched eyes. One green, one brown.

"If it's all right, I'd like to heal your injuries," said Eris. "May I?"

Tyn found herself nodding, still gazing down at the Compass. The border keeper carefully drew up the torn sleeve of her shirt.

At the end of the garden, the river flowed by, scattering the light. A heaviness settled over Tyn's limbs. Kan Buyak's sword was broken. Lfae was back, the tribe was safe, and the realm defended. And yet she craved to be anywhere else. She shut her eyes.

Live and remember.

The border keeper went still. A second later, the hard clink of metal on tile sounded behind them. Tyn turned. She recognised that noise. One of Lfae's medallions had fallen.

"Trouble," she said. "The barracks."

Eris stood. She stared at the trees beyond the river, her eyes narrowed. When Tyn tried to rise, she motioned for her to be still. In the distance, Tyn heard muffled shouting.

Show yourself, traitor!

The leaves rustled, and Vehn emerged from the grove. The First Spear looked haggard and drained, out of breath. She bled from a cut on her forehead. When she saw Tyn, her composure slipped for a second; her expression passing from relief to pain. She opened her mouth to speak.

"First Spear," said Lfae.

The demon stood in the doorway to the conservatory, tall and proud and beautiful. Vehn paled a little at the sight of them, but she did not shrink. With brittle courage, she held her head up and walked toward her ruler.

"I had to know." She spoke clearly. "I felt the death, and knew it would have been either Tyn or Rion."

Lfae's face revealed nothing. Tyn stood up. Eris put a hand on her shoulder.

"Rion, then." Vehn stopped a few feet from the house. She swallowed. "Did he suffer?"

"No," said Lfae. "He felt nothing."

Vehn nodded. Then she knelt, lowering her face towards the ground and pressing her fists together.

"I accept your punishment," she said.

Tyn pulled away from the border keeper. "No."

"I opened the channel for Kan Buyak so that he could assassinate the Ahri-dweller, the empane-protected." Vehn spoke into the ground. "I let Kan Buyak use a Spinelight Gate, which enabled him to access the Sanctum. As such, I take full responsibility for every death that followed."

"Kan Buyak lied to her." Tyn staggered over the grass and planted herself between Vehn and Lfae. "She was only trying to save you."

"Stand down, Tyn," said Lfae.

She refused to move.

"Second Spear, that was an order."

"Ever since you left, the First Spear has tried to fix her mistakes. She served you better than anyone else. She was always prepared to sacrifice herself, for you and for the realm."

"Don't," muttered Vehn.

Tyn met her ruler's eyes. "I vouch for her. If she is a traitor, then so am I."

Lfae sighed. They shook their head.

"I'm not going to hurt Vehn," they said.

Tyn wavered.

"I promise." They walked forward. "But I do need to talk to her in private."

Tyn glanced down at Vehn. Her chest hurt. This felt wrong, after everything they had been through together. Vehn had suffered enough.

"You have my word, Tyn," said Lfae.

Reluctantly, she moved aside. Vehn stayed on the ground. At her neck, her vertebrae pressed up against her skin.

Lfae bent their knees and crouched before her. They reached out and adjusted Vehn's hair where it had fallen across her forehead. The gesture was tender.

"Will you come inside?" they asked quietly.

Vehn lifted her head from the grass. Her eyes were wet. She nodded. Lfae offered her their hand and she took it, letting them help her to her feet.

"I'm sorry," she said.

Lfae leaned closer to her and whispered something. Vehn shivered, and all at once it seemed like the tension left her body, as if the weight she had been carrying for weeks had slipped away. When Lfae walked back to the conservatory, she followed them.

But at the entrance, she turned and looked at Tyn. Her lips parted like she wanted to say something or ask a question. No words came out.

"I'll be waiting for you," said Tyn.

Vehn pressed her fists together in acknowledgement.

Chapter Twenty-Eight

Tyn spent a lot of time alone. The tribe folded her back into its embrace, quietly and without fuss, and she drew comfort from the presence of her friends. Yet she could not quite forget the cut on Vehn's forehead when the First Spear had appeared in Lfae's garden, or the sound of the medallion striking the floor.

She wandered through Tahmais. She took Pax down to the plain, rode far and fast, and slept beneath the stars. She visited the Tedassa College; slipped through a side entrance and trailed the library stacks, picking up books at random, reading about any trivial and obscure subject, anything to distract her, even if only for a little while.

God Instruments and Their Makers found its way back to her. One day she returned from sparring, and the book lay open on her desk. There was no sign that it had recently been set alight; only the old, faded scorch marks remained. She threw it in the river.

At night she dreamed of falling, and woke up sweating and sick beside Matir. He held her and talked her back to sleep. Rion haunted her in those hours. She could not speak about his death, not with the rest of the tribe—they had scarcely had the chance to meet him. Only Vehn would understand, and the First Spear had been banished.

"You miss her," murmured Matir in bed one night. "Even now."

Tyn stayed silent. She shifted closer to him, and he put an arm around her. The moon shone silver through the gaps between the shutters.

"Everything feels so fragile," she said finally. "Like the realm could break apart around me. Vehn makes me feel . . . less like that."

Matir kissed the top of her head.

"She'll come back," he said.

"I know."

The lamp on his bedside table burned yellow and warm. Crickets chirped outside, and the night was still.

"People are talking about you in other realms, you know," said Matir. "They are calling you the God-Feared, after Kan Buyak fled from you."

"He was running away from the border keeper."

"And yet, people still talk."

Tyn sighed.

"As a title goes, I think it's quite good." There was gentle amusement in Matir's voice, a lightness. "Tyn the God-Feared, Breaker of Swords. It has a nice ring to it."

"Stop already."

"Make me, oh fearsome one."

Despite everything, he could still make her laugh. She drifted off to sleep beside him. In the morning, she left before he woke up.

Buyak's ghost lingered around the walkways of the grove. The god trailed alongside Tyn; the whispered shriek of his Sword echoed between the leaves. It would be a clear day; the deep blue sky was cloudless above her head.

Lfae was waiting for her at the door of their house. They wore a dark grey tunic and a necklace of amethyst and bronze.

Their expression was calm.

"I was wondering when you would come," they said.

"You could have summoned me."

"I figured I should leave it up to you, Upstart." They offered her a hand. "Walk with me?"

The Sanctum wall rippled with colour, amber slowly running into brown, black, and gold. Tyn followed Lfae as they climbed up the stairs to the parapet. For some reason, the height of the Sanctum wall did not bother her the way it used to. Perhaps because Lfae was with her. Perhaps because it no longer seemed so far to fall. She walked behind her ruler, and gazed out over the streets of the city, tracing its patterns through her memory.

"Vehn said that you named me your successor," she said.

Lfae stopped.

"Is it true?"

The demon exhaled, then turned and rested their elbows against the balustrade. The wind caressed their hair.

"I probably should have told you," they said.

The sounds of the city were growing louder. Behind them, the Sanctum remained quiet.

"Why?" she asked.

"Why didn't I tell you, or why did I name you inheritor of the realm?" They laced their fingers together, considering their answer. "For a variety of reasons, I suppose. I tried to keep it secret because naming a successor is usually what a ruler does when they think they might die. Given the circumstances, I did not want to cause any unnecessary alarm. Then, if people knew, they might treat you differently—at best, they would be more distant, at worst, they might try to harm you. That's the nature of the role. I also knew that my choice would exacerbate the conflict between you and Vehn, and drive the tribe further apart. And I was afraid you might not like the idea. You certainly would have resisted it."

Tyn allowed their words to sink in, considering them carefully.

"It confused me when I found out," she said. "I assumed that Vehn was mistaken. Why not her?"

"It's difficult to answer that."

"You do still care for her, don't you? She felt that—that she might have lost you, at some point."

Lfae smiled sadly. "Then she's a fool. But my fool, nonetheless. I made my feelings for her clear before I sent her to the Crux Fortress."

Tyn looked away.

"You're not going to forgive me for that, are you?"

"She should be here."

"It's temporary, Tyn. For the tribe to take her back, they need to believe that I punished her. It will take time, but she won't be there forever."

"But how long?"

They shrugged. "Months, probably. Go visit her. She would appreciate that, even if it kills her to show it. But to return to the original question, I didn't name Vehn or any of the other tribe leaders as successor, because I wanted it to be you."

"And you said that Vehn was a fool."

They snorted.

"It's not sentimentality," they said. "Not entirely. You're simply the person most likely to disobey me. When you believed I would hurt Vehn, you refused to stand aside. If I had pressed the issue, I suspect you would have tried to fight me. Correct?"

"No!"

"Oh, be honest. I could see it on your face." They were trying not to smile. "Which would have been a terrible idea, by the way. God-Feared or not, you definitely wouldn't beat me in direct combat."

Tyn winced.

"You push back when you think I am unjust," said Lfae. They resumed their watch of the city. "And infuriating though that can be, I value your integrity. So when I considered who would serve the best interests of the realm, you were the only one who seemed right. But I am sorry I never asked you about it. I'm sorry you found out the way you did."

She shook her head slightly.

"Did you really think you were going to die?" she asked, her voice low.

They glanced at her. The light of the sunrise made them appear impossibly beautiful, but, beneath the radiance, Tyn could still find traces of the face she had seen in the College Preserve.

"It was a possibility. Still is a possibility," they replied. "But I won't go down easily."

She nodded. A flock of red-winged starlings rose from the roofs over the Sunlit Downs and flew towards the plain.

"There's something I need to ask," said Tyn. "I've been thinking about it for a while."

A gust of wind blew a lock of Lfae's hair over their shoulder. It streamed over the balustrade like a banner.

"I want to leave the Spears," she said.

The change in her ruler's expression was subtle—not quite surprise, but something gentler and more sad. They did not speak.

"The tribe will always be a part of me," said Tyn. "But I have the sense that there's a gap between myself and everyone else, and I'll never quite return to the time when I belonged."

"Is it because of Rion?"

It was the first time she had heard them say his name. A dull ache settled over her.

"He's part of it, yes. But it's also—" She hesitated. After going over the idea so many times in her own head, it was strange that she still struggled to express it aloud. "I don't know if I ever truly wanted to be Second Spear. I was proud of it and it gave me purpose. I cherished serving at your side. But in the back of my mind, there was always a part of me that felt like an imposter."

"Oh, Tyn."

"It's true."

"But unfounded. You earned your place. The fact that I also happened to grow fond of you is . . ." They fluttered their hand irritably.

She smiled. "For a demon ruler, you're quite soft."

"I'll only tolerate so much insubordination from you, Upstart." They straightened. "You would forfeit the role of Second Spear?"

"If you'll allow it."

"And then, I imagine, you plan to join the border keeper in bringing down Buyak. And trying to save Vasethe."

She coloured.

"If you'll allow it," she said in a smaller voice.

"Have you discussed the matter with her?"

"Not . . . in detail."

"But your heart is set on it." They pursed their lips. "I'll admit, the idea of sending you outside the reach of my protection is uncomfortable. Especially since the last time I left you behind, Buyak almost killed you."

"He is weaker now."

"I wouldn't count on that." They sighed, then shook their head. "If it's what you feel you need to do, then go. You have my support. However, I have a condition."

She braced herself.

"You have to swear that you'll come back." Lfae gestured to the Sanctum, to the city. "Because I will be waiting for you."

Tyn lowered her eyes.

"Not just me, obviously," Lfae added. "The rest of the tribe will miss you too. And I suspect Matir in particular might object if you vanished completely."

Tyn blanched. "What—"

They smirked.

"How does everyone know about that?" she demanded.

"A better question is how you ever thought it was a secret. It's been a running joke in the tribe for years."

"So they *all* know?" She suddenly felt dizzy, and it had nothing to do with the height of the wall.

"Perhaps not the newest Spears."

She wasn't sure if she could ever show her face at the barracks again. "And they all pretended—"

"Like I said, something of a running joke." Lfae put a hand on her shoulder. "Do you swear that you will return?"

Tyn breathed out.

"Yes," she said. "I'm your dweller. Tahmais will always call me back home."

"Then go well, Tyn the God-Feared." Lfae's voice was solemn, but their eyes were smiling. "And come back safe."

She lifted her head.

"I will," she said.

Acknowledgements

Thank you to my agent, Jennifer Jackson, for your tireless support over the last three years. I'm so grateful for your kindness, patience, and humour.

Thank you to the whole team at Tordotcom Publishing, and most especially to Ruoxi Chen, Sanaa Ali-Virani, Caroline Perny, Lauren Hougen, Christine Foltzer, and Irene Gallo. I'm so lucky to work with you all.

Thank you to Emma Laubscher for being an excellent friend. Thank you to my father, Stephen Hall. I hope you enjoy this one.

Thank you to Sylvia Hall for the long hours and late nights you spent on this book. It's better because of you. Thank you for your support and love, always.

Finally, thank you to Tessa Hall. You were the first person to read this story, and your enthusiasm has fueled me ever since.

About the Author

Sylvia Hall

KERSTIN HALL is the author of the novella *The Border Keeper* and the novel *Star Eater*. She lives in Cape Town, South Africa.

TOR·COM

Science fiction. Fantasy. The universe.

And related subjects.

*

More than just a publisher's website, *Tor.com* is a venue for **original fiction, comics,** and **discussion** of the entire field of SF and fantasy, in all media and from all sources. Visit our site today—and join the conversation yourself.